THE KEY WEST READER

THE
KEY WEST
READER:

THE BEST OF KEY WEST'S WRITERS
1830~1990

EDITED AND WITH AN INTRODUCTION BY
GEORGE MURPHY

FOREWORD BY LES STANDIFORD

Tortugas Ltd.

The editor would like to thank the following people for their encouragement, support, advice, assistance, and generosity: John Boisonault, John Malcolm Brinnin, Benjamin "Dink" Bruce, Philip Caputo, Lola French, Charles Gearhart, Richard Heyman, Rust Hills, Liz Lear, Isabeall Logan, Sandy McKinney, Gerry Montgomery and the staff at *Island Life*, James Nagle, Susan Olson, Bets Reynolds, Susie Solares, Grant Spradling, Sandra Taylor, Gerry Tinlin, David Vincent, and especially Thomas Sanchez.

Cover: *A Norther—Key West*, 1886: Winslow Homer.
American, 1936-1910. Watercolor, 333 x 496 mm.
Gift of Mr. and Mrs. John D. Rockefeller 3rd.
Achenbach Foundation for Graphic Arts, 1979.7.54
Copyright © The Fine Arts Museums of San Francisco.

Book Design by George Murphy

The Key West Reader: The Best of Key West's Writers, 1830-1990
    Copyright © 1989 by George Murphy

Printed in the U.S.A.

Library of Congress Catalog Card Number: 89-051565

ISBN: 0-9624184-0-4   Clothbound
      0-9624184-1-2   Trade Paper Edition

Tortugas, Ltd.
Box 2626, Key West, FL 33045

Acknowledgements

"Death of a Pirate" is reprinted from *Ornithological Biography, Volume II* (pp.185-189) by John James Audubon

"A Norther–Key West" and "The Bight" from *The Complete Poems, 1927-1979* by Elizabeth Bishop. Copyright © 1979, 1983 by Alice Helen Methfessel. Reprinted by permission of Farrar, Straus and Giroux, Inc.

"Letter from Key West" © 1989 by John Malcolm Brinnin. Reprinted by permission of the author.

"The Ahab Complex," Copyright © 1988 by Philip Caputo. Reprinted from *Florida Keys Magazine* by permission of the author.

"Audit in Key West" and "Tuesday: Four Hundred Miles" Copyright © 1989 by John Ciardi. Reprinted by permission of Judith Ciardi.

"Imperial Addictions" Copyright © 1985 by Alexander Cockburn. Reprinted from *The Nation* by permission of the author.

"O Carib Isle" "Key West" and "–And Bees of Paradise" reprinted from *THE COMPLETE POEMS AND SELECTED LETTERS AND PROSE OF HART CRANE*, edited by Brom Weber, by permission of Liveright Publishing Corporation. Copyright 1933, © 1958, 1966 by Liveright Publishing Corporation.

"Under the Tropic" Copyright © 1966 by John Dos Passos. Reprinted from *The Best Times* by permission of New American Library.

"Letter from Key West" From *Selected Letters of Robert Frost* edited by Lawrance Thompson. Copyright © 1964 by Lawrance Thompson and Holt, Reinhart and Winston, Inc. Reprinted by permission of Henry Holt and Company, Inc.

"Porpoise" from *The Theory and Practice of Rivers* (Winn Books). Copyright © 1985 by Jim Harrison. Reprinted by permission of the author.

"Letter to Yesenin, #18" and "Awake" reprinted from *Selected and New Poems* (Delta) Copyright © 1973, 1982 by Jim Harrison. Reprinted by permission of the author.

"from A Good Day to Die" from *A Good Day to Die* (Delta/Seymour Lawrence) © 1973 by Jim Harrison. Reprinted by permission of the author.

"from To Have and Have Not" reprinted with permission of Charles Scribner's Sons, an imprint of MacMillan Publishing Company from *To Have and Have Not* by Ernest Hemingway. Copyright © 1937 by Ernest Hemingway; copyright renewed © 1965 by Mary Hemingway.

"Who Killed the Vets?" Copyright © 1935 by Ernest Hemingway; copyright renewed © 1989 by The Hemingway Foundation. Reprinted by permission of The Hemingway Foundation. Originally appeared in *The Masses*.

"Letter to Maxwell Perkins" copyright © 1989 by The Hemingway Foundation. Reprinted by permission of the Hemingway Foundation.

for
Isabeall Logan

CONTENTS

Letter From Key West

30 December 1934
Key West

[...] Look at where I am. I say it is for Mrs. Frost's health and she says it is for mine. This is Cayo Huaso as the Spaniards named it. It might have been translated into Bone Key. Instead it was corrupted into Key West...

Neither of us likes it very much yet. But after all it is a part of the earth. (a small part, two or three miles long by a mile or so wide, about a dozen times the size of my farm in South Shaftsbury but all cut up into speculators' house lots about the size of family lots in a graveyard.) And whatever thinkers may say against the earth, I notice no one is anxious to leave it for either Heaven or Hell...

It is a very very dead place because it has died several times. It died as a resort of pirates, then as a house of smugglers and wreckers, then as a cigar manufactury (The Cubans moved over here to get inside the tariff wall) then as a winter resort boomtown. Franklin D himself has taken it personally in hand to give it one more life to lose. FERA is all over the place. This town has been nationalized to rescue it from its own speculative excesses. The personal interest of Roosevelt in his second coming has been invoked and both mayor and governor have abdicated till we can see what absolute authority can do to restore the prices of the speculators' graveyard plots and make Key West equal to Miami...

It is tropical all right but it is rather unsanitary and shabby. It has a million dollars worth of concrete sidewalks with no houses by them. It has three races not very well kept apart by race-prejudice, Cubans, Negroes and Whites. The population once 25,000 has shrunk to 12,000. We live not twenty feet from the water of very quiet seas. What with coral shoals and other little keys, the wind has to be a West Indian hurricane to get up much waves. We are fifty miles at sea and the lowest temperature ever recorded was forty degrees above zero. I sleep under one sheet and wear one thickness of linen. People that know say it is a Honolulu five thousand miles nearer home. A third of the people at least speak Spanish but there is not a Spanish book in the poor public library. Neither is there a book with a star map. I went to make sure if the new big star we had raised was Canopus, Sirius' rival...

Ever Yours,

Robert Frost

FOREWORD

The publication of any collection as closely tied to a place as *The Key West Reader* raises the question of "regionalism" in American Literature. Ours is a vast country which comprises a number of distinct areas where social, economic, and environmental factors conflate in a fashion that distinguishes the artifacts created there. Critics influenced by the concept have identified "Southern" writers, the "New York School" of poetry, and "Western" writing, to name just a few. There are anthologies of "Texas" writers, "California" writers, writers of the Piedmont, and many, many others.

In most cases, the work so designated is physically set in the region at hand. Just as important are the subtleties of thought and values, character qualities and behavioral tics, the "world view" suggested by the work. In the American Southwest are endless vistas, few fences, and crystalline air that shrouds nothing. Whether or not such a specific, physical landscape figures in a "Western" story, attitudes developed by an author who lives in such space may find their way into a piece of writing in a thousand subtle ways. There, solitude is often taken for granted—roads are relatively few and rarely curve. It is difficult for writers not to be awed by all the land which lays itself out before them; created characters may well reflect a humility, clarity and straightforwardness born of this environment. Contrast such work with that born of a South where the line of sight is generally a mile or less and usually ends with a neighbor's land, where the air is hazy, freighted with moist, mysterious scent, where roads twist and turn through the hills, forests, and swamps that are the apotheosis of a Jungian dream. There's mystery in both worlds, of course, but "darkness," for example, is not a concept readily associated with a "Arizonan" story.

No one would argue for the worth of a piece simply because it paints an accurate picture of a landscape, but who can imagine the power of Hawthorne divorced from New England or

Faulkner from his South. Either artist might have achieved as much had he been born in Nevada, but imagine what visions of *that* landscape we would have had.

Ultimately then, the validity of any regional collection is to be found in the validity of the individual inclusions. In *The Key West Reader*, the reasons for the selections are well documented, and the power of the place is undeniable throughout. In each case the material is clearly anchored in this island at the end of the American Dream, alternately raffish and elegant, sometimes as cruel as it is beautiful, where sailors and shrimpers, literati and glitterati still mingle.

While no single work can be said to "sum up" the Key West experience," that is a sign of the complexity of this place. A much truer and more accurate vision of Key West is gathered and accumulated through the selections. There are certain constants: the water, of course, the relative solitude, the exotic tropical languor (and the underlying inexorable decay), the quirkiness of the inhabitants, the natural beauty of sun and sea, but underlying it all is the mythic quality of "island-ness," as powerful here as it was for Shakespeare and his Caliban. Despite the narrow ribbon of concrete that ties it—across 42 other islands—to the mainland, Key West is an island, and the road *in* leads nowhere else. It is the insulating buffer of Gulf, Gulf Stream, Caribbean, and Atlantic that has maintained Key West as a place apart, a place where mystery is ever abundant. In our literary cosmos, islands have always been sought-after places, havens shielded from the concerns of a larger world, microcosms of the social order, where life proceeds more elementally, certainly with more intensity. There are even islands, as Alison Lurie's piece, "The Truth About Lorin Jones" makes clear, where the dead may be restored to life.

Moreover, we have in Key West an island that is perched at the very edge of America. Poet Richard Hugo once said that most writers find "the edge" a most comfortable vantage point from which to work. Whether on the edge of normalcy or the edge of the continent, the writer gains the necessary perspective from which to create the most incisive work. Such insight is abundant in this volume—we learn, from selections as various as Wallace Stevens' "The Idea of Order at Key West" to Hunter S. Thompson's Gonzo Journalism, not only how we live in Key West but in the world as well.

One more thing is noteworthy. If this book is to be considered "regional" in nature, it is unique in that the writers whose work is collected are none of them Key West natives. They have found in the island a second, sometimes a spiritual, home and perhaps as a result of discovering the place at a time of relative maturity, have come to appreciate it all the more. Whether the elements of the work lay in beauty or in the benign brutality of a world almost too rich for humankind, the attitude that is constant is of a gift received. As John Dos Passos put it, speaking of the grand Hemingway days: "[we] made a point of spending as much time as we could at Key West... No doctor's prescription was ever pleasanter to take."

●●●

The collection is a signal achievement in Florida letters and one of importance for our national literary heritage as well. Key West is certainly the only city in Florida (and one of the few in the United States) to have enjoyed a century-long reputation as a place where writers gather. It is the result of a unique confluence of the factors of history, climate, physical beauty, cultural diversity, and unabashed romantic appeal, all of which is captured across the breadth of this collection. And what is more, the editorial choices reflect consistent literary excellence.

Anyone with the slightest spirit of adventure, may well, after reading the selections of Alison Lurie, John Leslie, Jim Harrison or Tom McGuane, be overcome with the desire to get behind the wheel or on the plane and head out toward the romance, mystery, sexuality, and danger that seemingly palpitates in this "last resort." Those interested in the history of American letters will be equally intrigued by the selection from Thomas Sanchez's fiction as well as the accounts of of Audubon, Caputo, Dos Passos, and Hemingway which make it clear that Key West has always been a real life repository of the stuff from which fables spring. Readers who have come to know and love Key West will find in the work of Richard Wilbur, Judith Kazantzis, Elizabeth Bishop, James Merrill and others a moving tribute to the power of language and to a rare place in the geography of the American consciousness.

In short, we have here a significant work—topography, climate, and culture coalesced into language working at its highest levels, offering, in the terms of William Carlos Williams, a glimpse of the universal in a fascinating particular.

Les Standiford
Director, Creative Writing Program
Florida International University

INTRODUCTION

It's difficult to fully or accurately describe the allure of Key West. By virtue of its geographical detachment from the rest of the United States, it is and always has been something of a retreat, an outpost, a hideout. Its early history is rich with pirates and with wreckers who lured vessels onto the reefs so that they might plunder their cargos. The island has been Caribbean Basin headquarters for the U.S. Navy since the Civil War. The abundance of sea-turtles and natural sponges made it an industrial island for a time. Later, Cuban and Bahamian immigrants made it the cigar capital of the world. When the overseas railroad was built, it became a boom—and then a bust—resort town as the gateway to Havana. President Harry S. Truman found Key West the perfect getaway and frequently vacationed at his "Little White House," now a museum. Sportsfishermen found the waters thriving with game. In the late forties, Navy divers on maneuvers discovered "pink gold," the night-crawling Gulf shrimp that opened up a completely new fishing industry. Later, less than twenty years ago, drug smugglers openly unloaded cargos of marijuana bales on public docks. Since that time, it has become a major drug interdiction fleet center for the Caribbean Basin and is now home to major Naval Air, and Coast Guard bases. As well, it was the gateway to America for the Cuban Mariel Boatlift.

Over recent years, it has also become a haven or hideout of a different sort, for both dropouts and high-rollers, environmentalists and developers, runaways and roustabouts of all persuasions. Add to this its geographical detachment from the rest of the country and its laissez-faire attitudes and you have a melting pot where vichyssoise and gumbo have been somehow successfully blended, a true democracy, a café society.

Literally and figuratively, Key West is also the end of the road, the tip of the American funnel. In the early 1980's, the city even seceded from the Union, an event celebrated annually. For many, the island represents the dream of romance, the beauty of nature, and, in the words of a catchy tourism phrase much richer and more accurate than I suspect its authors imagined, it is the "last resort."

But, beyond this unique history and environment, what

was it that attracted so many *writers* to Key West?

In the 1920's, John Dos Passos arrived in Key West at the end of a whimsical railroad ride and later recommended the island to Ernest Hemingway as a place that "looked like something in a dream."

Wallace Stevens wrote that the island was "the sweetest doing nothing contrived." He contrasted it with his Connecticut home as a "summer without end," a place whose "mind had bound me round."

Hemingway visited Key West in 1928 and returned to live here in 1931. His years here—until 1939—were among his most productive and it was here that he forged the larger-than-life image of himself which endures to this day.

In the late 1930's, Elizabeth Bishop, on a fishing trip, found the island perfect for a new home and, later, in turn, piqued the interest of other writers.

In 1941, Tennessee Williams arrived and stayed because, as he simply put it, "I like to swim."

John Malcolm Brinnin first came to a Key West which, in the 1940's, was in economic depression and which he called "a mess" but which he still loves and returns to each winter.

In the mid-sixties, Richard Wilbur arrived and has wintered here ever since. Ten years later, John Ciardi purchased a home in the same compound.

Thomas McGuane, who moved here in the late sixties, has spoken of Key West combining "sentimental wooden architectural dreams" with what he called the "scrambled edge" of American culture, a curious combination of elements which he shared with Jim Harrison, naturalist Russell Chatham, and Jimmy Buffett, among others.

McGuane also, indirectly at least, influenced the arrival of Philip Caputo, who finished *A Rumor of War* on McGuane's ranch in Montana. Caputo had been a foreign news correspondent in Moscow when that first book met with great success. Drawn by the island's architecture, he found the tropics - and especially sport fishing - irresistible. His record-breaking 569 pound blue marlin still hangs on the wall in the Full Moon Saloon.

Alison Lurie first visited in 1978, staying at *Shenandoah* Magazine editor Jim Boatwright's home, and soon after bought a home.

Boatwright also brought David Jackson to Key West. In 1979, he, in turn, brought James Merrill to the island which is now his winter home.

Thomas Sanchez, who moved here in 1981, sees Key West as an ever-changing metaphor, "the end of the American road, but also the beginning of the American dream." In a recent interview, Sanchez noted, "The Spanish first called it the island of bones, because it was littered with human bones bleached in the sun, bones of Indians left from lost battles with man and nature, bones of shipwrecked souls. For Cubans who emigrated in the last century, Key West was *Stella Maris*, Star of the Sea, filled with the bright promise of a future not ruled by a dictatorial past. The island is human metaphor, but reality is that at any moment a hurricane can wipe the slate clean."

Joy Williams and *Esquire* fiction editor Rust Hills, who have been visiting for the past five years, have also recently relocated here. Joy wrote of the Florida Keys that they "sparkle downward, warm and bright, full of light and air and a bit of intrigue."

Though each writer, no doubt, arrived in Key West for different reasons, some commonly shared motivations can be found: the climate, the architecture, the vegetation, the remoteness, the people and, with it all, the possibility for solitude — and work!

Privacy is greatly valued—and honored—on the island. Visitors are sometimes disappointed to learn that Key West has no celebrity saloon where "the writers" congregate.

Precisely.

Key West is still, for writers, a haven, a retreat where nature has conspired to create the most sensual distractions: that lizard climbing the bougainvillea, a cat wandering in through the picket fence, the brief but deafening rainstorm thundering on the tin roofs of the neighborhood, the eye-opening *café con leche* at the neighborhood Cuban *grocería*, the indescribable grasp of sunrise on the unearthly-red poinciana trees, the fresh fish weighed and sold each afternoon at the waterfront, and moments of magic when, for example, at the edge of the harbor, Black Vincent closes his eyes to a northern breeze and, from the *soul*, plays a Bach concerto on his steel drums—or the school of bottlenose dolphin which, at midnight one New Year's Eve, leaped, over and over again through the harbor, in apparent ecstasy, at the finalé of the annual fireworks show.

For some writers included here, as you shall see, such distractions became inspiration.

Of course there are stories of escapades and incidents: gossip, legend, curiosity and scandal.

In one notorious story, Ernest Hemingway responded to an unpleasant comment from poet Wallace Stevens—who was at that time not only a novice at boxing but also a portly man, twenty year's Hemingway's senior, who made his living as an insurance executive—with fists, bruising his face and blackening his eye.

Tennessee Williams could be observed arriving daily at the Sands Beach Club and completely disrobing, leaving his clothes casually draped on a favorite rock, to wade into the Atlantic for his afternoon swim.

It is said that Maxwell Anderson's play *Key Largo* (later a legendary Bogart film) was to have been called *Key West* until local smugglers pointed out that their anonymity might be compromised by his unwise choice of titles.

Another favored anecdote features Truman Capote who, while having a drink with Tennessee Williams, complied with a woman's request to autograph her navel with an eyebrow pencil. When her enraged husband saw the handiwork, he approached their table, unzipped his fly, and said "Since you're autographing everything, how'd you like to autograph *this?*" Capote paused and said, "Well, I don't know if I can *autograph* it, but perhaps I could *initial* it."

In the end, the claim is often made that Key West, per capita, is populated by more published writers than any other city in the world. Whether or not this is fact is ultimately irrelevant. What is certainly true is that many of Key West's writers are among the great talents of this nation. They have been recipients of innumerable literary prizes and awards, including eight Pulitzer Prizes and the Nobel Prize for Literature.

Just as the waters of the Florida Straits are rich with Spanish gold, so too is the history of Key West rich with literary treasures, many of which are contained here. For lovers of language and literature, Key West will always be *Stella Maris*.

When I arrived in Key West in 1984, I had been editing a literary Magazine, *Tendril*, for eight years and had published a number of poetry collections and anthologies. I'd had no idea of the scope of the island as a writer's community until I'd visited the *Author's Room* at the wonderful East Martello Museum where Bets Reynolds provided me with a historical list that she'd been compiling. From that time, I've been searching the stacks and gathering what is collected here, and much more.

Much of what has been written here over the years could, perhaps, have been written anywhere. But, as I read, I began to find that many of the writers were indeed affected by the island itself. They wrote about its geography, its history, and its people, both real and imagined.

This collection could certainly have been much longer and I apologize to those writers whose work is not included but what *is* contained here are those selections and works that I felt spoke to the island itself in some way, either literally or figuratively, work that contained some of the magic that is Key West.

The earliest piece is from John James Audubon who, though known for his ornithological research and art, was also a fine writer who kept journals of his travels. "Death of a Pirate" is his recounting of a tale he was told late at night on an island in the Keys in 1832 by a sailor standing watch over his expeditionary party.

Elizabeth Bishop is considered *the* American poet's poet, a genius, whose pure, inspired, and precise work has greatly influenced many other important contemporary poets. More, perhaps, than any other Key West writer, she fell in love with the tropics and, upon her departure from Key West, moved further *out*, to Brazil. "A Norther—Key West" is, in part, a tribute to Winslow Homer whose painting of the same name graces our cover.

Obviously, "Poem for Elizabeth Bishop," is something of a love letter from poet/biographer John Malcolm Brinnin who, when he first came to Key West, made a pilgrimage to the house of his friend and found himself inspired—and amusingly mistaken.

Though most readers know Philip Caputo for his fiction, "The Ahab Complex," which recounts his journey to Cuba where he landed a record-breaking 569 pound blue marlin, is the best essays on fishing I have ever read.

John Ciardi is one of the few American poets whose deep and resonant voice—on National Public Radio broadcasts—became familiar. Since his death in 1987, the Key West community of writers has felt the loss of his vigorous presence. The two poems collected here were offered by his widow, Judith, as representative of his best work from Key West.

Alexander Cockburn, who is perceived by many as political and social conscience of *The Nation*, for which he writes a column, here observes, with a historic and political eye, the legendary salvaging of the Spanish treasure ship *Nuestra Señora de Atocha*.

It is argued that there is no conclusive evidence that Hart Crane ever actually visited Key West before he took up residence in Vera Cruz. Such is hard to believe, however, when confronted with his *A Key West Sheaf* Series. His suicide leap from the *S.S. Orziba* nearby in the Gulf of Mexico remains a mysterious connection to the island as well.

Stephen Crane's "The Open Boat," which is ranked with America's finest short works, is a fictionalized account of the thirty-hours he spent in a ten-foot dinghy on open seas after *The Commodore*, a ship on which he was smuggling arms to Cuba, went down.

"Under the Tropic," John Dos Passos' memoir, recounts his fishing days with Hemingway, especially the events of a trip to Bimini which bear a striking similarity to *The Old Man and The Sea*.

Jim Harrison is one of those rare American writers who has successfully mastered both poetry and prose. A gritty and courageous writer, Harrison has found the Keys a rich source of imagery and characterization. Included here are three poems and an excerpt from a novel that captures the darker and more dissolute side of the Keys.

The impact of Ernest Hemingway's prose is inestimable. Always larger than life, the legend at times seems larger than the man, as big as he was. Nonetheless, it can be fairly said that he changed the style of American literature. Included here are two accounts of the great hurricane of 1935 which washed out the great Overseas Railroad and changed the face of the Keys forever, a devastating act of God as seen through the eyes of the one of the masters of American letters.

John Hersey once said that "fiction can be stronger than truth... The important bulletins are already forgotten by the time yesterday's newspaper is used to line the trash can... The things we remember for longer periods are emotions and impressions and illusions and images and characters: the elements of fiction..." Though "The Captain" is set on a Key West shrimp boat geographically removed, the *truth* of this story is here also, on any shrimp boat you see motoring into the Gulf.

Much of foreign-born Judith Kazantzis' poetry is set in the Keys, where she has made a new home. The clear and strong influence of the island is evidenced in these two poems. As has always been true, it is the dawn which brings truth—not the setting of the sun—and contained herein is an ideal motto for the city's seal, *je ne regret rien*.

John Leslie, is a voice we shall be hearing more from soon. *Blood on the Keys* is a mystery in the tradition of another Floridian, John D. MacDonald. This excerpt, though brief, captures a day in the lives of Key West's disappearing fishermen, and hints at the illicit alternatives available to those trapped between a tourist economy and the limits of the sea.

In *The Truth About Lorin Jones*, Alison Lurie not only accurately re-creates Key West's locales and lifestyle but also manages to brilliantly capture the essence of some of its very real sexual energies in a tale of identities confused on a number of levels.

Chet Pomeroy, the protagonist of Thomas McGuane's *Panama* epitomizes what McGuane has seen here as the sociological fringe that has come to the end of the road, of A1A, only to face the fact that they could go no further.

James Merrill's poetry has been called romantic, lyrical, autobiographical, and mystical. He is one of the great masters of form, making structure both integral, precise, and, most important, invisible. "Clearing the Title" recounts, in a poem so much larger than its apparent subject matter, the acquisition of his Key West home.

Thomas Sanchez author of the epic novel of the American Indian Nation—*Rabbit Boss*— has worked ten years on another epic. Spanning centuries and continents, *Mile Zero* is perhaps the definitive Key West novel, in Sanchez's words, a "cosmic *Cannery Row*." The excerpt contained here gives a glimpse into the lives of the cigarmakers, slavers, turtlers, sharkers, and spongers who are such a rich part of the city's history.

"The Idea of Order at Key West" is considered the single most important poem of Wallace Stevens' significant and influential life's work. It can be seen as an anthem for the work of a poet, making order out of chaos, or as one biographer called it, "a hymn to the ardor of the poet - to give order to the world by his command of language."

Hunter Thompson, the original Gonzo Journalist, is a truly unique voice in America. Since the publication of his get-into-the-story-even-if-it-kills-you book on the Hell's Angels motorcycle gang, and his Rolling Stone accounts of presidential elections, his influence on contemporary journalism cannot be overestimated. A perennial renegade, Thompson once took out an ad in the local Yellow Pages for a boat charter company called *Gonzo Tours* which offered for charter "the dark underbelly of the Florida Keys" on "fast boats at night." The reports included here span a day or two of much-too-typical high-seas chaos.

"Fishing for Blues" and "The Pelican," like all of Richard Wilbur's poetry, is defined by a combination of elegance, intelligence, and accessibility. The former Poetry Consultant to the Library of Congress has been a long-time resident of Key West. These two pieces are from his Pulitzer Prize winning *New and Selected Poems*.

Joy Williams, who has also authored the definitive *The Florida Keys: A History and Guide,* had, as this book was being finished, just bought a home in Key West. "The Route," from her new collection of stories *Escapes*, is populated— as are many of her stories—by the sort of offbeat characters commonly found on the streets of her new home's town.

Tennessee Williams is considered by many to be America's finest playwright. Key West is home to a Fine Arts Center named in his honor and his influence on the lives of other writers and as a member of the island community is undeniably significant. "Mr. Williams," or Tom, as he was called, was highly visible and deeply respected as a citizen of Key West. Many readers are unaware of his talents as a poet. As such, "The Diving Bell," collected here, stands as an strong example of his "other" craft.

As to the inclusion of my own poem, "Rounding Ballast Key," I have, in this instance, thrown aside my long-standing rule to never print my own work. I offer it, humbled by the talent surrounding me, as a recounting of a day's events which led me, in part, to choose Key West as my home.

Though no historical listing of all the many "Key West Authors" could ever to be complete, and though I hesitate here for fear of its inevitable oversights. What follows, nonetheless, is a list, in no particular order, of many of the notable American writers, editors, and publishers who have lived on or spent time on this island: Philip Burton, Robert Stone, Thornton Wilder, Ellie Welt, Joseph Lash, S. J. Perelman, Robert Aaron Wright, Gore Vidal, McKinlay Cantor, Jerry Herman, David Halberstam, Marsha Norman, Jayne Anne Phillips, Burt Garnett, Russell Chatham, James Boatwright, Christopher Isherwood, Lorian Hemingway, Sherwood Anderson, Dan Gerber, Irving Weinman, Mark Twain, Benedict Theiland, Rollie McKenna, Zane Grey, Diedre English, Frank Conroy, Dotson Rader, Richard Bach, Bill Grose, Stephen King, William Manville, Maxwell Anderson, James Fenimore Cooper, Carlos Baker, Sallie Bingham, George Plimpton, Frank Taylor, Lynn Kaufelt, Francois Sagan, James Leo Herlihy, Ramona Stuart, Bob Shacochis, Christopher Buckley, Jack London, Lisa Alther, Rust Hills, Ann Beattie, James T. Farrell, Morgan Dennis, Marie Clair Blais, Edward Hower, Alex Wilder, Jane O'Reilly, William Wright, Harold Robbins, James Plath, Ralph Ellison, Budd Shulberg, Archibald MacLeish, Carl Bernstein, Nancy Friday, Truman Capote, James Kirkwood, Gay Talese, Carson McCullers, Love Dean, James McLendon, Hilary Hemingway, Kirby Congdon, Dan Wakefield, Mary Lee Settle, William F. Buckley Jr., Dean and David Heller, Seymour Lawrence, Richard Brautigan, James Nagle, Martin Kane, Kathryn Proby, Alice Munroe, David Loovis, David Kaufelt, James W. Hall, Gahan Wilson, Shel Silverstein, Ernie Pyle, Evan Rhodes, Susan Nadler, Bob Reiss, Howard Sackler, and Peter Taylor.
Enjoy.

George Murphy
The "Sea Dog" Houseboat
Key West, 1989

KWR

John James Audubon

Death of a Pirate

In the calm of a fine moonlight night, as I was admiring the beauty of the clear heavens, and the broad glare of light that glanced from the trembling surface of the waters around, the officer on watch came up and entered into conversation with me. He had been a turtler in other years, and a great hunter to boot, and although of humble birth and pretensions, energy and talent, aided by education, had raised him to a higher station. Such a man could not fail to be an agreeable companion, and we talked on various subjects, principally, you may be sure, birds and other natural productions. He told me he once had a disagreeable adventure, when looking out for game, in a certain cove on the shores of the Gulf of Mexico; and, on my expressing a desire to hear it, he willingly related to me the following particulars, which I give you, not perhaps precisely in his own words, but as nearly so as I can remember.

"Towards evening, one quiet summer day, I chanced to be paddling along a sandy shore, which I thought well fitted for my repose, being covered with tall grass, and as the sun was not many degrees above the horizon, I felt anxious to pitch my mosquito bar or net, and spend the night in this wilderness. The bellowing notes of thousands of bull-frogs in a neighbouring swamp might lull me to rest, and I looked upon the flocks of blackbirds that were assembling as sure companions in this secluded retreat.

I proceeded up a little stream, to insure the safety of my canoe from any sudden storm, when, as I gladly advanced, a beautiful yawl came unexpectedly in view. Surprised at such a sight in a part of the country then scarcely known, I felt a sudden check in the circulation of my blood. My paddle dropped from my hands, and fearfully indeed, as I picked it up, did I look towards the unknown boat. On reaching it, I saw its sides marked with stains of blood, and looking with anxiety over the gunwale, I perceived to my horror, two human bodies covered with gore. Pirates or hostile Indians I was persuaded had perpetrated the foul deed, and my alarm naturally increased; my heart fluttered, stopped, and heaved with unusual tremors, and I looked towards the setting sun in consternation and despair. How long my reveries lasted I cannot tell; I can only recollect that I was roused from them by the distant groans of one apparently in mortal agony. I felt as if refreshed by the cold perspiration that oozed from every pore, and I reflected that though alone, I was well armed, and might hope for the protection of the Almighty.

Humanity whispered to me that, if not surprised and disabled, I might render assistance to some sufferer, or even be the means of saving a useful life. Buoyed up by this thought, I urged my canoe on shore, and seizing it by the bow, pulled it at one spring high among the grass.

The groans of the unfortunate person fell heavy on my ear, as I cocked and reprimed my gun, and I felt determined to shoot the first that should rise from the grass. As I cautiously proceeded, a hand was raised over the weeds, and waved in the air in the most supplicating manner. I levelled my gun about a foot below it, when the next moment, the head and breast of a man covered with blood were convulsively raised, and a faint hoarse voice asked me for mercy and help! A death-like silence followed his fall to the ground. I surveyed every object around with eyes intent, and ears impressible by the slightest sound, for my situation that moment I thought as critical as any I had ever been in. The croaking of the frogs, and the last blackbirds alighting on their roosts, were the only sounds or sights; and I now proceeded towards the object of my mingled alarm and commiseration.

Alas! the poor being who lay prostrate at my feet, was so weakened by loss of blood, that I had nothing to fear from him. My first impulse was to run back to the water, and having done so, I returned with my cap filled to the brim. I felt at his heart, washed his face and breast, and rubbed his temples with the contents of a phial, which I kept about me as an antidote for the bites of snakes. His features, seamed by the ravages of time, looked frightful and disgusting; but he had been a powerful man, as the breadth of his chest plainly shewed. He groaned in the most appalling manner, as his breath struggled through the mass of blood that seemed to fill his throat. His dress plainly disclosed his occupation:—a large pistol he had thrust into his bosom, a naked cutlass lay near him on the ground, a red silk handkerchief was bound over his projecting brows, and over a pair of loose trousers he wore fisherman's boots. He was, in short, a pirate.

My exertions were not in vain, for as I continued to bathe his temples, he revived, his pulse resumed some strength, and I began to hope that he might perhaps survive the deep wounds he had received. Darkness, deep darkness, now enveloped us. I spoke of making a fire. "Oh! for mercy's sake," he exclaimed, "don't." Knowing, however, that under existing circumstances, it was expedient for me to do so, I left him, went to his boat, and brought the rudder, the benches, and the oars, which with my hatchet I soon splintered. I then struck a light, and presently stood in the glare of a blazing fire. The pirate seemed struggling between terror and gratitude for my assistance; he desired me several times in half English and Spanish to put out the flames, but after I had given him a draught of strong spirits, he at length became more composed. I tried to staunch the blood that flowed from the deep gashes in his shoulders and side. I expressed my regret that I had no food about me, but when I spoke of eating he sullenly waved his head.

My situation was one of the most extraordinary that I have ever been placed in. I naturally turned my talk towards religious subjects, but, alas, the dying man hardly believed in the existence of God. "Friend," said he, "for friend you seem to be, I have never studied the ways of Him of whom you talk. I am an outlaw, perhaps you will say a wretch—I have been for many years a Pirate. The instructions of my parents were of no avail to me, for I have always believed that I was born to be a most cruel man. I now lie here, about to die in the weeds, because I long ago refused to listen to their many admonitions. Do not shudder when I tell you—these now useless hands murdered the mother whom they had embraced. I feel that I have deserved the pangs of the wretched death that hovers over me; and I am thankful that one of my kind will alone witness my last gaspings."

A fond but feeble hope that I might save his life, and perhaps assist in procuring his pardon, induced me to speak to him on the subject. "It is all in vain, friend—I have no objection to die—I am glad that the villains who wounded me were not my conquerors—I want no pardon from *any one*—Give me some water, and let me die alone.

With the hope that I might learn from his conversation

something that might lead to the capture of his guilty associates, I returned from the creek with another capful of water, nearly the whole of which I managed to introduce into his parched mouth, and begged him, for the sake of his future peace, to disclose his history to me. "It is impossible," said he, "there will not be time; the beatings of my heart tell me so. Long before day, these sinewy limbs will be motionless. Nay, there will hardly be a drop of blood in my body; and that blood will only serve to make the grass grow. My wounds are mortal, and I must and will die without what you call confession."

The moon rose in the east. The majesty of her placid beauty impressed me with reverence. I pointed towards her, and asked the Pirate if he could not recognise God's features there. "Friend, I see what you are driving at," was his answer,—"you, like the rest of our enemies, feel the desire of murdering us all.— Well—be it so—to die is after all nothing more than a jest; and were it not for the pain, no one, in my opinion, need care a jot about it. But, as you really have befriended me, I will tell you all that is proper."

Hoping his mind might take a useful turn, I again bathed his temples and washed his lips with spirits. His sunk eyes seemed to dart fire at mine—a heavy and deep sigh swelled his chest and struggled through his blood-choked throat, and he asked me to raise him for a little. I did so, when he addressed me somewhat as follows, for, as I have told you, his speech was a mixture of Spanish, French and English, forming a jargon, the like of which I had never heard before, and which I am utterly unable to imitate. However I shall give you the substance of his declaration.

"First tell me, how many bodies you found in the boat, and what sort of dresses they had on." I mentioned their number, and described their apparel. "That's right," said he, "they are the bodies of the scoundrels who followed me in that infernal Yankee barge. Both rascals they were, for when they found the water too shallow for their craft, they took to it and waded after me. All my companions had been shot, and to lighten my own boat I flung them overboard, but as I lost time in this, the two ruffians caught hold of my gun wale, and struck on my head and body in such a manner, that after I had disabled and killed them both in the boat, I was scarce able to move. The other villains carried off our schooner and one of our boats, and perhaps ere now have hung all my companions whom they did not kill at the time. I have commanded my beautiful vessel many years, captured many ships, and sent many rascals to the devil. I always hated the Yankees, and only regret that I have not killed more of them.—I sailed from Matanzas.—I have often been in concert with others. I have money without counting, but it is buried where it will never be found, and it would be useless to tell you of it." His throat filled with blood, his voice failed, the cold hand of death was laid on his brow, feebly and hurriedly he muttered, "I am a dying man, farewell."

Alas! It is painful to see death in any shape; in this it was horrible, for there was no hope. The rattling of his throat announced the moment of dissolution, and already did the body fall on my arms with a weight that was insupportable. I laid him on the ground. A mass of dark blood poured from his mouth; then came a frightful groan, the last breathing of that foul spirit; and what now lay at my feet in the wild desert?—a mangled mass of clay!

The remainder of that night was passed in no enviable mood; but my feelings cannot be described. At dawn I dug a hole with the paddle of my canoe, rolled the body into it, and covered it. On reaching the boat I found several buzzards feeding on the bodies, which I in vain attempted to drag to the shore. I therefore covered them with mud and weeds, and launching my canoe, paddled from the cove with a secret joy for my escape, overshadowed with the gloom of mingled dread and abhorrence.

Elizabeth Bishop

A Norther—Key West

Like little blackbirds in the street
the little Negroes lift their feet,
    the sidewalks freeze;

the tin roofs all look frozen, too,
the flowers blackened, and how blue
    the big palm trees!

While steadily the norther churns
the pale-green sea until it turns
    to lime milk sherbet,

and careful mother Mizpah Oates
brings out the ancient winter coats
    for Hannibal and Herbert,

once worn by an immense white child.
She drives her gentle children wild
    by her obtuseness.

Hannibal weeps. Oh, tragedy!
The waist hangs almost to his knee!
    Oh, worldliness!

The Bight
[On my Birthday]

At low tide like this how sheer the water is.
White, crumbling ribs of marl protrude and glare
and the boats are dry, the pilings dry as matches.
Absorbing, rather than being absorbed,
the water in the bight doesn't wet anything,
the color of the gas flame turned as low as possible.
One can smell it turning to gas; if one were Baudelaire
one could probably hear it turning to marimba music.
The little ocher dredge at work off the end of the dock
already plays the dry perfectly off-beat claves.
The birds are outsize. Pelicans crash
into this peculiar gas unnecessarily hard,
it seems to me, like pickaxes,
rarely coming up with anything to show for it,
and going off with humorous elbowings.
Black-and-white man-of-war birds soar
on impalpable drafts
and open their tails like scissors on the curves
or tense them like wishbones, till they tremble.
The frowsy sponge boats keep coming in
with the obliging air of retrievers,
bristling with jackstraw gaffs and hooks
and decorated with bobbles of sponges.
There is a fence of chicken wire along the dock
where, glinting like little plowshares,
the blue-gray shark tails are hung up to dry
for the Chinese-restaurant trade.
Some of the little white boats are still piled up
against each other, or lie on their sides, stove in,
and not yet salvaged, if they ever will be, from the last bad storm,
like torn-open, unanswered letters.

The bight is littered with old correspondences.
Click. Click. Goes the dredge,
and brings up a dripping jawful of marl.
All the untidy activity continues,
awful but cheerful.

John Malcolm Brinnin

Letter from Key West
For Elizabeth Bishop

Elizabeth my dear,
                    I found your house,
just as you said I would, by turning right
where "weedy" Southard Street falls off to grass
(one pensive little heron—legs as thin
as wire—watched me, but did not take flight)
beside the old building with the cup cake domes.
Even, I think, without your careful postings,
the place would have quivered, as if in quotation marks—
in much the same way, say, that one clean line
of yours will, on a page, dwell by itself,
simple, pretty and mysterious.

"Arrived at the site," as guidebooks say, "we pause
amidst a picturesque profusion of. . ."
Nothing of the sort. It's all there—open.
The house, four-square and delicate, sits snug—
a small white-shuttered castle in a keep
almost, yet not quite, filling up a space
left to a sprawl of cacti and rock roses.
That pyramid roof. Remember how the sun
shoots from its eaves like a Masonic eye?
(*My* fancy, dear—too gaudy to be yours.)
There's a sign tacked onto one of the slim pillars
—a smutch of black lopsided lettered crayon—
declaring *Alloe for Sale*, but otherwise
you might have closed your front door yesterday.

(What's this bereaved enchantment makes a man
pilgrim to places he has never left?
I see you circa 1936,
seated on that same white second step
in a straw hat, your chin on your right hand,
hardly smiling, yet, for all the grain
in that dim photograph, clearly at home.)

I have some doubts: that diamond on the gate,
upright—one of those you see on playing cards—
is it some unexplained motif of yours?
The Gothic frill along the overhang—
carpenter Gothic, I mean. Did that come later?
The green cast-iron railing by the stairs?
Everything else bespeaks you: purity
of line, strict measure, grace in miniature.
(The angle of the shutters, I might add,
allows for looking out but not—ha ha—
unless one stands there tip-toe, looking in.)
TOM MESA is the name on the mailbox.
(A Cuban cowboy? A strayed Navajo?)
Whatever he is, he's immaculate,
if not so hot on draughtsmanship, or spelling.

I don't see why you'd leave it, all in all,
unless—but who am I to speculate?—
even so modest a shape of painted wood
will jail the same spirit it might signify?
"Think of the long trip home," I hear you saying.
"Should we have stayed at home and thought of here?"
"Here" meaning, I see, here, there, anywhere.
I'm glad you turned my steps your way.
                                        Love,
                                            John

P.S. I've just re-read your letter. (Gulp.)
The house *you* lived in is the one next *door*.
It's now invisible behind big trees,
except for one high window, facing north.

Philip Caputo

The Ahab Complex

Like the Antarctic and the Amazon Basin, the Gulf
Stream is one of the last places on earth where nature holds
dominion and man is a mere intruder. Though remote stretches of it
flow through the open seas or past uninhabited coast, other parts
of it can be reached without mounting a major expedition funded by
the National Geographic Society. A short boat ride from the
gimcrack highrises of Miami will put you on it; it rushes just
outside the trash-flecked green of Havana Harbor, within sight
of the Mafia-built hotels where Meyer Lansky used to count his
chips, and where, now, starch-fattened Russians dance clumsily to
conga drums and the bray of Latin brass. Across the Florida Straits
from Havana, the Stream courses within 20 miles of Key West,
the island city that's as much a refuge for smugglers, gunrunners
and redneck shrimpers as it is for young men who bump bottoms in
discos where slide projectors flash pictures of unnatural acts on the
walls.

Despite its proximity to these, and other, centers of
civilization, the Stream is much safer from conquest and
exploitation than either Antarctica or the Amazon. Man cannot
build highways or time-share condominiums on it; he can't dam it,
sink offshore rigs into it, mine it, fence it, subdivide it, my God, its
flow is so powerful that he can't even properly pollute it. The only
imprints he makes on it are evanescent: the wakes that froth and
roll, then vanish in the mighty ocean current Hemingway called

"the great blue river".

What a place it is, so long that its waters cool the Yucatan Peninsula and warm the harbors of Norway; so strong that its volume of flow in the Florida Straits, only a small part of the Stream, is equal to that of one thousand Mississippi Rivers; so mysterious that oceanographers have yet to chart its maze of cross-currents and under-currents, eddies and meanders.

And it is as much a home to wild giants as the Serengeti: mako and great white sharks, broadbill sword-fish, blue marlin and bluefin tuna weighing half a ton breed and hunt in the Stream. It is also a highway for these roving monsters, which follow its course for enormous distances: tuna and swordfish travel it from New England to the Bahamas; marlin that mated in its Caribbean reaches have swum with it across the Atlantic and turned up off the coast of West Africa. None of these great fish, like, say, the great cats, can be oggled and photographed in parks and preserves. Anyone who wishes to see them must fish for them in the Stream, either commercially or for sport. The latter is by far preferable; although these species are caught on primitive handlines in some parts of the world—in Cuba, for instance, men still hook and fight giant marlin as Santiago did in *The Old Man and the Sea*—most modern commercial fishing is an industrial enterprise that gives the fish little chance to escape and no chance to demonstrate its power.

On the other hand, big-game fishing with sporting tackle not only gives a person a chance to see these huge brutes, it offers the sportsman or woman the experience of feeling the awesome strength of a large predator without suffering serious injury or death in the process. He or she will suffer from sore muscles, exhaustion, dehydration, dizziness, blistered fingers, swollen hands, perhaps a few minor cuts and bruises, and, in some instances, a torn ligament or two; but I've never heard of an angler being wounded or killed by a marlin or giant tuna. Big marlin and swordfish have rammed, and sometimes sunk, fishing boats with their bills; mako sharks have lunged over gunwales and nearly torn small craft to pieces; however, these have been freak incidents. Thus, danger-junkies, like some of the weirdos I knew in Vietnam, would do better to find their amusement hunting polar bears with a .22. Of course, going far off-shore in a small fishing vessel can be very charming for those who are charmed by risk. Sometimes, as when a nor'wester packing 50-knot winds blows up out of nowhere, hurling mountainous seas at your boat, the experience can be so damned charming that you'd do anything not to be charmed anymore. Enough. Big game fishing is not an inherently dangerous sport.

It is, like other forms of angling, fragmented into various cults, cliques and castes. Within its circle is a smaller circle of billfishermen—those who pursue sailfish, swordfish, and the four species of marlins—and within that a still smaller circle of anglers who hunt the giant blue marlin to the exclusion of all other fish. Given the abundance of gamefish—there are around fifty species—this sort of purism may seem foolish, perhaps a little crazy. Bill Robinson, formerly a first mate on a Key West charterboat, calls it "an expensive form of mental illness." To refine Robinson's analysis, marlin fishermen suffer from a rare psychological disorder that I call the Ahab Complex—an obsession to pursue and conquer a monster of the depths regardless of the consequences to one's bank account, career and family life.

To be sure, a number of fish in the Gulf Stream qualify as monsters. Each of them possesses one or two qualities attractive to anglers, but in none of them is found the fusion of power, speed, endurance, size, agility and an immeasurable virtue, character, that is found in the blue marlin. Of the four species of marlin, the Atlantic-Pacific blue, the Pacific black, the striped and the white, the first two are by far the largest. There is some debate as to which, the blue or the black, is bigger; a black weighing over 2,200 pounds was harpooned off Australia, but commercial fishermen have reported catching Pacific blues of over 2,500 pounds. The Atlantic blues of the Gulf Stream are smaller, though fish of half a ton are not unheard of. The current world's record on rod and reel is 1,282 pounds, and specimens of 1,500 pounds have been caught commercially. Their massiveness alone makes them awesome fish, but they are also among the fastest creatures in the sea, capable of sustained runs of over 35 miles an hour and short bursts of 60. This feat is nothing short of phenomenal: the resistance of water is seventy times that of air. The combination of size and speed makes the marlin one of the lords of the open ocean. With its sword-like bill, it can easily kill large prey (marlin have been found with 150-pound tuna in their stomachs), or defend itself against almost anything that swims. The swift mako shark is its only natural enemy, but even the mako generally cannot catch a healthy marlin. If it does, it's in for a fight: commercial fishermen in the Bahamas have reported witnessing combats between the two fish. The makos lost every time. That makes sense, because marlin bills strike with tremendous impact. They have pierced 22 inches of solid wood. A bill retrieved from a floating ball of raw rubber revealed a depth penetration of 13 inches; there is no bullet on earth capable of penetrating submerged rubber that far.

When it comes to endurance, swordfish and giant tuna may

have the marlin beat, but not by much. That also makes sense, for the marlin is the embodiment of the principle that only the fit survive. First of all, no creature on earth that starts off so small—in the larval stage they are one inch long—grows so big. Secondly, out of every million eggs laid by a female, only ten reach maturity, so, when an angler hooks one that's lasted long enough to tip the scales at 500 pounds, he has definitely not tied into a creature that's made of sugar candy. A short fight with one will last about an hour; two or three is more likely. The longest on record, with a huge black off Australia's Great Barrier Reef, went on for thirty hours. (The fish threw the hook and the angler was hospitalized.)

The marlin's agility is another of its prized attributes. Its spectacular aerial displays—you have to imagine an animal bigger than a grizzly and capable of more mid-air twists and turns than an acrobat—mesmerize anglers. Sportsmen value nobility in a fight, and fish that jump, for some reason, are considered more "noble" than those that don't. Given their size and royal coloration—dark blue, purple and silver—blue marlin are downright majestic when they lunge out of the water.

All four species are rare, which, of course, makes them much sought after. The blue is the rarest of all, not in terms of numbers (no one can make even a wild guess as to how many there are) but in terms of concentration. Blacks, stripers and whites tend to travel in schools. The blue is a loner, wandering the oceans in male-female pairs, occasionally in "wolfpacks" of four fish. In the Atlantic, they're scattered from the northernmost edges of the Stream to as far south as Cape Horn; and because little is known of their habits and migratory patterns, the angler who goes in quest of them must be willing to cover vast stretches of water and put in anywhere from 12 to 72 hours of fishing time just to hook one. If he manages to, he has, on an average, only two chances in five of catching it. Blues are as unpredictable as they're elusive. They have the strength and stamina of blacks, the speed and nimbleness of stripers and whites. In a fight they employ a wide repertoire of combative skills: they streak away from the boat with stunning acceleration, then turn on a dime and come at the boat, greyhounding as they come; they jump out of the water ten or twelve times in a row, corkscrewing in mid-air to wrap the leader around their bills or tails; they beat the waves to a froth with their heads, "walk" on their tails, sound 100 fathoms, and, sounding, sulk in the depths, loggy as sharks or bulldog—shake their heads from side to side to throw the hook. Sometimes, in their frenzy, they ram their bills through the hull. And sometimes, rarely, but it has happened, they come to the boat, apparently beaten; then, as the mate takes hold of the wire leader, they sense their peril, and making a valedictory leap for freedom, impale the mate or cause the wire to snap like a steel whip that amputates his ear, fingers or hand.

Even when gaffed, the fish can behave erratically. One summer off Key West, an angler aboard Captain Steve Magee's charterboat hooked a blue so large that Magee is reluctant to estimate its size. The fish was alongside an hour and forty-five minutes later. As the mate, Robinson, held onto the leader, literally as a man holds a rope in a tug-of-war, Magee struck the huge marlin with a flying gaff. The fish roared under the boat, the great sickle-shaped tail raising a wall of water that washed over the deck, knocking off Magee's and Robinson's hats and sunglasses. The fish broke loose. Robinson hauled up the empty gaffhead. It was made of quarter-inch steel and it had been opened up like a coathanger.

Having discussed the fish, I'll now turn to a somewhat less impressive creature, the fishermen. I use the masculine because big-game angling is a largely masculine sport. I don't mean masculine in the sense of *machismo*, although the sport is associated with he-men celebrities like Ernest Hemingway and Lee Marvin. Despite the size and ferocity of the quarry and the heftiness of the tackle (some big-game rigs weigh 22 pounds), you don't have to be a middle linebacker or drink kerosene as an apertif to catch the monsters. Yes, Lee Marvin has caught plenty of big fish; so did Bing Crosby. So have a lot of women, for the sport requires skill, stamina and determination, not brute strength. Female anglers have boated marlin of over 1,000 pounds. In the Florida Keys, the local record of 527 pounds was established by a 5-foot, 2-inch, 100 pound woman who fought the fish for three hours. The reason why this sort of fishing is dominated by men lies not in the masculine body but within the masculine mind.

"Women can do as good a job catching marlin as men," said charter captain Frank Kerwin. "But women can take it or leave it. They'd rather catch something for dinner. Let a man just hook one and he goes crazy. He doesn't want to fish for anything else."

Norman Wood is a man who hooked one and went crazy. He does not fit the tough-guy stereotype of the big-game angler, and hasn't lost his mental faculties. An amiable, easy-going Georgian who is now a real estate developer in the Florida Keys, Wood is quite sane except when he's twenty miles out in the Gulf Stream aboard his fishing boat, the *Petticoat III*. That is when the obsession takes over. On a recent voyage, the *Petticoat* ran into a school of dolphin, a prized gamefish that is also excellent table fare. Wood's wife, Shirley, began reeling them in for dinner. The

skipper fumed impatiently on the flying bridge, then called to the
cockpit below:

"That's enough. Let's get back to fishing."

Mrs. Wood replied that she was fishing.

"Dolphin aren't fish," Wood shot back. "Marlin are fish."

It began several years ago, when he caught his first blue.

"I'd been a light-tackle angler up till then. First I thought
bonefishing was the ultimate. Then tarpon fishing," he said. "But
that marlin weighed 365 pounds, and when I saw it make twelve
or fourteen leaps out of the water, I didn't want to fish for
anything else."

And he hasn't. Since then, Wood has caught something
like 67 blue marlin (all but a few of which were released).

It would be an exaggeration to say that all men get excited
about the sport. There are plenty of male sportsmen who find it
intolerable, mostly because the fish are hunted by trolling. Artist
Russell Chatham, an expert fly-fisherman, once described trolling
as the next most boring thing to an "unsuccessful bridge club
luncheon." He went on to say that, when a fish is finally hooked
"and you are faced with the appalling prospect of an hour in the
fighting chair, you simply would rather have a beer."

To an extent, Chatham exaggerates in the opposite
direction. Trolling—trailing baits or lures behind a slow-moving
boat—needn't be dull; nonetheless, it is probably the least
interesting method of angling next to still-fishing with a worm.
"The peasant...with patient angle trolls the finny deep," said
Oliver Goldsmith; and the monotony of it often pummels the
sharpest mind into a peasant-like stupor. Which is not to say that
marlin fishermen are peasants. No peasant I know of could afford
the outlay. The sport is no longer reserved for men who could
comfortably play high-stakes poker with the Emir of Kuwait, but
it does require a considerable supply of ready cash as well as the
time freedom that money buys.

What kind of men are willing to pay large sums and
endure hours of tedium simply to catch a big fish? Are they trying
to compensate for some real or imagined inadequacy? You bet. But
let's get one thing straight: I don't mean sexual inadequacy. No
cocktail-party Freudianism, all right? No baloney about rods
being phallic symbols and the overcoming of large fish a surrogate
for sexual conquest for men. None of that nonsense, OK? For those
of you who insist on believing that something dark and weird is
going on here, I'll toss out a tidbit: all giant marlin, those over 300
pounds, are females. Yes, they are ladies. While you ponder the
implications of that fact, I'll get on with my point. The
inadequacy of which I speak is the inadequacy, the limitations

imposed on men by their human natures. The human male is a predator, but he's a puny one compared to the competition. The blue marlin is to the Gulf Stream what the lion is to the Serengeti: it is the living symbol of its world, the beauty, might and mystery of the Stream made flesh. Like the lion, it is a creature that seizes the masculine imagination and arouses in the masculine heart an urge to pursue and capture because it has been endowed by nature far more generously than men have been, with those virtues that men prize. Catching one of these great fish is, furthermore, a team effort. It is common to say that the angler caught the fish, but in fact he caught it with the assistance of a skilled captain and mate. The camaraderie, the union of several men in a single quest, is probably some sort of throwback to those primitive hunting bands from which masculine society is thought to have evolved. In that sense, marlin fishermen are diametric opposites of fly fishermen. Fly fishing is a solitary sport that calls for a contemplative, cerebral nature; for its object is to outwit a fish. Marlin do not need to be outwitted because intelligence and wariness are not among their attributes. (When you weigh half a ton and are armed with a sword capable of piercing two feet of solid wood, you don't need to be smart or careful.) The satisfaction is in outlasting or outdoing the fish. The pleasures of the sport are athletic as opposed to intellectual in nature. Marlin fishermen relish an engagement that calls forth all of the physical resources, and the elation, the somehow pleasant pain, the cleansing exhaustion that come after a hard-fought battle.

The Hemingway blue marlin tournament sponsored by the Cuban government in 1978 was my big-game initiation. I have mixed feelings about fishing tournaments, which turn a non-competitive activity into competitive blood sport; but signing up for the 1978 tourney was the only way an American could fish the waters Hemingway had made legendary. Along with two fishing partners, Jack London and Dave Finkelstein, a 6-foot, 7-inch captain named Garrett Anger, and a 5-foot, 6-inch mate, Dick Stammers, I made the crossing in the *Candide II*, a much-abused 31-foot Bertram that London, Finkelstein and I had picked up for $19,000.

I had become reasonably competent at most forms of light-tackle angling, which I'd found to be what sportfishing is supposed to be: fun. Marlin fishing, on the other hand, was proving an awful disappointment. Trolling seemed an activity you could train for by sitting in front of a TV and watching test patterns all day. In three days of it, we'd hooked one fish, a docile, middling-sized male that came to the boat in five minutes, then sounded and cut the line on the running gear. No epic battle. No spectacular leaps. Nothing. The difference between expectation and performance was like winding up in bed with a Hollywood sex symbol and discovering that she's a bad lover.

On the fourth day, London and Finkelstein were so fed up that they decided to stay ashore and see something of Castro's Havana. Already showing symptoms of the Ahab Complex, I went out with Garrett and Stammers. We prowled the waters off Cojimar, a fishing village several miles east of Havana. There, in 800 fathoms, the Stream met an onshore current, creating an upwell that, a Cuban handliner told us, brought plankton up from the bottom, squid that fed on the plankton, and marlin that fed on the squid. You know, the old food-chain trick. It worked for Hemingway. Fishing out of Cojimar in 1933 Papa caught the blue marlin that still stood as the Cuban national record on rod and reel: 468 pounds.

By noon, we were cooking in the microwave of a Cuban August. A breeze made the heat bearable. On the other side of the ledger, the breeze was blowing against the Stream, churning the water into a four-foot chop. Gazing astern, I saw, behind the *Candide's* wake, a shadow like the shadow of an immense, torpedo-shaped bird, a shadow rising from the purple-blue of 800 fathoms. Stammers, sitting on the port side gunwale, jumped to his feet.

"Marlin!"

The port outrigger line snapped from the pin with a crack like that of a starter's pistol, the rod bending and the line ratcheting off the reel. Then the rod straightened. The mangled carcass of the bonito we'd been trolling flopped in the seas perhaps a hundred yards behind us.

"It's off," Stammers mourned, cranking in the line to put on a fresh bait.

"On the right!" Garrett bellowed from the bridge. "It's a horse! On the right!"

The monstrous shadow reappeared behind the mackerel trolling on the starboard outrigger. The marlin, as marlin often do when enraged or in a feeding frenzy, "lit up". The fish turned a brilliant, electric blue from gill to tail; it looked as if a gigantic police mars light had flashed in the water. A split-second later, the mackerel vanished in a furious boil, and the line was disappearing at an alarming rate. At full throttle, 25 knots, the *Candide* could not have pulled it off the reel any faster. Inexperienced, I tried to pull the rod from the holder without lightening the drag. It was like trying to yank a stop sign out of the ground; the forces of the drag, the boat moving in one direction, and the fish in the other, had jammed it into the holder.

"Back off the drag!" Garrett yelled from the bridge. He gunned the boat forward to take slack out of the line. "Back it of!"

But when you see perhaps 200 yards of 80 pound test line, pulled against a drag resistance of 25 pounds, evaporate in seconds, you're certain that the reel will be stripped if you lighten the drag an ounce.

Somehow I wrestled the rod free, and was shocked, even a little frightened, as the powerful fish jerked me across the deck to the transom, my arms and shoulders feeling as if I'd grabbed hold of a ski rope attached to a Chris Craft. Locking my knees under the gunwale, leaning far back, I saved the tackle, and maybe myself from going overboard.

"BACK THE GODDAMNED DRAG!"

I managed to, then maneuvered myself into the fighting chair, the rod butt into the gimbal. Raising the rod tip, I struck the fish hard three or four times, the speed of the boat helping me set the hook deep into the marlin's bony mouth. Still the line was peeling off with a sound like...well you can duplicate the sound by expelling a deep breath through clenched teeth as hard as you can, flicking your tongue behind your teeth at the same time. I did not see the fish, only the line going out a shallow angle: 300 yards, 350, 400, 450. Stammers got me into the shoulder harness, which took the strain off my arms and allowed me to fight the fish with my back and legs, my feet braced against the chair's footrest. Keeping the rod tip high, I tried to slow the marlin, and might as well have tried, with rod and reel, to slow a 1,000-cc Harley-Davidson.

"You settled down yet?" Garrett called from the bridge. "You gonna listen to your skipper? I should have been backing down on this fish yesterday. It's halfway back to Key West by now."

Backing down—pursuing a running fish stern first—is a maneuver performed by a captain to prevent a reel from being stripped while at the same time avoiding the dangerous bellies that form in a line when chasing the fish head on. This tactic also spares the angler the hideous job of retrieving several yards of line on his own power. This marlin was running against the seas, which meant we had to back into them. What seemed like a ton of water crashed over the transom as soon as Garrett threw the clutches into reverse. Through the blur of salt spray, I saw the marlin's head come up, a gargantuan head, with a bill that resembled a cavalry lance, beating the waves into a froth.

Light-tackle fishing had been fun, but fighting the marlin was shocking, scary, surreal. Garrett and Stammers were talking to me like cornermen to a fighter. Reel, reel, reel. Rod tip's too low. Raise it. That's it. Level wind, watch the line, damnit, it's piling up. That's it. You've got slack. Take up the slack when it's trying to throw the hook. Reel, reel, reel. All the while, the fish's head was thrashing the water a long way off, the cockpit awash, the engines whining at full astern, and I, pouring sweat, guided the line onto the reel with my left hand, cranking with my right until I was winded as a sprinter at the end of a race.

I'd retrieved all but 100 yards of line when the fish made its first sound, a shallow one. Rod tip low, I thumbed the reel spool, then raised the rod, the line within a few pounds of breaking strain. To catch a marlin, or any big gamefish, you must break its will in much the same way a horseman breaks the will of a wild stallion. It's done by putting maximum pressure on the line, a procedure which eventually convinces the fish to come to the boat. The big blue was a long way from being convinced. It didn't budge, it held down, wing-like pectoral fins outspread, creating incredible resistance. Reel, thumb the spool, raise the rod. Muscles strained, tendons pulled. Try again. Thumb the spool so you don't pull drag and lose line. Now lift. Pressure, pressure. Try to turn its head. Can't. Feels like I'm hooked to a submarine.

I was leaning well back in the chair, throwing my weight against the weight of the fish, the harness straps pulled taut, rod and line quivering from the tension, when the rod whipped to one side, cracking my wrist against the chair's armrest. Then to the other side. Then back again. Whap, whap, whap. The marlin was bulldogging, and the power in those swipes of its head was intimidating. Get control of this fish. It isn't just beating you, it's beating you up.

The line hissed off the reel again, its angle decreasing sharply.

"Coming up," Garrett shouted. "Take up the slack when it jumps."

The fish was not far astern when it broke water. It came out like a plane lifting off a runway, the blue-black javelin of its bill, the head with one big saucer-shaped eye that seemed to be examining us, the massive cobalt shoulders topped by a stubby, pointed dorsal fin, the pectoral fins swept back against a silver belly shining like a mirror in the sun, then the rest of its body, all 12-odd feet of it, water streaming from flanks as royal blue as the Stream and barred by stripes glowing a neon lavender. It came out with its curved tail scything the air, its body shuddering not with the quick desperate spasms of a tarpon or sailfish but with a slow, stately grace, shuddering and arching into a crescent. The fish dived bill first, sliding into the seas as smoothly as a high diver, its tail vanishing in a plume of spray. It was up again in an instant. This time it jumped straight out of the mystery of the Stream, a missile rather than a plane, a blue, purple-striped missile rocketing up until the tips of its tail-fin were ten feet above the surface. It seemed to hang in midair for a moment, the powerful, sinuous twists of its body as lovely as anything I'd ever seen; then it flung itself over on its side, the splash of its impact like the burst of a six-inch shell.

"Jee-sus," said Garrett. "It'll go six hundred."

The fish jumped three more times, and there was in each soaring leap a union of power and grace that arrested my heart and brought a tightness to my throat. For the next 15 minutes the marlin leaped and made long runs that made the reel hot as an iron; it greyhounded across the ocean in one direction, turned, and went off in the other; it pounded the seas with its head to dislodge the hook; it tailwalked, its tail whipping up a whirling mist like a waterspout before it flung itself on its side to run again. Such an explosion of energy would have exhausted any ordinary fish; and I understood why the ancient Greeks believed billfish were warrior-gods of the sea, the swordsmen of Achilles who had been transformed into fish after they'd drowned themselves in grief over their hero's death.

At the end of an hour, I felt as if I had played four quarters of football, but the marlin showed no signs of tiring. Garrett was backing down hard when the impeller on the starboard engine's raw water pump froze, causing the engine to overheat. He had to shut it down, and, on one engine, pursue the fish head on. The line bellied dangerously. I reeled until it came tight again. The fish, which seemed to sense we were crippled, sounded. I tightened the drag as much as I dared, and rising off the seat, threw all my 165 pounds against the marlin. It did not slow for a second, running line down as fast as it had run it out, the reel so hot that Stammers had to pour fresh water on it to keep the drag washer from scorching. A third of the line was gone by the time the fish stopped, about 100 fathoms below. That is when the most honest phase of the fight began: honest because, when a marlin sounds, the angler cannot rely on a boat to help him retrieve the line he's lost. On his own power, he must fight the fish for it, sometimes an inch or two at a time.

The marlin and I fell into a gruelling contest. I would pump it toward the surface until the 100-foot marker (a strand of dental floss wrapped around the line) appeared. Then, sensing the boat, the fish would bulldog, extend its pectorals, and hold so fast I felt I was snagged on a coral head. Then, with contemptuous ease, the marlin would sound once more. All I could do was watch the line slant ever downward into the fiery blue, down through the leaning pillars of sunlight and sparkling blooms of plankton.

I think it was on the fish's third sounding that I felt a sense of utter defeat. I was fairly strong and well-conditioned, but it was demoralizing to see the fish stripping line from me as though I were a child. Also, it was appalling to think that I would have to fight for every inch once again. The marlin began to assume mythic proportions in my mind; maybe the ancients were right. The bloody fish was a god. Deity or no, I was convinced it could not be beaten, at least not by me. I guess the only thing that stopped me from handing the rod to Stammers was the fear of disgrace.

I was sitting in my customary position, bent into a question mark, the sun working me over with the zeal of a Chicago cop clubbing a radical, when Stammers said:

"Two hours."

I was aware only of the rod, the taut line, the solid, immovable weight below, and a numbness in my back. Closing my eyes, which burned from sweat and crusted salt, I imagined how the great fish looked, long and streamlined as it held in the current. I think I loved it then, loved it for its might and stubborn valor, and regretted my own lack of nobility, my vanity. That fish was a record-breaker, and after all I'd been through, I wanted it. Wanted it more than anything. Silently I asked forgiveness for what I was going to do. I'm sorry. I can't help it. If I catch another, I'll release it. And the one after that. And the next, but not this one. I want this one.

Thumbing the spool and lifting again, I felt an odd lightness, which for a very long, sickening second, I mistook for a pulled hook. When the line came tight, I realized I'd turned the marlin's head. Lifting, I turned it again and the piety I'd felt a moment before was overcome by a triumphant, savage glee. (And I wonder if that excitement of dominating the indomitable is one of the darker attractions of the sport.) Instead of inches, I gained yards at a time. I wound the marker onto the reel. Stammers put on the gloves with which he could wire the fish. The double line popped to the surface and went onto the reel, and then the fish was on the surface, lying exhausted on its side, and it looked as though it went on forever.

Garrett, bounding down from the bridge, unlimbered one of our two flying gaffs. Stammers got a wrap on the wire. In advance I decided to be calm and sportsmanlike when they screwed up and lost the fish. Garrett hit the fish hard and high up. Though it had seemed spent, the marlin smacked the hull with its tail and dived under the boat, thrashing with its last strength. Garrett hauled it up by the gaff rope, and Stammers struck with the second gaff. The great fish, bleeding, rolled once and again, the blood green in the water, rolled a third time and died. We tail-roped it and struggled for fifteen minutes to winch it aboard. I slumped in the chair, staring dumbly at its length, two feet longer than the cockpit deck, the massiveness of its blue shoulders, fading to slate, the stripes whose glow was dimming. I was sore from my neck to my ankles, my wrists bruised, hands swollen and blistered, but I could have flown.

On one engine, it took us over two hours to limp back to Barlovento Harbor, where the fish was weighed: 569 pounds. It beat Hemingway's record and won the tournament, and I was thrown in the water by Garrett and Stammers—a ritual always performed when an angler catches his first marlin.

Being a person with some unfortunate insecurities, one who seems to require visible proof of his achievements in the way of framed awards, plaques and trophies, I had the fish mounted and found a wall at the Full Moon Saloon to hang it on. It hangs there now, its grand colors restored by the taxidermist's art, 12 feet, 3 inches of fish suspended above a document certifying that it established a new blue marlin record for Cuba. Yes, folks, irrefutable proof that I am no gee-hawing bass fisherman, but a 24-karat big-game *conquistador*.

Today, five years and some two dozen marlin battles later, I'm a bit conscience stricken, it was all for pride and vanity. At least looney Captain Ahab had the decency to die with Moby Dick. I now prefer to tag and release marlin, boating them only when they're exhausted and the choice is between killing them quickly with a gaff or leaving them to the sharks, an act as unconscionable as leaving a wounded animal in the brush. After all, if the essence of big-game fishing is the contest, then the angler has proved his point when the marlin comes to the boat, beaten. There is no real justification for killing it. It's only fair to point out that these fine ethics of mine haven't been tested. None of the marlin I've caught since that first one has exceeded 250 pounds, so it was easy to let them go. I seriously doubt I would have the saintliness required to release an 800 or 1,000 pound fish. Of course, the surest way to avoid any moral dilemmas is to stop fishing for them, spend my weekends playing golf or watching 22 men bash each other for possession of an oval-shaped ball.

That isn't likely. I haven't become a marlin purist—there are simply too many other types of fishing I love—but I go for the big blues when they make their runs through the Florida Straits in the Spring and the Fall. Yes, it can be extremely monotonous, but one of the pleasures of marlin fishing is not knowing exactly where the fish are or when they'll strike, or the sudden, unexpected appearance of that shadow in the blue water, then the huge shoulders and the dorsal fin cutting a wake, the bill slashing and the captain hollering from the bridge, *"Marlin."*

Another pleasure is simply going far out on the stream, where the land and the lighthouses drop beneath a horizon as straight as a ruler. The great blue river can be tranquil as a trout pond one day; the next it's wild with mounded seas, spray blowing off the crests of the waves like snow off mountain tops. Sometimes the Stream is riotous with life; at other times you swear it's part of the Dead Sea. Always it makes you aware of what is genuine and what is false, what is important and what is trifling. For when you are on it, you know that everything happening in it, from the silent blooms of plankton to vast migrations of fish to the lethal ballets of hunter and prey, was happening long before all your ancestors were born and will be happening long after all your descendants are dead.

John Ciardi

Audit at Key West

You could put silver dollars on my eyes
and say I died of inflation. Strictly speaking
this isn't expense but unexpendibility.

Like being a crooked cop: I was last night
on late TV but woke here unnegotiable.
How am I to sell out when no one's buying?

Somewhere a naked boy without bus fare,
and with nowhere to go, is bending over the bed
of a girl about to inherit her own body.

There are always investment opportunities.
But who breaks even? I might have been born rich
but couldn't afford the taxes. Perry was.

He died with a silver dogtag in his mouth.
In the cleft of his teeth. Everyone, Doc said, has one.
Eddie could spit like a B.B. gun through his.

But I don't want to start over. Suppose I could
spit bullets—what's a target? Last month in Frankford
we took flowers to the graveyard. A hundred names

spoke from their stones but we knew no one in town.
The house had been sold to strangers. The world is divided
into those who managed to buy in time, and their children

who can no longer afford to and must wait
for their parents to die. I'm willing in no hurry.
I have a book to finish. I'll put the contract

in the children's names. If there are royalties—
sometimes there are—at least I'll die a tax cheat
thumbing my clogged skull at the sons of bitches.

I carry a donor's card for what's left over
that could be any good to anyone.
If anything is. I doubt there is much left,

but the eyes aren't bad. Someone might still see something.
I'll leave a picture in them.—There, my Cuban
neighbor's fighting cock posed on the roof ridge,

a bomb of lit red fuses sputtering day.

Tuesday:
Four Hundred Miles

Yesterday at the motel desk in Ocala
I could not remember my zip. Today
I can speak Etruscan. It came back.

It won't be called. It comes. And sometimes
my oath to Caesar, which need not be binding
in Ocala, but break it on the causeway

past Marathon Key and the sea is impassable:
you will be taken back, nailed upside down
to the cross, and be made to remember

sacred Marcia who stole from her parents
to run from honor with you. She died
of bad air from the marshes, but first knew

all the words to all the songs
she took with her. I can't even remember
the tunes, till they start uncalled.

It comes and goes and I stay wary.
I have grown a beard but keep moving
and avoid most public places. Old comrades

can see through hair, and it is death
to be recognized. I did not call
my life to these evasions, nor Marcia

to that fevered bed. It came.
Between Ostia and the Keys. In the new car
whose license number I can never remember.

Alexander Cockburn

Imperial Addictions

The scene on a Key West dock on Sunday, July 21,1985, was as apt an illustration of the relationship between the developed and underdeveloped world as you could find by merely swiveling your head 180 degrees.

Being unloaded in front of me from a boat to an old flat-bed truck were ten silver bars and two paint buckets full of seventeenth century coins, part of the vast hoard uncovered the day before off the Marquesas, thirty-five miles to the southwest. Glancing a couple hundred yards south from these relics of Spanish imperial exploitation of the Americas, I could see the construction equipment of the crews that are diligently upgrading the U.S. Navy's wharves and fueling facilities, backup for a North American imperial armada proceeding against Nicaragua.

On a sunny day I would have been able to see Fat Albert too, thus rounding off the thought-provoking vista of colonial relations then and now, but for once Fat Albert, the spy blimp hovering over the Lower Keys, was concealed by clouds, unable to monitor whatever drug commerce was taking place that day in the Florida straits. The same dock that now carried the silver bars also saw the Mariel refugees land in 1980. Thus, what with the Navy ships and the intercepting craft of the U.S. Coast Guard, the Key West scene united three forms of export that trouble the United States—cocaine, refugees and revolution.

Mel Fisher and his team of treasure seekers had been looking for this silver for sixteen years, and the day before, a young diver from Iowa named Greg Wareham finally came upon the mother lode fifty-four feet down. That Saturday was also the opening of the Florida lobster season, and along with several thousand people up and down the Keys, we'd been diving for them off a boat. Catching Florida "bugs" is a bit like interviewing a nervous politician. You see the horny antennae waving cautiously from a dark hole in a coral head. You dive down, and out comes the bug, declining to make any statement on the record and trying to sidle away down the corridor. The next thing is to get your scoop net behind the bug and then waggle a stick in its face, as if it were a microphone. The bug leaps back toward its hole and, if all goes well, straight into your net, where it thrashes about shouting for lawyers. Its only chance is that the Florida Marine Patrol will deem it to be less than legal size, throw it back and fine you $500 in the bargain.

We'd caught seventeen of them by the time, late in the day, we heard much shouting on the radio about "a reef of silver" sixty feet long; later still, a diver described the silver ingots stacked like logs of wood, with our friends the Florida crayfish living comfortably in the crevices and not pleased to be witnessing the largest treasure find in U.S. history.

On the dock on Sunday afternoon the ingots looked unimpressive, blackened by silver sulfide, like charred logs, seventy pounds in weight and fifteen inches long, crusted with barnacles from 363 years under the waves after the Nuestra Señora de Atocha went down in a hurricane on September 6, 1622. Each ingot has a number or marking on it, and since the Spanish ran the first modern bureaucratic empire, Fisher's people will be able to check from a copy of the ship's original manifest which mine each ingot came from and whether it was the property of Philip IV or a private asset being sent home by a businessman or priest to Castile. Silver bar number 569, for example, was sent by Capt. Duarte Marquez, based in Cartagena, Nueva Granada, to his partners in Spain as their slice of the profit on the 1,400 West African slaves sold in Cartagena that year.

Most of the silver on the Atocha came from the great mine at Potosi, 4,000 feet up on the *altiplano* of what was Peru and is now Bolivia. The Spanish boom town there had 160,000 inhabitants, 14 gambling houses, 120 white prostitutes for the carriage trade. At the mine some 13,000 Indians, forced laborers, dragged the ore out of shafts as deep as 2,000 feet. At the bottom of the shafts they gasped in the heat, and on the bleak *altiplano*, clad in rags, they trembled in the cold. As a Spanish official named Luis Capoche remarked at the time, "The only relief they have from their labors is to be told that they are dogs, beaten on the pretext of having brought up too little metal, taken too long, or that what they have brought up is earth or that they had stolen some metal." Most of the Indians died fairly rapidly of silicosis. After 1585, when an Englishman invented the amalgamating process of refining silver, they died of mercury poisoning too, adding their corpses to the body count: 150 years after the arrival of Columbus in 1492, the number of Indians in the Americas had dropped from about 70 million to 12 million.

By the time the Atocha set sail from Havana in 1622 the Spanish Empire was in serious decline, freighted with debt, its economy rotted by this same silver from Potosi and the mines near Mexico City, just as oil has distorted and rotted the economies of nations like Mexico today. Spanish economists of the late sixteenth and early seventeenth centuries groaned piteously as they accurately predicted that these constant boosts in the money supply from New Granada and New Spain would unleash a savage price explosion and concomitant inflation. The economy tilted from manufacture to service. The lower classes staggered under an increasing tax burden, and the upper classes frisked in conspicuous consumption as Spain became an entrepôt between the New World and the manufacturing nations to the north. "Spain," one economist lamented, "is the foreigners' Indies; they treat us like Indians." The international bankers of the time, underwriting the imperial deficit, paced the docks of Cadiz, with first lien on whatever treasure survived the winds, the waves and the pirates.

The Atocha loaded up first in Porto Bello, on the northern side of the Panamanian isthmus. The manifest lists among other things thousands of coins from the sale of papal indulgences and fines levied by local courts, along with 21,323 pieces of eight as part of the royal settlement to the heirs of Christopher Columbus. From Porto Bello the ship headed to Cartagena to take on gold mined by the African slaves. When it left Havana, on September 4, it carried 1,032 silver ingots, 255,000 silver coins and 161 pieces of gold (excluding personal contraband), all worth about a million pesos, along with 265 people, many of them grandees, six of them "persons of no consequence," that is, slaves.

But the fleet left too late, for September is the middle of hurricane season in these waters. The winds picked up and the Atocha went down two days later, and there were only five survivors: a seaman, two apprentices, two persons of no consequence and no grandees at all. The King, the heirs of Columbus. The international bankers and the partners of Duarte Marquéz paced the dock of Cadiz in vain.

Now the treasure extracted with such misery in Potosi

will continue its vigorous twentieth-century career as an outcrop of the U.S. tax system. The indefatigable Fisher, who successfully fought off the claims of the Federal government and the State of Florida on the booty, amassed about 700 investors in the treasure hunt, both large and small, who, over the years, have sent in their dollars and taken their writeoffs. As the silver comes up, a great tax shelter starts to go down. Although the market value of the metal in each silver ingot is about $7,000, the historical value of the bar can be much more; still, the value of the hoard is not necessarily anywhere near the $3 billion to $4 billion at first touted by the irrepressible Fisher. An investor can donate his ingot to a museum and take whatever write-off an appraising committee persuades the I.R.S. to stand for. The royal tax men of Philip IV who took the King's 20 percent cut in Potosi yield to the artistry of the U.S. Federal tax code and those who know how to use it.

The flatbed truck trundled the bars and coins off to their new life in another late imperial economy. I looked south toward the Navy base, where a paradigm of the U.S. national security obsession is conveniently on display. Beyond the men and machinery industriously strengthening the wharf for ships headed for Central America looms the remains of Fort Zachary Taylor. It was part of a string of forts planned down the East Coast shortly after the War of 1812. Engineers and building crews toiled for more than fifty years to bring it to completion, and in the hour of its glory, it loomed over Key West, with tremendous cannon pointed in the general direction of Cuba. But what with time overruns, the fort was by then obsolete, and U.S. Army sappers demolished a large part of it at the outbreak of the Spanish-American War. It has just been opened as a state park, representing the most southerly military boondoggle in the continental United States. I was able to tell a recent group of visitors there that they should thank me for the amenity, since my ancestor Adm. Sir George Cockburn was one of the leaders of the British in 1812 and thus it was the Cockburn Threat that prompted the construction of the fort. By way of response, Cullen Chambers, the park ranger there, has proposed that I be ritually tarred and feathered each July 4 as entertainment for the locals.

Above Fort Taylor swoop U.S. Navy jets from the airfield at Boca Chica, a few miles up the road. There is so much hardware flying above southern Florida that plummeting chunks of propellers, engines and assorted military garbage are a recognized hazard for the terrestrials. Nearer at hand, the eye travels past an old white building—a southern White House, in fact, in which Harry Truman lingered and to which John Kennedy repaired at the time of the Bay of Pigs invasion—out to sea, where officials of the Customs Service and the Coast Guard labor mightily to prevent the landing of a commodity much more valuable than the Spanish silver: cocaine.

The Spanish spent much time and effort trying to make sure that their silver got safely in past the pirates and the reefs, whereas U.S. officials struggle to keep the cocaine out. This must be the first time a state has passed up so rich an excise opportunity. The Spanish crown got its tax of a *quinto*, or fifth, of all bullion minted. The U.S. Treasury gets nothing from the cocaine trade, though the employment of all those agents is a jobs program of sorts. As far as the countries servicing the addicted metropolitan centers are concerned, cocaine is surely a better bargain than silver. Silver, in the lust to find it and the rush to extract it, contributed considerably to the deaths of more than 50 million Indians. In the case of cocaine, the relations of production and distribution are a considerable improvement, though not anything we would want to see in actually-existing or utopian socialism.

Back in the metropole, silver didn't do Spain much good in the end, as it addicted and stupefied the economy. With cocaine, it's a mixed story. On the one hand, as Jesse Jackson constantly points out, its effect on ghettos has been bad—like many other forms of commodity circulation under capitalism. On the other hand, the cocaine trade has picked up the slack from trickle-down social spending in the 1960's, the free market's answer to straightforward government handouts. Nothing's perfect. It would probably be better to hook slot machines in every community into a computer bank of the leading economic indicators and adjust the payouts according to the needs of Keynesian stimulus or contraction. The "dignity of labor" crowd wouldn't like it, but it would be a pretty democratic way of coping with the demand side of the economy.

In the interim, the cocaine and marijuana trade has played a valiant countercyclical role in the Reagan years, as anyone making a study of the retail economy of small American towns will speedily discover. Of course, it would be rational for the Feds to legalize cocaine and take its *quinto*, but that would mean dealing with the supplying countries in a rational and constructive way, which, as the vista in Key West makes clear, is not a likely proposition.

Hart Crane

Key West:
An Island Sheaf

The starry floor,
The wat'ry shore,
Is given thee 'til the break of day.
                      -Blake

O Carib Isle!

The tarantula rattling at the lily's foot
Across the feet of the dead, laid in white sand
Near the coral beach — nor zigzag fiddle crabs
Side-stilting from the path (that shift, subvert
And anagrammatize your name) — No, nothing here
Below the palsy that one eucalyptus lifts
In wrinkled shadows — mourns.

                    And yet suppose
I count these nacreous frames of tropic death,
Brutal necklaces of shells around each grave
Squared off so carefully. Then
To the white sand I may speak a name, fertile
Albeit in a stranger tongue. Tree names, flower names
Deliberate, gainsay death's brittle crypt. Meanwhile
Then wind that knots itself in one great death—
Coils and withdraws. So syllables want breath.

But where is the Captain of this doubloon isle
Without a turnstile? Who but catchword crabs
Patrols the dry groins of the underbrush?
What man, or What
Is commissioner of mildew throughout the ambushed senses?
His Carib mathematics web the eyes' baked lenses!

Under the poinciana, of a noon or afternoon
Let fiery blossoms clot the light, render my ghost
Sieved upward, white and black along the air
Until it meets the blue's comedian host.

Let not the pilgrim see himself again
For slow evisceration bound like those huge terrapin
Each daybreak on the wharf, their brine caked eyes;
—Spiked, overturned; such thunder in their strain!
And clenched beaks coughing for the surge again!

Slagged of the hurricane—I, cast within its flow,
Congeal by afternoons here, satin and vacant.
You have given me the shell, Satan,—carbonic amulet
Sere of the sun exploded in the sea.

Key West

Here has my salient faith annealed me.
Out of the valley, past the ample crib
To skies impartial, that do not disown me
Nor claim me, either, by Adam's spine—nor rib.

The oar plash, and the meteorite's white arch
Concur with wrist and bicep. In the moon
That now has sunk I strike a single march
To heaven or hades—to an equally frugal noon.

Because these millions reap a dead conclusion
Need I presume the same fruit of my bone
As draws them towards a doubly mocked confusion
Of apish nightmares into steel-strung stone?

O, steel and stone! But gold was, scarcity before.
And here is water, and a little wind...
There is no breath of friends and no more shore
Where gold has not been sold and conscience tinned.

—And Bees of Paradise

I had come all the way here from the sea,
Yet met the wave again between your arms
Where cliff and citadel—all verily
Dissolved within a sky of beacon forms—

Sea gardens lifted rainbow-wise through eyes
I found.

       Yes, tall, inseparably our days
Pass sunward. We have walked the kindled skies
Inexorable and girded with your praise,

By the dove filled, and bees of Paradise.

Stephen Crane

The Open Boat

I

None of them knew the color of the sky. Their eyes glanced level, and were fastened upon the waves that swept toward them. These waves were the hue of slate, save for the tops, which were of foaming white, and all of the men knew the colors of the sea. The horizon narrowed and widened and dipped and rose, and at all times its edge was jagged with waves that seemed thrust up in points like rocks.

Many a man ought to have a bath-tub larger than the boat which here rode upon the sea. These waves were most wrongfully and barbarously abrupt and tall, and each froth-top was a problem in small-boat navigation.

The cook squatted in the bottom, and looked with both eyes at the six inches of gunwale which separated him from the ocean. His sleeves were rolled over his fat forearms, and the two flaps of his unbuttoned vest dangled as he bent to bail out the boat. Often he said. "Gawd! that was a narrow clip." As he remarked it he invariably gazed eastward over the broken sea.

The oiler, steering with one of the two oars in the boat, sometimes raised himself suddenly to keep clear of water that swirled in over the stern. It was a thin little oar, and it seemed often ready to snap.

The correspondent, pulling at the other oar, watched the waves and wondered why he was there.

The injured captain, lying in the bow, was at this time buried in that profound dejection and indifference which comes, temporarily at least, to even the bravest and most enduring when, willy-nilly, the firm fails, the army loses, the ship goes down. The mind of the master of a vessel is rooted deep in the timbers of her, though he command for a day or a decade; and this captain had on him the stern impression of a scene in the grays of dawn of seven turned faces, and later a stump of a topmast with a white ball on it, that slashed to and fro at the waves, went low and lower, and down. Thereafter there was something strange in his voice. Although steady, it was deep with mourning, and of a quality beyond oration or tears.

"Keep'er a little more south, Billie," said he.

"A little more south, sir," said the oiler in the stern.

A seat in this boat was not unlike a seat upon a bucking bronco, and, by the same token, a bronco is not much smaller. The craft pranced and reared and plunged like an animal. As each wave came, and she rose for it, she seemed like a horse making at a fence outrageously high. The manner of her scramble over these walls of water is a mystic thing, and, moreover, at the top of them were ordinarily these problems in white water, the foam racing down from the summit of each wave, requiring a new leap, and a leap from the air. Then, after scornfully bumping a crest, she would slide and race and splash down a long incline, and arrive bobbing and nodding in front of the next menace.

A singular disadvantage of the sea lies in the fact that, after successfully surmounting one wave, you discover that there is another behind it, just as important and just as nervously anxious to do something effective in the way of swamping boats. In a ten-foot dinghy one can get an idea of the resources of the sea in the line of waves that is not probable to the average experience, which is never at sea in a dinghy. As each slaty wall of water approached, it shut all else from the view of the men in the boat, and it was not difficult to imagine that this particular wave was the final outburst of the ocean, the last effort of the grim water. There was a terrible grace in the move of the waves, and they came in silence, save for the snarling of the crests.

In the wan light the faces of the men must have been gray. Their eyes must have glinted in strange ways as they gazed steadily astern. Viewed from a balcony, the whole thing would, doubtless, have been weirdly picturesque. But the men in the boat had no time to see it, and if they had had leisure, there were other things to occupy their minds. The sun swung steadily up the sky, and they knew it was broad day because the color of the sea changed from slate to emerald-green streaked with amber lights, and the foam was like tumbling snow. The process of the breaking day was unknown to them. They were aware only of this effect upon the color of the waves that rolled toward them.

In disjointed sentences the cook and the correspondent argued as to the difference between a life-saving station and a house of refuge. The cook had said: "There's a house of refuge just north of the Mosquito Inlet Light, and as soon as they see us they'll come off in their boat and pick us up."

"As soon as who see us?" said the correspondent.

"The crew," said the cook.

"Houses of refuge don't have crews," said the correspondent. "As I understand them, they are only places where clothes and grub are stored for the benefit of shipwrecked people. They don't carry crews."

"Oh, yes, they do," said the cook.

"No, they don't," said the correspondent.

"Well, we're not there yet, anyhow," said the oiler in the stern.

"Well," said the cook," perhaps it's not a house of refuge that I'm thinking of as being near Mosquito Inlet Light; perhaps it's a life-saving station."

"We're not there yet." said the oiler in the stern.

II

As the boat bounced from the top of each wave the wind tore through the hair of the hatless men, and as the craft plopped her stern down again the spray slashed past them. The crest of each of these waves was a hill, from the top of which the men surveyed for a moment a broad, tumultuous expanse, shining and wind-riven. It was probably splendid, it was probably glorious, this play of the free sea, wild with lights of emerald and white and amber.

"Bully good thing it's an on-shore wind," said the cook. "If not, where would we be? Wouldn't have a show."

"That's right," said the correspondent.

The busy oiler nodded his assent.

Then the captain, in the bow, chuckled in a way that expressed humor, contempt, tragedy, all in one. "Do you think we've got much of a show now, boys?" said he.

Whereupon the three were silent, save for a trifle of hemming and hawing. To express any particular optimism at this time they felt to be childish and stupid, but they all doubtless possessed this sense of the situation in their minds. A young man thinks doggedly at such times. On the other hand, the ethics of their condition was decidedly against any open suggestion of hopelessness. So they were silent.

"Oh, well," said the captain, soothing his children, "we'll get ashore all right."

But there was that in his tone which made them think; so the oiler quoth, "Yes! if this wind holds."

The cook was bailing. "Yes! if we don't catch hell in the surf."

Canton-flannel gulls flew near and far. Sometimes they sat down on the sea, near patches of brown seaweed that rolled over the waves with a moment like carpets on a line in a gale. The birds sat comfortably in groups, and they were envied by some in the dinghy, for the wrath of the sea was no more to them than it was to a covey of prairie-chickens a thousand miles inland. Often they came very close and stared at the men with black, bead-like eyes. At these times they were uncanny and sinister in their unblinking scrutiny, and the men hooted angrily at them, telling them to be gone. One came, and evidently decided to alight on the top of the captain's head. The bird flew parallel to the boat, and did not circle, but made short sidelong jumps in the air in chicken fashion. His black eyes were wistfully fixed upon the captain's head. "Ugly brute," said the oiler to the bird. "You look as if you were made with a jack-knife." The cook and the correspondent swore darkly at the creature. The captain naturally wished to knock it away with the end of the heavy painter, but he did not dare do it, because anything resembling an emphatic gesture would have capsized this freighted boat; and so, with his open hand, the captain gently and carefully waved the gull away. After it had been discouraged from the pursuit the captain breathed easier on account of his hair, and others breathed easier because the bird struck their minds at this time as being somehow gruesome and ominous.

In the meantime the oiler and the correspondent rowed; and also they rowed. They sat together in the same seat, and each rowed an oar. Then the oiler took both oars; then the correspondent took both oars; then the oiler; then the correspondent. They rowed and they rowed. The very ticklish part of the business was when the time came for the reclining one in the stern to take his turn at the oars. By the very last star of truth, it is easier to steal eggs from under a hen than it was to change seats in the dinghy. First the man in the stern slid his hand along the thwart and moved with care, as if he were of Sèvres. Then the man in the rowing-seat slid his hand along the other thwart. It was all done with the most extraordinary care. As the two sidled past each other, the whole party kept watchful eyes on the coming wave, and the captain cried: "Look out, now! Steady, there!"

The brown mats of seaweed that appeared from time to time were like islands, bits of earth. They were traveling, apparently, neither one way nor the other. They were, to all intents, stationary. They informed the men in the boat that it was making progress slowly toward the land.

The captain, rearing cautiously in the bow after the dinghy soared on a great swell, said that he had seen the lighthouse at Mosquito Inlet. Presently the cook remarked that he had seen it. The correspondent was at the oars then, and for some reason he too wished to look at the lighthouse; but his back was toward the far shore, and the waves were important, and for some time he could not seize an opportunity to turn his head. But at last there came a wave more gentle than the others, and when at the crest of it he swiftly scoured the western horizon.

"See it?" said the captain.

"No," said the correspondent, slowly; "I didn't see anything."

"Look again," said the captain. He pointed. "It's exactly in that direction."

At the top of another wave the correspondent did as he was bid, and this time his eyes chanced on a small, still thing on the edge of the swaying horizon. It was precisely like the point of a pin. It took an anxious eye to find a lighthouse so tiny.

"Think we'll make it, Captain?"

"If this wind holds and the boat don't swamp, we can't do much else," said the captain.

The little boat, lifted by each towering sea and splashed viciously by the crests, made progress that in the absence of seaweed was not apparent to those in her. She seemed just a wee thing wallowing miraculously, top up, at the mercy of five oceans. Occasionally a great spread of water, like white flames, swarmed into her.

"Bail her, cook," said the captain, serenely.

"All right, Captain," said the cheerful cook.

III

It would be difficult to describe the subtle brotherhood of men that was here established on the seas. No one said that it was so. No one mentioned it. But it dwelt in the boat, and each man felt it warm him. They were a captain, an oiler, a cook, and a correspondent, and they were friends—friends in a more curiously iron-bound degree than may be common. The hurt captain, lying against the water-jar in the bow, spoke always in a low voice and calmly; but he could never command a more ready and swiftly obedient crew than the motley three of the dinghy. It was more than a mere recognition of what was best for the common safety. There was surely in it a quality that was personal and heartfelt. And after this devotion to the commander of the boat, there was this comradeship, that the correspondent, for instance, who had been taught to be cynical of men, knew even at the time was the best experience of his life. But no one said that it was so. No one mentioned it.

"I wish we had a sail," remarked the captain. "We might try my overcoat on the end of an oar, and give you two boys a chance to rest." So the cook and the correspondent held the mast and spread wide the overcoat; the oiler steered; and the little boat made good way with her new rig. Sometimes the oiler had to scull sharply to keep a sea from breaking into the boat, but otherwise sailing was a success.

Meanwhile the lighthouse had been growing slowly larger. It had now almost assumed color, and appeared like a little gray shadow on the sky. The man at the oars could not be prevented from turning his head rather often to try for a glimpse of this little gray shadow.

At last, from the top of each wave, the men in the tossing boat could see land. Even as the lighthouse was an upright shadow on the sky, this land seemed but a long black shadow on the sea. It certainly was thinner than paper. "We must be about opposite New Smyrna," said the cook, who had coasted this shore often in schooners. "Captain, by the way, I believe they abandoned that life-saving station there about a year ago."

"Did they?" said the captain.

The wind slowly died away. The cook and the correspondent were not now obliged to slave in order to hold high the oar; but the waves continued their old impetuous swooping at the dinghy, and the little craft, no longer under way, struggled woundily over them. The oiler or the correspondent took the oars again.

Shipwrecks are *apropos* of nothing. If men could only train for them and have them occur when the men had reached pink condition, there would be less drowning at sea. Of the four in the dinghy none had slept any time worth mentioning for two days and two nights previous to embarking in the dinghy, and in the excitement of clambering about the deck of a foundering ship they had also forgotten to eat heartily.

For these reasons, and for others, neither the oiler nor the correspondent was fond of rowing at this time. The correspondent wondered ingenuously how in the name of all that was sane could there be people who thought it amusing to row a boat. It was not an amusement; it was a diabolical punishment, and even a genius of mental aberrations could never conclude that it was anything but a horror to the muscles and a crime against the back. He mentioned to the boat in general how the amusement of rowing struck him, and the weary-faced oiler smiled in full sympathy. Previously to the foundering, by the way, the oiler had worked double watch in the engine-room of the ship.

"Take her easy now, boys," said the captain. "Don't spend yourselves. If we have to run a surf you'll need all your strength, because we'll sure have to swim for it. Take your time."

Slowly the land arose from the sea. From a black line it became a line of black and a line of white—trees and sand. Finally the captain said that he could make out a house on the shore. "That's the house of refuge, sure," said the cook. "They'll see us before long, and come out after us."

The distant lighthouse reared high. "The keeper ought to be able to make us out now, if he's looking through a glass," said the captain. "He'll notify the life-saving people."

"None of those other boats could have got ashore to give word of the wreck," said the oiler, in a low voice, "else the lifeboat would be out hunting us."

Slowly and beautifully the land loomed out of the sea. The wind came again. It had veered from the northeast to the southeast. Finally a new sound struck the ears of the men in the boat. It was the low thunder of the surf on the shore. "We'll never be able to make the lighthouse now," said the captain. "Swing her head a little more north, Billie."

"A little more north, sir," said the oiler.

Whereupon the little boat turned her nose once more down the wind, and all but the oarsman watched the shore grow. Under the influence of this expansion doubt and direful apprehension were leaving the minds of the men. The management of the boat was still most absorbing, but it could not prevent a quiet cheerfulness. In an hour, perhaps, they would be ashore.

Their backbones had become thoroughly used to balancing in the boat, and they now rode this wild colt of a dinghy like circus men. The correspondent thought that he had been drenched to the skin, but happening to feel in the top pocket of his coat, he found therein eight cigars. Four of them were soaked with sea-water; four were perfectly scatheless. After a search, somebody produced three dry matches; and thereupon the four waifs rode in their little boat and, with an assurance of an impending rescue shining in their eyes, puffed at the big cigars, and judged well and ill of all men. Everybody took a drink of water.

IV

"Cook," remarked the captain, "there don't seem to be any signs of life about your house of refuge."

"No," replied the cook. "Funny they don't see us!"

A broad stretch of lowly coast lay before the eyes of the men. It was of low dunes topped with dark vegetation. The roar of the surf was plain, and sometimes they could see the white lip of a wave as it spun up the beach. A tiny house was blocked out black upon the sky. Southward, the slim lighthouse lifted its little gray length.

Tide, wind, and waves were swinging the dinghy northward. "Funny they don't see us," said the men.

The surf's roar was here dulled, but its tone was nevertheless thunderous and mighty. As the boat swam over the great rollers the men sat listening to this roar. "We'll swamp sure," said everybody.

It is fair to say here that there was not a life-saving station within twenty miles in either direction; but the men did not know this fact, and in consequence they made dark and approbrious remarks concerning the eyesight of the nation's life-savers. Four scowling men sat in the dinghy, and surpassed records in the invention of epithets.

"Funny they don't see us."

The light-heartedness of a former time had completely faded. To their sharpened minds it was easy to conjure pictures of all kinds of incompetency and blindness and, indeed, cowardice. There was the shore of the populous land, and it was bitter and bitter to them that from it came no sign.

"Well," said the captain, ultimately, "I suppose we'll have to make a try for ourselves. If we stay out here too long, we'll none of us have strength left to swim after the boat swamps."

And so the oiler, who was at the oars, turned the boat straight for the shore. There was a sudden tightening of muscles. There was some thinking.

"If we don't all get ashore," said the captain—"if we don't all get ashore, I suppose you fellows know where to send news of my finish?"

They then briefly exchanged some addresses and admonitions. As for the reflections of the men, there was a great deal of rage in them. Perchance they might be formulated thus: "If I am going to be drowned—if I am going to be drowned—if I am going to be drowned, why, in the name of the seven mad gods who rule the sea, was I allowed to come thus far and contemplate sand

and trees? Was I brought here merely to have my nose dragged away as I was about to nibble the sacred cheese of life? It is preposterous! If this old ninny-woman, Fate, cannot do better than this, she should be deprived of the management of men's fortunes. She is an old hen who knows not her intention. If she has decided to drown me, why did she not do it in the beginning, and save me all this trouble? The whole affair is absurd . . . . But no; she cannot mean to drown me. She dare not drown me. She cannot drown me. Not after all this work!" Afterward the man might have had an impulse to shake his fist at the clouds. "Just you drown me, now, and then hear what I call you!"

The billows that came at this time were more formidable. They seemed always just about to break and roll over the little boat in turmoil of foam. There was a preparatory and long growl in the speech of them. No mind unused to the sea would have concluded that the dinghy could ascend these sheer heights in time. The shore was still afar. The oiler was a wily surfman. "Boys," he said swiftly, "she won't live three minutes more, and we're too far out to swim. Shall I take her to sea again, Captain?"

"Yes; go ahead!" said the captain.

This oiler, by a series of quick miracles and fast and steady oarsmanship, turned the boat in the middle of the surf and took her safely to sea again.

There was a considerable silence as the boat bumped over the furrowed sea to deeper water. Then somebody in gloom spoke: "Well, anyhow, they must have seen us from the shore by now."

The gulls went in slanting flight up the wind toward the gray, desolate east. A squall, marked by dingy clouds, and clouds brick-red, like smoke from a burning building, appeared from the southeast.

"What do you think of those life-saving people? Ain't they peaches?"

"Funny they haven't seen us."

"Maybe they think we're out here for sport! Maybe they think we're fishin'. Maybe they think we're damned fools."

It was a long afternoon. A changed tide tried to force them southward, but wind and wave said northward. Far ahead, where coast-line, sea, and sky formed their mighty angle, there were little dots which seemed to indicate a city on the shore.

"St. Augustine?"

The captain shook his head. "Too near Mosquito Inlet."

And the oiler rowed, and then the correspondent rowed; then the oiler rowed. It was a weary business. The human back can become the seat of more aches and pains than are registered in books for the composite anatomy of a regiment. It is a limited area, but it can become the theater of innumerable muscular conflicts, tangles, wrenches, knots, and other comforts.

"Did you ever like to row, Billie?" asked the correspondent.

"No," said the oiler;"hang it!"

When one exchanged the rowing-seat for a place in the bottom of the boat, he suffered a bodily depression that caused him to be careless of everything save an obligation to wiggle one finger. There was cold sea-water swashing to and fro in the boat, and he lay in it. His head, pillowed on a thwart, was within an inch of the swirl of a wave-crest, and sometimes a particularly obstreperous sea came inboard and drenched him once more. But these matters did not annoy him. It is almost certain that if the boat had capsized he would have tumbled comfortably out upon the ocean as if he felt sure that it was a great, soft mattress.

"Look! There's a man on the shore!"

"Where?"

"There! See 'im? See 'im?"

"Yes, sure! He's walking along."'

"Now he's stopped. Look! He's facing us!"

"He's waving at us!"

"So he is! By thunder!"

"Ah, now we're all right! Now we're all right! There'll be a boat out here for us in half an hour."

"He's going on. He's running. He's going up to that house there."

The remote beach seemed lower than the sea, and it required a searching glance to discern the little black figure. The captain saw a floating stick, and they rowed to it. A bath towel was by some weird chance in the boat, and tying this on the stick, the captain waved it. The oarsman did not dare turn his head, so he was obliged to ask questions.

"What's he doing now?"

"He's standing still again. He's looking, I think. . . . There he goes again—toward the house. . . . Now he's stopped again."

"Is he waving at us?"

"No, not now; he was though."

"Look! There comes another man!"

"He's running."

"Look at him go, would you!"

"Why, he's on a bicycle. Now he's met the other man. They're both waving at us. Look!"

"There comes something up the beach."

"What the devil is that thing?"

"Why, it looks like a boat."

"Why, certainly, it's a boat."

"No; it's on wheels."

"Yes, so it is. Well, that must be the life-boat. They drag them along shore on a wagon."

"That's the life-boat, sure."

"No, by—, it's—it's an omnibus."

"I tell you it's a life-boat."

"It is not! It's an omnibus. I can see it plain. See? One of these big hotel omnibuses."

"By thunder, you're right. It's an omnibus, sure as fate. What do you suppose they are doing with an omnibus? Maybe they are going around collecting the life-crew, hey?"

"That's it, likely. Look! There's a fellow waving a little black flag. He's standing on the steps of the omnibus. There come those other two fellows. Now they're all talking together. Look at the fellow with the flag. Maybe he ain't waving it!"

"That ain't a flag, is it? That's his coat. Why, certainly, that's his coat."

"So it is; it's his coat. He's taken it off and is waving it around his head. But would you look at him swing it!"

"Oh, say, there isn't any life-saving station there. That's just a winter-resort hotel omnibus that has brought over some of the boarders to see us drown."

"What's that idiot with the coat mean? What's he signaling, anyhow?"

"It looks as if he were trying to tell us to go north. There must be a life-saving station up there."

"No; he thinks we're fishing. Just giving us a merry hand. See? Ah, there, Willie!"

"Well, I wish I could make something out of those signals. What do you suppose he means?"

"He don't mean anything; he's just playing."

"Well, if he'd just signal us to try the surf again, or to go to sea and wait, or go north, or go south, or go to hell, there would be some reason in it. But look at him! He just stands there and keeps his coat revolving like a wheel. The ass!"

"There come more people."

"Now there's quite a mob. Look! Isn't that a boat?"

"Where? Oh, I see where you mean. No, that's no boat."

"That fellow is still waving his coat."

"He must think we like to see him do that. Why don't he quit it? It don't mean anything."

"I don't know. I think he is trying to make us go north. It must be that there's a life-saving station there somewhere."

"Say, he ain't tired yet. Look at 'im wave!"

"Wonder how long he can keep that up. He's been revolving his coat ever since he caught sight of us. He's an idiot. Why aren't they getting men to bring a boat out? A fishing-boat—one of those big yawls—could come out here all right. Why don't he do something?"

"Oh, it's all right now."

"They'll have a boat out here for us in less than no time, now that they've seen us."

A faint yellow tone came into the sky over the low land. The shadows on the sea slowly deepened. The wind bore coldness with it, and the men began to shiver.

"Holy smoke!" said one, allowing his voice to express his impious mood, "if we keep on monkeying out here! If we've got to flounder out here all night!"

"Oh, we'll never have to stay here all night! Don't you worry. They've seen us now, and it won't be long before they'll come chasing out after us."

The shore grew dusky. The man waving a coat blended gradually into this gloom, and it swallowed in the same manner the omnibus and the group of people. The spray, when it dashed uproariously over the side, made the voyagers shrink and swear like men who were being branded.

"I'd like to catch the chump who waved the coat. I feel like soaking him one, just for luck."

"Why? What did he do?"

"Oh, nothing, but then he seemed so damned cheerful."

In the meantime the oiler rowed, and then the correspondent rowed, and then the oiler rowed. Gray-faced and bowed forward, they mechanically, turn by turn, plied the leaden oars. The form of the lighthouse had vanished from the southern horizon, but finally a pale star appeared, just lifting from the sea. The streaked saffron in the west passed before the all-merging darkness, and the sea to the east was black. The land had vanished, and was expressed only by the low and drear thunder of the surf.

"If I am going to be drowned—if I am going to be drowned—if I am going to be drowned, why, in the name of the seven mad gods who rule the sea, was I allowed to come thus far and contemplate sand and trees? Was I brought here merely to have my nose dragged away as I was about to nibble the sacred cheese of life?"

The patient captain, drooped over the water-jar, was sometimes obliged to speak to the oarsman.

"Keep her head up! Keep her head up!"

"Keep her head up, sir." The voices were weary and low.

This was surely a quiet evening. All save the oarsman lay heavily and listlessly in the boat's bottom. As for him, his eyes were just capable of noting the tall black waves that swept forward in a most sinister silence, save for an occasional subdued growl of a crest.

The cook's head was on a thwart, and he looked without interest at the water under his nose. He was deep in other scenes. Finally he spoke. "Billie," he murmured dreamfully, "what kind of pie do you like best?"

V

"Pie!" said the oiler and the correspondent, agitatedly. "Don't talk about those things, blast you!"

"Well," said the cook, "I was just thinking about ham sandwiches, and—"

A night on the sea in an open boat is a long night. As darkness settled finally, the shine of the light, lifting from the sea in the south, changed to full gold. On the northern horizon a new light appeared, a small bluish gleam on the edge of the waters. These two lights were the furniture of the world. Otherwise there was nothing but waves.

Two men huddled in the stern, and distances were so magnificent in the dinghy that the rower was enabled to keep his feet partly warm by thrusting them under his companions. Their legs indeed extended far under the rowing-seat until they touched the feet of the captain forward. Sometimes, despite the efforts of the tired oarsman, a wave came piling into the boat, an icy wave of the night, and the chilling water soaked them anew. They would twist their bodies for a moment and groan, and sleep the dead sleep once more, while the water in the boat gurgled about them as the craft rocked.

The plan of the oiler and the correspondent was for one to row until he lost the ability, and then arouse the other from his sea-water couch in the bottom of the boat.

The oiler plied the oars until his head drooped forward and the overpowering sleep blinded him; and he rowed yet afterward. Then he touched a man in the bottom of the boat, and called his name. "Will you spell me for a little while?" he said meekly.

"Sure, Billie," said the correspondent, awaking and dragging himself to a sitting position. They exchanged places carefully, and the oiler, cuddling down in the sea-water at the cook's side, seemed to go to sleep instantly.

The particular violence of the sea had ceased. The waves

came without snarling. The obligation of the man at the oars was to keep the boat headed so that the tilt of the rollers would not capsize her, and to preserve her from filling when the crests rushed past. The black waves were silent and hard to be seen in the darkness. Often one was almost upon the boat before the oarsman was aware.

In a low voice the correspondent addressed the captain. He was not sure that the captain was awake, although this iron man seemed to be always awake. "Captain, shall I keep her making for that light north, sir?"

The same steady voice answered him. "Yes. Keep it about two points off the port bow."

The cook had tied a life-belt around himself in order to get even the warmth which this clumsy cork contrivance could donate, and he seemed almost stove-like when a rower, whose teeth invariably chattered wildly as soon as he ceased his labor, dropped down to sleep.

The correspondent, as he rowed, looked down at the two men sleeping under foot. The cook's arm was around the oiler's shoulders, and, with their fragmentary clothing and haggard faces, they were the babes of the sea—a grotesque rendering of the old babes in the wood.

Later he must have grown stupid at his work, for suddenly there was a growling of water, and a crest came with a roar and a swash into the boat, and it was a wonder that it did not set the cook afloat in his life-belt. The cook continued to sleep, but the oiler sat up, blinking his eyes and shaking with the new cold.

"Oh, I'm awful sorry, Billie" said the correspondent, contritely.

"That's all right, old boy," said the oiler, and lay down again and was asleep.

Presently it seemed that even the captain dozed, and the correspondent thought that he was the one man afloat on all the oceans. The wind had a voice as it came over the waves, and it was sadder than the end.

There was a long, loud swishing astern of the boat, and a gleaming trail of phosphorescence, like blue flame, was furrowed on the black waters. It might have been made by a monstrous knife.

Then there came a stillness, while the correspondent breathed with the open mouth and looked at the sea.

Suddenly there was another swish and another long flash of bluish light, and this time it was alongside the boat, and might almost have been reached with an oar. The correspondent saw an enormous fin speed like a shadow through the water, hurling the crystalline spray and leaving the long glowing trail.

The correspondent looked over his shoulder at the captain. His face was hidden, and he seemed to be asleep. He looked at the babes of the sea. They certainly were asleep. So, being bereft of sympathy, he leaned a little way to one side and swore softly into the sea.

But the thing did not then leave the vicinity of the boat. Ahead or astern, on one side or the other, at intervals long or short, fled the long sparkling streak, and there was to be heard the whiroo of the dark fin. The speed and power of the thing was greatly to be admired. It cut the water like a gigantic and keen projectile.

The presence of this biding thing did not affect the man with the same horror that it would if he had been a picnicker. He simply looked at the sea dully and swore in an undertone.

Nevertheless, it is true that he did not wish to be alone with the thing. He wished one of his companions to awake by chance and keep him company with it. But the captain hung motionless over the water-jar, and the oiler and the cook in the bottom of the boat were plunged in slumber.

VI

"If I am going to be drowned—if I am going to be drowned—if I am going to be drowned, why, in the name of the seven mad gods who rule the sea, was I allowed to come thus far and contemplate sand and trees?"

During this dismal night, it may be remarked that a man would conclude that it was really the intention of the seven mad gods to drown him, despite the abominable injustice of it. For it was certainly an abominable injustice to drown a man who had worked so hard, so hard. The man felt it would be a crime most unnatural. Other people had drowned at sea since galleys swarmed with painted sails, but still—

When it occurs to a man that nature does not regard him as important, and that she feels she would not maim the universe by disposing of him, he at first wishes to throw bricks at the temple, and he hates deeply the fact that there are no bricks and no temples. Any visible expression of nature would surely be pelleted with his jeers.

Then, if there be no tangible thing to hoot, he feels, perhaps, the desire to confront a personification and indulge in pleas, bowed to one knee, and with hands supplicant, saying, "Yes, but I love myself."

A high cold star on a winter's night is the word he feels that she says to him. Thereafter he knows the pathos of his situation.

The men in the dinghy had not discussed these matters, but each had, no doubt, reflected upon them in silence and according to his mind. There was seldom any expression upon their faces save the general one of complete weariness. Speech was devoted to the business of the boat.

To chime the notes of his emotion, a verse mysteriously entered the correspondent's head. He had even forgotten that he had forgotten this verse, but it suddenly was in his mind:

> A soldier of the Legion lay dying in Algiers;
> There was lack of woman's nursing, there was dearth of
> woman's tears;
> But a comrade stood beside him, and he took that comrade's
> hand,
> And he said, "I never more shall see my own, my native land."

In his childhood the correspondent had been made acquainted with the fact that a soldier of the Legion lay dying in Algiers, but he had never regarded it as important. Myriads of his school-fellows had informed him of the soldier's plight, but the dinning had naturally ended by making him perfectly indifferent. He had never considered it his affair that a soldier of the Legion lay dying in Algiers, nor had it appeared to him as a matter for sorrow. It was less to him than breaking of a pencil's point.

Now, however, it quaintly came to him as a human, living thing. It was no longer merely a picture of a few throes in the breast of a poet, meanwhile drinking tea and warming his feet at the grate; it was an actuality—stern, mournful, and fine.

The correspondent plainly saw the soldier. He lay on the sand with his feet out straight and still. While his pale left hand was upon his chest in an attempt to thwart the going of his life, the blood came between his fingers. In the far Algerian distance, a city of low square forms was set against a sky that was faint with the last sunset hues. The correspondent, plying the oars and dreaming of the slow and slower movements of the lips of soldier, was moved by a profound and perfectly impersonal comprehension. He was sorry for the soldier of the Legion who lay dying in Algiers.

The thing which had followed the boat and waited had evidently grown bored at the delay. There was no longer to be heard the slash of the cutwater, and there was no longer the flame of the long trail. The light in the north still glimmered, but it was apparently no nearer to the boat. Sometimes the boom of the surf rang in the correspondent's ears, and he turned the craft seaward then and rowed harder. Southward, some one had evidently built a watch-fire on the beach. It was too low and too far to be seen, but it made a shimmering, roseate reflection upon the bluff back of it, and this could be discerned from the boat. The wind came stronger, and sometimes a wave suddenly raged out like a mountain-cat, and there was to be seen the sheen and sparkle of a broken crest.

The captain, in the bow, moved on his water-jar and sat erect. "Pretty long night," he observed to the correspondent. He looked at the shore. "Those life-saving people take their time."

"Did you see that shark playing around?"

"Yes, I saw him. He was a big fellow, all right."

"Wish I had known you were awake."

Later the correspondent spoke into the bottom of the boat.

"Billie!" There was a slow and gradual disentanglement. "Billie, will you spell me?"

"Sure," said the oiler.

As soon as the correspondent touched the cold, comfortable sea-water in the bottom of the boat and had huddled close to the cook's life-belt he was deep in sleep, despite the fact that his teeth played all the popular airs. This sleep was so good to him that it was but a moment before he heard a voice call his name in a tone that demonstrated the last stages of exhaustion. "Will you spell me?"

"Sure, Billie."

The light in the north had mysteriously vanished, but the correspondent took his course from the wide-awake captain.

Later in the night they took the boat farther out to sea, and the captain directed the cook to take one oar at the stern and keep the boat facing the seas. He was to call out if he should hear the thunder of the surf. This plan enabled the oiler and the correspondent to get respite together. "We'll give those boys a chance to get into shape again," said the captain. They curled down and, after a few preliminary chatterings and trembles, slept once more the dead sleep. Neither knew they had bequeathed to the cook the company of another shark, or perhaps the same shark.

As the boat caroused on the waves, spray occasionally bumped over the side and gave them a fresh soaking, but this had no power to break their repose. The ominous slash of the wind and the water affected them as it would have affected mummies.

"Boys," said the cook, with the notes of every reluctance

in his voice, "she's drifted in pretty close. I guess one of you had better take her to sea again." The correspondent, aroused, heard the crash of the toppled crests.

As he was rowing, the captain gave him some whisky and water, and this steadied the chills out of him. "If I ever get ashore and anybody shows me even a photograph of an oar—"

At last there was a short conversation.

"Billie! . . . Billie, will you spell me?"

"Sure," said the oiler.

VII

When the correspondent again opened his eyes, the sea and the sky were each of the gray hue of the dawning. Later, carmine and gold was painted upon the waters. The morning appeared finally, in its splendor, with a sky of pure blue, and the sunlight flamed on the tips of the waves.

On the distant dunes were set many little black cottages, and a tall white windmill reared above them. No man, nor dog, nor bicycle appeared on the beach. The cottages might have formed a deserted village.

The voyagers scanned the shore. A conference was held in the boat. "Well," said the captain, "if no help is coming, we might better try a run through the surf right away. If we stay out here much longer we will be too weak to do anything for ourselves at all." The others silently acquiesced in this reasoning. The boat was headed for the beach. The correspondent wondered if none ever ascended the tall wind-tower, and if then they never looked seaward. This tower was a giant, standing with its back to the plight of the ants. It represented in a degree, to the correspondent, the serenity of nature amid the struggles of the individual— nature in the wind, and nature in the vision of men. She did not seem cruel to him then, nor beneficent, nor treacherous, nor wise. But she was indifferent, flatly indifferent. It is, perhaps, plausible that a man in this situation, impressed with the unconcern of the universe, should see the innumerable flaws of his life and have them taste wickedly in his mind and wish for another chance. A distinction between right and wrong seems absurdly clear to him, then, in this new ignorance of the grave-edge, and he understands that if he were given another opportunity he would mend his conduct and his words, and be better and brighter during an introduction or at a tea.

"Now, boys," said the captain, "she is going to swamp sure. All we can do is to work her in as far as possible, and then when she swamps, pile out and scramble for the beach. Keep cool now, and don't jump until she swamps sure."

The oiler took the oars. Over his shoulders he scanned the surf. "Captain," he said, "I think I'd better bring her about, and keep her head-on to the seas, and back her in."

"All right, Billie," said the captain. "Back her in." The oiler swung the boat then, and, seated in the stern, the cook and the correspondent were obliged to look over their shoulders to contemplate the lonely and indifferent shore.

The monstrous inshore rollers heaved the boat high until the men were again enabled to see the white sheets of water scudding up the slanted beach. "We won't get in very close," said the captain. Each time a man could wrest his attention from the rollers, he turned his glance toward the shore, and in the expression of the eyes during this contemplation there was a singular quality. The correspondent, observing the others, knew that they were not afraid, but the full meaning of their glances was shrouded.

As for himself, he was too tired to grapple fundamentally with the fact. He tried to coerce his mind into thinking of it, but the mind was dominated at this time by the muscles, and the muscles said they did not care. It merely occurred to him that if he should drown it would be a shame.

There were no hurried words, no pallor, no plain agitation. The men simply looked at the shore. "Now, remember to get well clear of the boat when you jump," said the captain.

Seaward the crest of a roller suddenly fell with a thunderous crash, and the long white comber came roaring down upon the boat.

"Steady now," said the captain. The men were silent. They turned their eyes from the shore to the comber and waited. The boat slid up the incline, leaped at the furious top, bounced over it, and swung down the long back of the wave. Some water had been shipped, and the cook bailed it out.

But the next crest crashed also. The tumbling, boiling flood of white water caught the boat and whirled it almost perpendicular. Water swarmed in from all sides. The correspondent had his hands on the gunwale at this time, and when the water entered at that place he swiftly withdrew his fingers, as if he objected to wetting them.

The little boat, drunken with this weight of water, reeled and snuggled deeper into the sea.

"Bail her out, cook! Bail her out!" said the captain.

"All right, Captain," said the cook.

"Now, boys, the next one will do for us sure," said the

oiler. "Mind to jump clear of the boat."

The third wave moved forward, huge, furious, implacable. It fairly swallowed the dinghy, and almost simultaneously the men tumbled into the sea. A piece of life-belt had lain in the bottom of the boat, and as the correspondent went overboard he held this to his chest with his left hand.

The January water was icy, and he reflected immediately that it was colder than he had expected to find it off the coast of Florida. This appeared to his dazed mind as a fact important enough to be noted at the time. The coldness of the water was sad; it was tragic. This fact was somehow mixed and confused with his opinion of his own situation so that it seemed almost a proper reason for tears. The water was cold.

When he came to the surface he was conscious of little but the noisy water. Afterward he saw his companions in the sea. The oiler was ahead in the race. He was swimming strongly and rapidly. Off to the correspondent's left, the cook's great white and corked back bulged out of the water; and in the rear the captain was hanging with his one good hand to the keel of the overturned dinghy.

There is a certain immovable quality to a shore, and the correspondent wondered at it amid the confusion of the sea.

It seemed also very attractive; but the correspondent knew that it was a long journey, and he paddled leisurely. The piece of life-preserver lay under him, and sometimes he whirled down the incline of a wave as if he were on a hand-sled.

But finally he arrived at a place in the sea where travel was beset with difficulty. He did not pause swimming to inquire what manner of current had caught him, but there his progress ceased. The shore was set before him like a bit of scenery on a stage, and he looked at it, and understood with his eyes each detail of it.

As the cook passed, much farther to the left, the captain was calling to him. "Turn over on your back, cook! Turn over on your back and use the oar."

"All right, sir." The cook turned on his back, and paddling with an oar, went ahead as if he were a canoe.

Presently the boat also passed to the left of the correspondent, with the captain clinging with one hand to the keel. He would have appeared like a man raising himself to look over a board fence if it were not for the extraordinary gymnastics of the boat. The correspondent marveled that the captain could still hold to it.

They passed on nearer to shore,—the oiler, the cook, the captain,—and following them went the water-jar, bouncing gaily over the seas.

The correspondent remained in the grip of this strange new enemy, a current. The shore, with its white slope of sand and its green bluff, topped with little silent cottages, was spread like a picture before him. It was very near to him then, but he was impressed as one who, in a gallery, looks at a scene from Brittany or Algiers.

He thought: "I am going to drown? Can it be possible? Can it be possible? Can it be possible?" Perhaps an individual must consider his own death to be the final phenomenon of nature.

But later a wave perhaps whirled him out of this small deadly current, for he found suddenly that he could again make progress toward the shore. Later still he was aware that the captain, clinging with one hand to the keel of the dinghy, had his face turned away from the shore and toward him, and was calling his name. "Come to the boat! Come to the boat!"

In his struggle to reach the captain and the boat, he reflected that when one gets properly wearied drowning must really be a comfortable arrangement—a cessation of hostilities accompanied by a large degree of relief; and he was glad of it, for the main thing in his mind for some moments had been horror of the temporary agony; he did not wish to be hurt.

Presently he saw a man running along the shore. He was undressing with most remarkable speed. Coat, trousers, shirt, everything flew magically off him.

"Come to the boat!" called the captain.

"All right, Captain." As the correspondent paddled, he saw the captain let himself down to bottom and leave the boat. Then the correspondent performed his one little marvel of the voyage. A large wave caught him and flung him with ease and supreme speed completely over the boat and far beyond it. It struck him even then as an event in gymnastics and a true miracle of the sea. An overturned boat in the surf is not a plaything to a swimming man.

The correspondent arrived in water that reached only to his waist, but his condition did not enable him to stand for more than a moment. Each wave knocked him into a heap, and the undertow pulled at him.

Then he saw the man who had been running and undressing, and undressing and running, come bounding into the water. He dragged ashore the cook, and then waded toward the captain; but the captain waved him away and sent him to the correspondent. He was naked—naked as a tree in winter; but a halo was about his head, and he shone like a saint. He gave a strong pull, and a long drag, and a bully heave at the correspondent's hand. The correspondent, schooled in the minor formulæ, said, "Thanks, old man." But suddenly the man cried, "What's that?" He pointed a swift finger. The correspondent said, "Go."

In the shallows, face downward, lay the oiler. His forehead touched sand that was periodically, between each wave, clear of the sea.

The correspondent did not know all that transpired afterward. When he achieved safe ground he fell, striking the sand with each particular part of his body. It was as if he had dropped from a roof, but the thud was grateful to him.

It seems that instantly the beach was populated with men with blankets, clothes, and flasks, and women with coffee-pots and all the remedies sacred to their minds. The welcome of the land to the men from the sea was warm and generous; but a still and dripping shape was carried slowly up the beach, and the land's welcome for it could only be the different and sinister hospitality of the grave.

When it came night, the white waves paced to and fro in the moonlight, and the wind brought the sound of the great sea's voice to the men on shore, and they felt that they could then be interpreters.

John Dos Passos

Under the Tropic

Some of the best times in those years were with Hem and Pauline in Key West. The time that stands out was in late April and early May of 1929. . .

It is hot in April in Key West when the trade wind drops. We trolled back and forth between the wharves and an old white steamboat that had gone on a reef in a hurricane. She had lost her stack and the engines had been taken out. Waldo painted a picture of her that still hangs in the upstairs hall at Spence's Point. When Charles took his boat up into a bight away from the town, an unbelievable sweetness of blossoming limes came out along with the mosquitoes from among the mangroves.

Hem had brought along a couple of bottles of champagne which perched on the ice that kept the mullet fresh in the bait bucket. The rule was that you couldn't have a drink until somebody caught a fish. The sun set in a wash of gaudy pinks and ochres. We kept fishing on into the moonlight. I'm not sure whether we caught any tarpon that night, but we certainly had one hooked because I remember the arc of dark silver against the moon's sheen on the water when the fish jumped.

The tarpon seemed only to bite when the tide was low and the water warm in the channels. When they stopped striking and we had finished the champagne Charles said with a yawn that he had to go to work at the store at seven o'clock next morning and headed us in to the dock.

If we hadn't pulled in a tarpon I was probably just as glad because catching tarpon always seemed a waste to me. I hated to see the great silver monsters lying in the dust on the wharf. They aren't fit to eat. About the only use is for mounting. Some people make knicknacks out of the dried scales. Sheer vanity catching tarpon.

We went to the Asturian's for a bite before going to bed. Frenchfried yellowtail and bonito with tomato sauce were his specialities. It was a delight to be able to chatter amiably on all sorts of topics without tripping over that damn Party line. No taboos. Everybody said the first thing that came into his head. After the ideological bickerings of the New York theater Key West seemed like the Garden of Eden.

Hem was the greatest fellow in the world to go around with when everything went right. That spring was a marvelous season for tarpon. Every evening Charles would take us out tarpon fishing and we would fish and drink and talk and talk and talk far into the moonlit night. Days, after Hem and I had knocked off our stint—we were both very early risers—we would go out to the reef with Bra.

Bra was a Conch. That's what they called white people from Spanish Wells in the Bahamas. His real name was Sanders. Hem, who had gotten to be a Conch right along with him, talked Captain Sanders into taking us out. Nobody had heard of a party boat. Fifteen dollars was considered a fair price for the day.

Fishingboats were still smacks whether they had sails or not. They carried a livebox built into the boat amidships to keep the fish alive. Key West had a iceplant, but at the fishmarket down at the wharf they would scoop up your yellowtails with a net out of a big vat when you bought them. Another great tank was full of green turtles. Shipping sea turtles was an important industry.

There was endless fascination in the variety of creatures you pulled up off the reef. Never much of a sports fisherman, I liked going along, just to be out on the varicolored water. I always announced that I fished for the pot. Although as competitive as a race horse, Hem wasn't yet so much the professional sportsman as to spoil the fun. Such was my enthusiasm for the great pale moonstruck snappers known locally as mutton fish that Katy got to calling me Muttonfish. It stuck for a while as a nickname.

•••

For several winters after that Katy and I made a point of spending as much time as we could at Key West. It wasn't quite under the tropic but it was mighty close to it. No doctor's prescription was ever pleasanter to take.

The railroad had folded and now you arrived by car-ferry from a point below Homestead on the mainland. There were three separate ferryrides and sandy roads through the scrubby keys between. It took half a day and was a most delightful trip, with long cues of pelicans scrambling up off the water and manofwar birds in the sky and boobygulls on the buoys, and mullet jumping in the milky shallows.

Hem and I kept planning a trip to Bimini, but it always had to be put off for some reason or other. The first time we started out we had hardly reached the purple water of the Gulf Stream when old Hem shot himself in the leg—in the fleshy part, fortunately—with his own rifle trying to shoot a shark that was making for a sailfish somebody had alongside and was trying to gaff. We had to turn back to take him to the sawbones at the hospital. Katy was so mad she would hardly speak to him.

Hem's leg had hardly healed when a package arrived for him from Oak Park. It was from his mother. It contained a chocolate cake, a roll of Mrs. Hemingway's paintings of the Garden of the Gods which she suggested he might get hung at the Salon when he next went to Paris, and the gun with which his father shot himself. Katy, who had known her of old, had explained to me that Mrs. Hemingway was a very odd lady indeed. Hem was the only man I ever knew who really hated his mother.

It was on the first of Hem's *Pilars* that we finally made it to the Bahamas. The big money fishing camp at Cat Cay had gone broke in the collapse of the first Florida boom and was still closed down. There were a few yachtsmen and sports fishermen about but the tiny island of Bimini proper was very much out of the world. There was a wharf and some native shacks under the coconut palms and a store that had some kind of a barroom attached, where we drank rum in the evenings, and a magnificent broad beach on the Gulf Stream side. There was an official residency and a couple of sunbeaten bungalows screened against the sandflies up on the dunes. Katy and I occupied one of them for a week to give Hem more room on the *Pilar*.

We had gotten to calling Hem the Old Master because nobody could stop him from laying down the law, or sometimes the Mahatma on account of his having appeared in a rowboat with a towel wrapped around his head to keep off the sun. He had more crotchety moments than in the old days, but he was a barrel of monkeys when he wanted to be. Life still seemed enormously comical to all of us. Nobody ever got so mad that some fresh crack didn't bring him around. We drank a good deal but only cheerfully. We carried things off with great fits of laughing.

If I'm not mistaken this trip to Bimini was the first time the Old Master really went out after tuna. He'd been reading Zane Grey's book about catching great tuna on the seven seas (and a surprisingly wellwritten book it is) and wanted to go Zane Grey one better.

We had caught a few smallish yellowfins along with some rainbowcolored dolphins on the way over across the Gulf Stream from the upper end of Hawk Channel. It was in the spring of the year and the wiseacres all claimed that the tuna were running.

Katy and I were delighted with the island. We never tired of walking on the beach and watching the highslung landcrabs shuttle like harness racers among the fallen coconuts. We did a lot of bathing in the comfortable surf on the great beach. Hem was scornful of our shell collection.

We got hold of an agreeable storytelling Negro with a small sailboat who took us sailing over the marly waters of the Great Bahama Bank and fishing for bonefish in the shallows between the coral heads. The Mahatma used to kid us about our taste for going out in rowboats together, said people did that before they were married, not after.

The Bimini Negroes were great fun. They made up songs about every incident of the day. Every little job like hauling a boat ashore was a choral event. It was the first time any of us had heard

My Mama don't want no peas no rice no coconut oil
All she wants is handy brandy and champagne.

They immediately made up songs about old Hem. I wish I remembered the words. All my recollections of that week are laced with the lilt of those Bimini songs.

Anyway while Katy and I were unashamedly sightseeing and sailing and rowing and dabbling in folklore—all occupations frowned on by serious fishermen—the Old Master was cruising the deep. He'd brought tuna rigs along and was trolling with that implacable impatient persistence of his.

We were ashore when the Old Master first tangled with his great tuna. It had been hooked early in the morning by a man named Cook who was caretaker at Cat Cay. It must have been an enormous fish because as soon as it sounded it ran out all the line. Cook's hands were cut to shreds when he turned it over to Ernest, who came alongside with the *Pilar* in the early afternoon. Hem went on playing it from Cook's boat and sent the *Pilar* in to fetch us so that we should see the sport. I've forgotten who was at the wheel but we cruised alongside while the battle continued.

Among the assembled yachtsmen there was a gentleman who had a large white yacht named the *Moana*. William B. Leeds, of a family famous in the international set, had invited the Old Master aboard for drinks a couple of days before. The Old Master had come away charmed by Bill Leeds' hospitality but even more charmed by the fact that Leeds owned a Thompson submachine gun. Just at that moment a submachine gun was what the Old Master wanted more than anything in the world.

From a boy he had been fond of firearms but now he was particularly interested in a submachine gun as a way of fighting the sharks. Bimini was infested with sharks that season. They even bothered us bathing on the beach, but particularly they had an exasperating way of cutting off a hooked fish just as you were about to get him into the boat. The Old Master tried potting them with his rifle but unless you shoot him right through his tiny brain a rifle bullet doesn't make much impression on a shark. The night before he fought the tuna he'd been trying all sorts of expedients over the rum collinses to get Leeds to part with his submachine gun. He kept suggesting that they match for it or that they cut a hand of poker for it or shoot at a target for it. I believe he even offered to buy it. But Leeds was holding on to his submachine gun which he told me later had been given to him by the inventor's son who was a good friend of his.

It was late afternoon by the time Katy and I got out to the scene of the battle. By dusk the tuna began to weaken. The Old Master was reeling in on him. Everybody was on the ropes but the tuna was still hooked. We were very much excited to be in for the kill. There was a ring of spectator boats around, including Leeds with his machine gun on the launch from the *Moana*.

It was getting dark. The wind had dropped but a nasty looking squall was making up on the horizon. In the last gloaming the Old Master inched the fish alongside. Nobody had seen him yet. One man was ready with the gaff. The rest of us, hunched on top of the cabin of the *Pilar*, peered into the water with our flashlights.

We all saw him at once, dark, silvery and immense. Eight hundred pounds, nine hundred pounds, a thousand pounds, people guessed in hornswoggled whispers. All I knew was that he was a very big fish. He was moving sluggishly. He seemed licked. The man with the gaff made a lunge and missed. The silver flash was gone. The reel whined as the fish sounded.

The Old Master's expletives were sibilant and low.

The fish took half the reel; then the Old Master began hauling in on him again. He didn't feel right. Somebody suggested he might be dead. Bill Leeds had been keeping the sharks at bay with his machine gun, but now he laid off for fear a ricochet might hit someone. The Old Master reeled and reeled.

The stormcloud ate up a third of the starry sky. Lightning flickered on its fringes. Most of the small boats had put back to shore.

Leeds from his launch was inviting us to take cover on his yacht but the Old Master was doggedly reeling in.

At last in a great wash of silver and spume the tuna came to the surface ten or fifteen yards astern of the boat. The sharks hadn't touched him. We could see his whole great smooth length. The Old Master was reeling in fast. Then suddenly they came. In the light of our flashlights we could see the sharks streaking in across the dark water. Like torpedoes. Like speedboats. One struck. Another. Another. The water was murky with blood. By the time we hauled the tuna in over the stern there was nothing left but his head and his backbone and his tail.

Getting Katy and me aboard the *Moana* was a real victory for Old Hem. He'd been trying to cotton up to Leeds on account of that machine gun, and maybe too because he thought Leeds was so stinking rich. Katy had taken a scunner to poor Leeds and declared she'd rather die than go aboard his yacht. There was an oily and rather pimpish old Spaniard in the party whom we called Don Propina. We'd both taken a scunner to him. Anyway Ernest won. The squall blew up so hard there was nothing for it but to take refuge on the yacht. We climbed up the gangplank in the first horizontal sheets of rain and sat wet and shivering under the ventilation ducts in the saloon. To serve us right for being so snooty we both caught colds in the head.

Leeds hospitably put us up for the night. We turned in early, so we never knew exactly how it happened; but when we shoved off from the yacht in the lovely early morning sunlight the Old Master had the submachine gun affectionately cradled in the crotch of his arm.

It must have been a loan because Bill Leeds wrote me later that he didn't make Hem a present of the machine gun until a couple of years after when the Old Master was leaving for the civil war in Spain. Leeds agreed that what we saw was a preview of *The Old Man and the Sea*, though the tales the Canary Islander told Hem in Havana certainly played their part. Nobody ever had much luck trying to trace a fish story to its source.

•••

It was probably the following spring that Hem and Waldo and I rented Bra's boat to go out to the Dry Tortugas. These are the westernmost islets of the string of coral islands that make up the Florida Keys. We'd made the long choppy trip across the banks hoping to catch up with one of the schools of big king mackerel that move east and north out of the Gulf of Mexico in the spring. We hadn't caught many big fish.

Waldo set up his easel at one of the embrasures of the vast stone fort and painted. I had my cot and notebook in another shady nook. The sun was hot and the tradewind cool. The place was enormous and entirely empty. We kept expecting to meet poor old Dr. Mudd coming out of one of the tunnels. No sound but the querulous shrieking of the terns. The water was incredibly clear, delicious for swimming. We saw no shark or barracuda, only a variety of reef fish: yellowtails, angelfish, searobbins, all sorts of tiny jewellike creatures we didn't know the names of swarming under the coralheads. A couple of days went by; it was one of the times I understood the meaning of the word halcyon.

Ernest had brought along Arnold Gingrich, who was just starting *Esquire*. The man was in a trance. It was a world he'd never dreamed of. He was mosquitobitten, half seasick, scorched with sunburn, astonished, half scared, half pleased. It was as much fun to see Ernest play an editor as to see him play a marlin.

Gingrich never took his fascinated eyes off Old Hem. Hem would reel in gently letting his prey have plenty of line. The editor was hooked. Sure he would print anything Hemingway cared to let him have at a thousand dollars a whack. (In those days it never occurred to us anyone got paid more than that. We lived outside of the world of agents and big time New York lunches.) Ernest was practicing up on skills he'd later apply to high literary finance. He got Gingrich so tame he even sold him a few pieces of mine for good measure.

Bra meanwhile was spending his time dredging up conches. Tourists had appeared in Key West. Bra had discovered to his amazement that tourists would buy the great rosy scalloped shells. He had the whole bow of the boat piled up with them. The night before we started back to Key West he made us one of the best conch chowders I ever ate. That with fried yellowtail seasoned with a brine and lime concoction he called Old Sour, made a royal feast. We washed it down with a little too much Bacardi rum.

We were tied up to a pier across from the fort. While we were eating and drinking, a couple of Cuban smacks that had been fishing in deep water for red snapper came alongside. They were a ragged sunbaked friendly crew. We handed around tin cups of

Bacardi. Hem's Spanish became remarkably fluent. From out of his beard Waldo produced that mixture of French, Italian, and bastard Castilian that had carried him for years through the Mediterranean countries. Bra, who disdained foreign tongues, made himself friendly with shrugs and grunts. Gingrich sat speechless and goggleeyed while we climbed around each other's boats jabbering like a band of monkeys.

There were feats of strength, tales of huge blue marlin hooked and lost, of crocodiles sighted in the Gulf and rattlesnakes twenty feet long seen swimming out to sea. Night fell absolutely windless. There was no moon. Our friends pushed their boats off, anchored a few hundred feet out and turned in. We moved out from the pier to catch what breeze there was. The stars looked big as Christmastree ornaments, clustered overhead and reflected in the sea. The three small craft seemed suspended in the midst of an enormous starstudded indigo sphere.

It was hot in the cabin. Weighed down with heat and Bacardi we lay sweating in the narrow bunks. Sleep came in a glare of heat.

We were wakened by a knocking on the deck. It was the elderly grizzled man who was skipper of one of the smacks. "Amigos, par despedirnos." Redeyed, with heads like lumps of lead, we scrambled on deck.

He pointed. Against the first violet streak in the east we could see a man on the bow of the smack shaking some liquid in a large glass carboy. They were sailing for Havana with the first breeze. They wanted to honor us with a farewell drink before they left.

Everybody climbed up on the narrow planking of the pier. Of course there was no ice. It was a warm eggnog made with a kind of cheep aguardiente that smelt like wood alcohol. Obediently we brought out our tin cups. We were hung over. We felt squeamish. It made us retch. We couldn't insult our amigos. We expected to die but they were our amigos and we drank it.

It was then that Ernest brought out his rifle and started to shoot. By this time it was silvery gloaming. You could feel the sun burning under the horizon. He shot a baked-bean can floating halfway to the shore. We threw out more cans for him. He shot bits of paper the Cubans spread out on wooden chips from their skiff. He shot several terns. He shot through a pole at the end of the pier. Anything we'd point at he would hit. He shot sitting. He shot standing. He shot lying on his belly. He shot backward, with the rifle held between his legs.

So far as we could see he never missed. Finally he ran out of ammunition. We drank down the last of the fishermen's punch.

The amigos shook hands. The amigos waved. They weighed anchor and hoisted the grimy sails on their smacks and steered closehauled into the east as the first breath of the trade lightened the heavy air.

We headed back to Key West. There was an oily swell over the banks on the way back. What wind there was settled into the stern. Bra's conches had begun to rot and stank abominably. The punch set badly. Our faces were green. Our lips were cold. Nobody actually threw up, but we were a pallid and silent crew until we reached the lee of the first low patches of mangroves that lay in the approaches of Key West.

Jim Harrison

Porpoise

Every year, when we're fly-fishing for tarpon
off Key West, Guy insists that porpoises
are good luck. But it's not so banal
as catching more fish or having a fashion
model fall out of the sky lightly on your head,
or at your feet depending on certain
preferences. It's what porpoises do to the ocean.
You see a school making love off Boca Grande,
the baby with his question mark staring
at us a few feet from the boat.
Porpoises dance for as long as they live.
You can do nothing for them.
They alter the universe.

Awake

Limp with night fears: hellebore, wolfbane,
Marlowe is daggered, fire, volts, African vipers,
the grizzly the horses sensed, the rattlesnake
by the mailbox — how he struck at thrown rocks,
black water, framed by police, wanton wife,
I'm a bad poet broke and broken at thirty-two,
a renter, shot by mistake, airplanes and trains,
half-mast hardons, a poisoned earth, sun will
go out, car break down in a blizzard,
my animals die, fistfights, alcohol, caskets,
the hammerhead gliding under the boat near
Loggerhead Key, my soul, my heart, my brain,
my life so interminably struck with an ax
as wet wood splits bluntly, mauled into
sections for burning.

From

Letters to Yesenin
"18"

Thus the poet is a beached gypsy, the first porpoise to
whom it occurred to commit suicide. True, my friend, even porpoises have
learned your trick and for similar reasons: losing hundreds of
thousands of wives, sons, daughters, husbands to the tuna nets.
The seventh lover in a row disappears and it can't be endured.
There is some interesting evidence that Joplin was a porpoise and
simply decided to stop breathing at an unknown depth. Perhaps the
navy has her body and is exploring ways to turn it into a weapon.
Off Boca Grande a baby porpoise approached my boat. It was a girl
about the size of my two year old daughter who might for all I know
be a porpoise. Anyway she danced around the boat for an hour
while her mother kept a safer distance. I set the mother at ease by
singing my infamous theme song: "Death dupe dear dingle devil flower
bird dung girl," repeating seven times until the mother approached
and I leaned over the gunnel and we kissed. I was tempted to swim
off with them but I remembered I had a date with someone who tripled
as a girl, cocaine dealer and duck though she chose to be the last,
alas, that evening. And as in all ancient stories I returned to the
spot but never found her or her little girl again. Even now mariners
passing the spot deep in the night can hear nothing. But enough
of porpoise love. And how they are known to beach themselves. I've
begun to doubt whether we ever would have been friends. Maybe. Not
that it's to the point—I know three one-eyed poets like myself
but am close to none of them. These letters might have kept me
alive—something to do you know as opposed to the nothing you chose.
Loud yeses don't convince. Neitzsche said you were a rope dancer
before you were born. I say yes before breakfast but to the smell
of bacon. Wise souls move through the dark only one step at a time.

Jim Harrison

from
A Good Day To Die

Double-anchored off Cudjoe Key: barely dawn and she's still asleep but I was awakened by water birds. So many. The first sight upward from the skiff's bottom was an osprey with a small snake hanging from her talons—back to the nest now in the rookery for breakfast. Almost chilly, in the mid-sixties at six A.M., but it will be eighty by noon. I wanted to get over to the Snipe Key basin and catch the incoming tide and what fish would be there looking off that huge sandspit toward the rank mangroves. She's snoring, when she said she'd never sleep as the boat's bottom was too hard and we had no air mattresses. Drone of a sponger off to work. How they stand in that narrow prow without falling off and it must be genetic. I talked to one for a half hour once and understood nothing. She's waking. Lukewarm coffee in the Thermos. The mosquitoes were bad in the night and sand fleas. Over the freeboard I see a small sand shark nuzzling around the prongs of the sea anchor.

"Let's go back," she says.

"I thought you wanted to fish."

"That was the margaritas you gave me."

I thought for a moment of kicking her ass out of the boat but that would be murder. We were sweating like piggies in that sleeping bag and I thought how in youth I had heard about our soldiers in the Orient getting rolled up in rugs with Chinese girls. Too hot and we didn't manage. After coming out at dusk with the markers not totally visible. Only a drunk or a master would try it and I was the former. I stood on the freeboard and cast a streamer but a barracuda snipped the leader when he struck.

I watched her dress with no interest. No panties, only white bells and a muslin blouse under which her breasts swung free and that was why I asked her out here. But she grew progressively dense after so much laughter. I tied on another tippet and small keel hook streamer. There is a long happy streak when half drunk: everything is possible on earth—love, sanity, enormous fish, fame. I met her in Captain Tony's, a saloon off Duval. A dozen drinks and some shrimp and picadillo in a Cuban restaurant. Then borrowed a friend's boat and took off from Garrison Bight with beer and a pint and a Thermos of coffee, some bread and cheese. I only stopped off Cudjoe because of darkness. I popped a beer; my head ached insanely and I wanted fresh water and aspirin but we had none.

"My friends will worry about me."

"Your friends won't be up for a few hours."

I pulled the anchors and coiled the dripping rope. She chewed on the bread and drank out of the Thermos, shivering. I checked the gas. The tank was nearly full but then I remembered Felipe had filled it while we bought the beer. I turned on the marine radio and picked up a Havana station which was playing some wild Latin music. I thought it would cheer her up. I checked the lower unit then pressed the powertilt and started the motor. Birds flew up by the thousands from a small key a hundred yards away. A few roseate spoonbills among them.

"Don't go fast, it will make me colder," she said over the idling motor. It would be nice to drag her by an anchor rope at forty knots. I pointed toward Snipe Key and accelerated.

"You're going the wrong way," she shouted.

"A shortcut." I intended to have a look at the basin if it meant binding and gagging her. I slowed down enough to reach for the chart under the seat so I could check for the markers. They are generally easy to see, with a cormorant perched on each one.

"Why don't you get back in the bag?"

She looked at me quizzically then crawled in. If the water had been choppy she would have been pounded senseless. I pushed the throttle up to full bore, covering the seven miles flat out at forty knots; but when I pulled up to the basin the water was too shallow to enter. I got out the tide book to see if the wait would be long but the book was inscrutable. Numbers. I looked at the far end of the basin through my binoculars to see if any bonefish were tailing but the water was flat and motionless.

"Why did you stop?" she asked, peeking out of the bag.

"So I wouldn't tear out the fucking lower unit."

"Don't get mad."

"We don't have enough water to get over the reef."

"Can we turn around?" She was sniffling now, in part

from her obvious hangover. She looked at me as if I were a madman, not altogether inaccurate as a judgment of character. It is hard enough to wake up in a motel room with a woman you don't really know. I began to try to remember her last name but drew a blank. Ansel. Atkins. Aberdeen. Angus. Cow. There was nothing to do but turn around and head back to Key West. I eased the boat around at low throttle in the shallow water, disturbing a small, beautiful leopard ray.

"Where are we going now?"

"The Japs have closed off the channel. Keep your head down."

Now her eyes were truly fearful. No gift for the surreal, a dull stenographer's brain.

"Have a beer," I suggested.

"I'd throw up."

The questioning eyes again, reminding me of a retarded collie pup I owned as a boy. Bit a bicycle tire and caught its teeth in the wire spokes. Back broken when flipped. How I mourned for puppies.

"You look like a puppy I owned once."

She made another snivel noise and receded into the sleeping bag. A giant turd. Burial at sea. I'll play taps on the kazoo when I dump the bag over. Full throttle again, following the markers to Key West, singing fly the friendly skies of united over the motor whine. Jingo songs stick in my head. Do all people sing when alone in their cars? Once in Boston I was bellowing out Patsy Cline's "The Last Word in Lonesome Is Me" and at a stoplight a truck driver clapped.

I entered Key West channel at full speed passing the Navy officers' housing with a sign of NO WAKE tacked to each dock. An early morning wake for each. A dawn riser stood on his lawn and mouthed a soundless "slow down" and I gave him the finger.

At the marina Felipe looked at us and said a pleasantry in Spanish while tying up the boat.

"Dumbo cunto stupido no fisho," I said pointing at my mate who was crawling out of the bag. Felipe giggled.

We drove in silence down Duval to the Pier House where she was staying. She got out and flounced to the motel door without a backward glance. Oh well.

• • • • •

I went back to my room and lolled around naked. I took a shower and examined my insect bites and my gritty bloodshot eyes. Was it all worth it? No. The soul of a clerk bent deeply over his arithmetic. Eve proffers the clerk an apple which turns out to be hollow and contains a howling succubus. I considered smoking a little dope but rejected the idea—after a nap I wanted to play pool and dope always took the edge off whatever competitive spirit I had left in the world. Stretched out on the cot my thoughts alternated between pool and fishing in an attempt to rid my brain of the girl. She would be in a perfect snit by now. Perhaps it had happened a hundred times. The clerk again. Maybe only seventy-seven. A rack of pool balls lay gleaming against green felt. The one-ball is yellow but then the color of the two-ball escaped me. The water was calm and very clear and shallow and some maniacs could see tarpon coming a quarter of a mile away. They would deliver their casts with graceful fluid motions while I would chop the air in panic. In Ecuador the Indian mate was too poor to buy Polaroid glasses but he saw the caudal fins of marlin long before my perfect eyes noticed anything. Benny played pool as if the cue stick emerged from his body. Not my own alcohol and geometry. She was an asshole and I couldn't have loved her at gun point.

The late afternoon sun flowing in a sheet through the window. Why didn't I draw the blinds. Sweating with the air apparently the same temperature as my blood's. I dressed quickly in a light khaki shirt and suntans and tennis shoes. Anonymity. I took a beer from my boat cooler but the ice cubes had melted and the beer was lukewarm. I drank it looking out at the white hotness of Duval Street. The world looked askew and foreign. The girl might be just getting up from an air-conditioned nap, stretching her admittedly attractive limbs and deciding to be more careful about whom she left bars with.

In Sloppy Joe's I drank three or four glasses of beer waiting for a used-car salesman from Denton, Texas, to show up. We played pool nearly every afternoon when I got through fishing and he finished hustling sailors into car deals they couldn't afford. I was pleased with the way beer made me feel like an ordinary sot. Maybe I was really a veteran or a pipefitter or carpenter. Seventh Airborne or something like that. After a case of Budweiser I might have voted for Goldwater. A retired chief petty officer, a passing acquaintance, sat down next to me and began rattling off complaints about the weather, his car, his wife's drinking, and then politics. When he was drunk he was not above trying to run over a hippie. I had once teased him about the Navy's combat readiness at Pearl Harbor and that after that debacle they were lucky to get their hands on a rowboat. He was on the verge of hitting me but I apologized and bought him several drinks.

The car salesman finally came in and we played a nearly wordless hour of eightball during which I lost twelve dollars. I won five of it back playing nineball but then he left saying that the "little woman" would have dinner ready. I had a disturbing image of a female midget before a stove stirring food with teeny-weeny hands. I went back to a stool at the bar and ordered a double bourbon straight up. I was tired of going to the bathroom every fifteen minutes to get rid of the beer. I glanced out through the large open doors to see if anyone interesting was wandering around but it was the dinner hour lull and dusk still came rather early in April. Then I noticed that there was a strange-looking guy sitting directly across the circular bar staring at me. He was large with fairly long hair, tanned and extremely muscular with a small eagle tattooed on his left forearm. But the right side of his face was distorted with a bleached twist of scar tissue and it drew his eye a few degrees off center. I instantly averted my glance. Perhaps a shrimper and they're always cutting each other up.

"What are you staring at?"

"Nothing. I was looking over your head at the street." Shot of adrenaline. A single drop of sweat moved down the inside of my leg.

He turned around and looked out the open door behind him and I drew in my breath. Then he swiveled quickly on his stool and stood up. "How about a game?"

"O.K."

He flipped me a quarter for the rack and walked over to the jukebox. By the time he chose his cue Jim Ed Brown had started singing "Morning," a song I rather liked about country style adultery. Who screws who in Mingo Country. It seemed to me that you had to be out in the country, traveling, or rather drunk to listen to such music.

"Eightball for a buck?"

"Fine with me."

He broke very hard and got two stripes and a solid but I quickly saw on the next shot that he was a slammer, a hard stroker who didn't play for shape. This sort of player can be very accurate but he plays with his balls, his manhood, and never leaves himself well for the next shot except by accident: a pointless arrogance, a kind of dumbbell "macho." His speech was Southern, either Alabama or Georgia, without the sing-song effect you hear in Mississippi. While he shot I thought of a record a teacher had played for us in college with Faulkner talking about fox hunting. The record was studiously fatuous with the great man's voice high pitched and lacking the timbre one would imagine in his heroes, say Bayard Sartoris.

I won a half dozen games in a row but he was only mildly irritated. He drew the money out of a bulky clip. There were twenties and fifties in quantity and I wondered idly why anyone would take the chance. But then I thought that it was unlikely that anyone would attack him.

"My muster pay." He had read my thoughts.

"Vietnam?"

"A year and a half's worth."

Now two sailors were watching us play, obviously sizing up our game for a challenge. One of them was small and wiry and was giggling while the other who was large and beefy merely stared. Then the big one put a quarter on the edge of the table which meant he was challenging the winner. I had just missed an easy shot and was irritable. It was bad etiquette to put a quarter up while someone was shooting. My partner took the quarter and deftly flipped it out into the street where it rolled rather electrically in a small circle. I held my breath.

"What are you, a smartass?" the big sailor said. My partner continued his shooting but then the sailor picked up the eightball and dropped it in a pocket. "That ends your game, smartass."

I felt a touch of vertigo and moved instinctively toward the door but curiosity stopped me. I couldn't see any sign in my partner's face of what he was going to do except that he chewed his gum more rapidly. He looked down at his left hand which held the cue stick and then at his right which was empty. Then with startling speed he clouted the sailor in the ear with the heel of his hand. The arc of the swing was wide but fast and the sailor collapsed on his butt with a yelp. There was a quick boot to his chest and then the cue stick pressed across his throat until he began to gag. I saw the other sailor looking at me but he only shrugged. Several barflies had gathered around us.

"We're playing pool now. When we're done you can play." He was letting his full weight rest on his knee on the sailor's chest. Then he stood abruptly and the sailor stumbled to the door.

"Those fucking creeps think they own this town." Now he was smiling and we sat back down at the table but the bartender was standing next to us.

"You guys are cut off."

"You don't know what those guys said." I found myself talking. "They said we were queers and we weren't allowed in the bar. Do we look like queers to you? What if someone called you a queer?"

The bartender paused, trying to figure out if I was bullshitting him, but then the chief petty officer who was now terribly drunk said he had heard the whole thing. We were allowed to stay and I gave the chief the victory sign and ordered him a drink. We played another game of pool but lost interest.

"What if that guy had known karate?"

"Nobody knows karate if you get a good one in first." He laughed and put another quarter in the jukebox.

We began drinking steadily and talked about everything excluding the war: baseball (Boog Powell who played for the Orioles was from Key West), music, fishing, the girls that now walked by the door with splendid regularity. Many of the girls were tourists or college girls down for Easter week but some were local conchs and Cubans. He liked the Cubans but I preferred the tourists as I considered Latin girls to be somewhat frightening and unreliable. For an instant I thought of the girl I had met the evening before—all that I had drunk made her seem interesting again. He said that his name was Tim and that he was from Valdosta, Georgia, and was staying a few weeks on Stock Island with his sister who was married to a Navy man he described as a "real jackoff." We were getting fairly drunk and I wanted something to eat before I lost control. We quarreled mildly about whether a pump or a double-barreled shotgun was better for bird shooting. I really wanted to ask him about the war but felt afraid to bring it up.

"I never ate in a French restaurant." He was looking over my shoulder at the only one in town. "Are we dressed up enough?"

"I've been in there. It costs a lot."

"I'll buy. I won a lot of this at poker in the hospital."

"How long were you there?"

"Two months."

This was the first reference to his face. It was sort of a mess at close range and I wondered why the Army hadn't done plastic surgery.

"I'm not going back to the hospital," he said, anticipating my question.

He asked me what I was doing in town and I said that I came every year for a month or two to fish. I rambled on about the fishing and admitted that it seemed that every year I became less capable at it to the point that I dreaded going out with those who fished well. I said that it had always struck me that unless you were able to become single minded about fishing and hunting you would fail. You were either obsessive and totally in control or you were nothing. He didn't appear interested in these subtleties. I suddenly thought that it would be fun to kick the shit out of someone in a few seconds, which was obviously one of his talents. I reflected on all the multifoliate ways you parry when you first meet someone.

When we got up to leave I noticed for the first time that the eagle on his tattoo had a beak that was drawn up into a maniacal smile and asked him about it.

"Just a joke to piss people off."

"They're going to dam up the Grand Canyon," I said halfway across Duval Street. Tim stopped and looked at me, puzzled. A car beeped.

"You're shitting me."

"Nope."

We entered the restaurant and the hostess with a quick knowing glance seated us in a corner as far from other customers as possible.

"Where'd you hear about that?" he said looking at the menu.

"I read about it. It's true." For a moment I had been lost. It had only been an errant comment.

"No kidding?"

"Word of honor," I said raising my two fingers in a mock cub scout sign.

"Jesus Christ, it will fill up with water." He was clearly troubled and I wanted to drop the subject.

I ordered drinks from the waiter who was obviously a homosexual. He raised his eyebrows at me as if I had scored and I was terribly embarrassed. But then I supposed that we didn't look like we quite fit together. Some homosexuals have an uncanny ability to figure people out by their immediate appearances.

"I don't understand this shit. You order for us."

I asked for two orders of steak au poivre and some endive, which seemed inoffensive. Then the waiter asked us if we wanted wine.

"Yeah, I want some fucking champagne," Tim said a bit loudly but the waiter was charmed.

We got out of the place with difficulty. The food was excellent, especially the endive which reminded me of New York, but the waiter tried to clip us when he returned the change. We had had a half dozen cups of Cuban coffee which had a nerve-jangling effect mixed with all the pepper and alcohol. The owner placated us at the door with assurances that it wasn't intentional on the waiter's part but I felt very melancholy pondering all the little cheats people pull on one another. Up on Big Pine Key a wealthy angler from Vermont had tried to cheat on a fishing record by filling the gullet of a bonefish with sinkers. He had bribed his guide to go along with the little project. A gesture at a corner of immortality and not at all concomitant with what you thought of the stern Yankees.

Meanwhile the waiter was standing sullen in the background.

"You ought to fire that cocksucker," Tim said loudly.

"Let's go." I pulled on his arm. His word had had a magical effect on the restaurant. We were being looked at in mute wonderment. I waved and grinned at some people I knew. I wanted to leave before the owner called the police. The local police were very authoritative. A few nights before I had seen one dragging a shrimper from a bar by the hair and the shrimper's eyes were buggy with pain. I was somehow sure that Tim wouldn't react gracefully to such treatment.

•••••

We walked around the corner and into Captain Tony's, which was dark and crowded. Behind the dancing area a jug band was playing and a guy with a pigtail was singing loudly and not very well. We moved down the length of the bar and sat near the pool table and jukebox.

"I wish I had one."

"One what?" It was hard to hear over the music. I tried to signal the barmaid.

"A pigtail."

"You're putting me on." This was a surprise—my ordinary conception of a Georgia cracker involved shooting treed blacks or messing around with old cars, though as time passed it seemed much easier for a black to get himself shot in Detroit than anyplace else. "You could grow one."

He was becoming plaintive and morose about the prospect of waiting for a pigtail. The barmaid came and I ordered two beers. She looked bored but took an unusual interest in Tim which made me slightly jealous as I had never been able to gather her attention. Tony always hires the most beautiful barmaids in Key West and the Navy pilots come in numbers, fall in love and are rejected. The barmaids, it seems, are in love with musicians and other worthless types who wear pigtails and are always broke. The barmaids are not interested in sleek pilots with thin mustaches and wallets full of flight pay. When the blond one whose name was Judy bent over the cooler to get our beer we were cleanly mooned. Polka-dot panties. But I knew she was hopeless because she lived with a rather affable freak who sold tacos from a pushcart.

I realized we had become less drunk and would have to start over again, a practice that is known as a double-header. I had clearly peaked out and was on my way down. I could scarcely swallow the beer, my head ached and I wanted a nap, full dress and under the covers. By myself. All the pepper on the steak had given me heartburn and I needed some Gelusil.

"That's really true?" Tim was staring into my eyes.

"What?"

"About the Grand Canyon?"

"It's at least in the planning stage." Now I truly regretted saying anything.

"I've never seen the Grand Canyon."

I was on the verge of saying it was very large then giggled at the idea. I had seen Glen Canyon years ago before it was literally drowned and liked it better but any comparison was absurd with such splendors. And besides I was a Chicken Little and tended to believe in nonsense. I had once read in a New York underground newspaper that an asteroid was going to hit Long Island Sound and the resultant tidal wave would kill everyone. I sat in our little apartment in Port Jefferson and brooded about the logic and scientific probabilities involved. I convinced my wife and she had nightmares of burning railroad cars and bloated sheep. When the appointed day went by without a single asteroid I was embarrassed.

"We probably ought to blow up the goddamn thing." Tim nodded in assent then spoke but I couldn't hear him over the band. I suddenly felt very bored and claustrophobic. "I got to go."

"Why? We're just getting started."

"I'm tired and I have to be up at six tomorrow to fish."

"I'll fix you up." He began searching his pockets then stood and looked blankly at me. "Ride with me to my sister's. I got some uppers."

I hesitated, weighing alternatives. Did I want to get blasted? If I did I wouldn't go fishing in the morning. With a hangover a two-foot chop sends me puking despite Merazine. Probably be too windy anyway—I had noticed the palms swaying on the side street. And maybe this guy was crazy too. I hadn't envied the sailor. I didn't like the idea of dropping speed with alcohol in my guts. Blood pressure soars. I looked at my watch—only nine o'clock—and remembered how much I had always disliked people who copped out on a good drunk. You would just get started talking and laughing and playing pool and they would go home to their wives. Pussy-whipped we called it. I couldn't go home to my wife. Six months now.

"Let's hear the rest of the set first." The jug band was getting better. A tall black woman was singing a Joplin tune, a graceful reverse gesture. She was well over six foot and wore a white silk sheath dress that allowed her hip bones to protrude. She was awesome.

"God I'd like some of that," Tim said.

I nodded agreement but admitted to myself that I

wouldn't dare try it. Now that I had decided to stick it out the beer went down easily and I thought how deftly the brain screws up the stomach and breathing. We played a few games of nineball for five dollars and I lost them all.

"You can owe me," he said.

I checked my wallet. I had two hundred back in the room but had to make it last. I put twenty-five dollars in my pocket each morning and stuck to this budget. I had nearly run out of people to borrow from. The liquor was obviously bothering my shooting more than his. It was between sets and the jukebox was playing a Beatles tune that had a phrase "we all shine on." I liked the music but the lyrics were so patently absurd. How like me to be questioning the rock lyrics when I should have been concentrating on pool. There goes the allowance.

"Let's go get that shit and come back."

Tim drove very fast but capably down the back streets until we caught Route 1 for the short trip to Stock Island. A Detroit jockey, a Dodge with four on the floor. His sister lived in a large mobile home and was watching the tube when we entered. *Marcus Welby, M.D.* She was frowsy and dilapidated, perhaps ten years older than Tim

"Pleased to meetcha," she said without getting off the couch. I sat and watched the Doctor with her while Tim went in the other room. It seems the Doctor was telling a young woman that her husband had to have a kidney transplant and they couldn't afford it. Her eyes flickered moistly as did Tim's sister's. Commercial. The room smelled of fried potatoes.

"Where you from?" she said turning from the set.

"Michigan."

"My husband he's from Flint. He's in Pensacola for a few days. Want a beer?" She was drinking hers straight from the can.

"No thanks."

Tim came in with a bottle of pop.

"Offer your friend a Coke, Timmy," The commercial was over and she was watching Marcus as he strode resolutely across a hospital parking lot.

"No. We're going. See you later."

"Be careful," she said.

I had been staring at a lamp in the corner that had a black plaster leopard as its base. From the leopard's skull protruded the stem and bulb and shade. The leopard had green pastel eyes and painted white snarling teeth and a chipped jaw.

When we got into the car he handed me two spansules which I dropped with a swing of pop. He dropped four.

"You're going to fuck up your head."

"Right," he said.

On the way back downtown we talked about college which I couldn't remember very well. He said that he had gone to Georgia Tech for two years before dropping out and enlisting. It wasn't too hard but it was boring and there had been too few cunt around the place. He had re-upped after his first year in Vietnam to get the extra volunteer pay and to avoid marriage. He thought he had got his girl pregnant but then she miscarried. It somehow sounded old fashioned.

We pulled up near Tony's and it was even more crowded than before. I talked to a head I knew vaguely and he gave me directions for a party on Sugarloaf Key after the bar closed. The speed had already taken effect and my system was winding up like a jet engine. I felt young and stupid. Tim looked calm enough though his eyes were a bit glittery. We bought drinks for two college girls from Ohio and asked them if they wanted to go to a party. They were suspicious. Too straight. And I was twenty-eight, clearly not a college student, and Tim's scar didn't seem to help.

"Why don't you go home and play with each other. See if we give a shit," he said. They were startled and moved quickly to the far end of the bar. Then we asked a hip-looking girl with long blond hair if she wanted a drink and she accepted and when we mentioned a party she said she already knew about it but would ride with us. She recognized me from the Cuban diner where I ate regularly. I was disappointed—she was vacant and simple-minded—but Tim was enthralled. A fat soiled-looking girl approached and our new friend offered her a ride. She was homely but her brain was absolutely vivacious compared to the beauty who kept saying she was "strung out" as if the condition were unique on earth.

On the way out to Sugarloaf Key we passed around several bombers that Tim took from under the dashboard. The grass was Colombian buds, dry and hot and powerful. I entered some sort of fantasy time warp where I was out on the flats at noon repeating and perfecting every bad cast I had made in five years. I now felt that my brain was a purring electric motor and that my fingers would fry people at touch. Usually with drugs there was a small undisturbed center in my brain that could view what was happening with clarity. But it had been swallowed by the unilaterally manic notion that my whole body was less than an inch thick and the only backing I had on earth was the back seat of a car. Now the warm air coming in the window reminded me of a thousand other summer nights and I was dazed and constricted. The fat girl began humming. I thought in self-defense of the pleasant time I had had when I dropped four hits of psilocybin, lay down in a creek for an hour and became a trout. An infatuation with poisons.

We pulled into a yard after some confused circling. The subdivision roads were made of crushed coral and the noise of the tires was nearly unbearable. It was a small place built on the principle of stilts in anticipation of tropical storms, with the lower half of the house given over to a utility room and a screened-in area and the upper half containing kitchen and bedrooms, the functional living space. The house abutted a canal; I knew you could go out the canal and through Tarpon Creek to get to the Gulf Stream or Loggerhead Key. The shrubbery was dense and there were about a dozen cars. The music was very loud and when we entered people seemed sprayed about everywhere in a semi-comatose state. I went upstairs to the kitchen and drank a lot of lukewarm water from the tap. All water is piped from the mainland but I didn't want to snoop in their refrigerator for the water bottle even in my advanced state of looniness. A group was sitting at the kitchen table talking intently and passing a joint. Smelled strange, perhaps laced with something. I went back downstairs looking for Tim but couldn't find him. Then I went outside to muffle the music a bit and some people were swimming beneath a dim boathouse light. The light attracted an enormous swarm of insects some of which looked as large as sparrows. I shed my clothes and jumped into the warm brackish water. No sharks I hoped but they rarely come into the canals: out on the flats at night tearing into mullet or anything that moves. I hung in the water, my hand grasping a tire that served as a boat buffer; dizzy, weightless, joyless. The pretty girl was next to me but her face was flat as a magazine cover. I reached out and touched her. She began giggling and I became more conscious though it was apparent that my body was made of rubber, an extension of the tire I held on to. I felt her sex, slippery in the water, and she squeezed her eyes shut. I held my breath and sank into the water and began nuzzling her but it required too much effort. She climbed up the ladder and I followed, a dazzling sight. We gathered our clothes and walked through the bushes to Tim's car and got into the back seat still wet with salt water. She took a joint from her purse and I lit it taking only two drags as I was so spaced I was sure the car was moving. Vague taste of hash. A single mosquito. I began kissing her again and she dropped the roach out the window and returned the gesture. Skin sticking to the Naugahyde with the glue of wet salt. But I was a small motor again, metallic. Part of my brain thought of my wife and how we hid behind sexuality when nothing else worked. Saline. Aqueous. I watched my lower half drift out to sea.

Ernest Hemingway

From
To Have and Have Not

He did not take the bicycle but walked down the street. The moon was up now and the trees were dark against it, and he passed the frame houses with their narrow yards, light coming from the shuttered windows; the unpaved alleys, with their double rows of houses; Conch town, where all was starched, well-shuttered, virtue, failure, grits and boiled grunts, under-nourishment, prejudice, righteousness, interbreeding and the comforts of religion; the open-doored, lighted Cuban bolito houses, shacks whose only romance was their names; The Red House, Chicha's; the pressed stone church; its steeples sharp, ugly triangles against the moonlight; the big grounds and the long, black-domed bulk of the convent, handsome in the moonlight; a filling station and a sandwich place, bright-lighted beside a vacant lot where a miniature golf course had been taken out; past the brightly lit main street with the three drug stores, the music store, the five Jew stores, three pool-rooms, two barbershops, five beer joints, three ice cream parlors, the five poor and the one good restaurant, two magazine and paper places, four second-hand joints (one of which made keys), a photographer's, an office building with four dentists' offices upstairs, the big dime store, a hotel on the corner with taxis opposite; and across, behind the hotel, to the street that led to jungle town, the big unpainted frame house with lights and the girls in the doorway, the mechanical piano going, and a sailor sitting in the street; and then on back, past the back of the brick courthouse with its clock luminous at half-past ten, past the whitewashed jail building shining in the moonlight, to the embowered entrance of the Lilac Time where motor cars filled the alley.

The Lilac Time was brightly lighted and full of people, and as Richard Gordon went in he saw the gambling room was crowded, the wheel turning and the little ball clicking brittle against metal partitions set in the bowl, the wheel turning slowly, the ball whirring, then clicking jumpily until it settled and there was only the turning of the wheel and the rattling of chips.

Who Murdered the Vets?

A First-Hand Report On The Florida Hurricane

I have led my ragamuffins where they are peppered; there's not three of my hundred and fifty left alive, and they are for the town's end, to beg during life.   -Shakespeare

Yes, and now we drown those three.

Whom did they annoy and to whom was their possible presence a political danger?

Who sent them down to the Florida Keys and left them there in hurricane months?

Who is responsible for their deaths?

The writer of this article lives a long way from Washington and would not know the answers to those questions. But he does know that wealthy people, yachtsmen, fishermen such as President Hoover and President Roosevelt, do not come to the Florida Keys in hurricane months. Hurricane months are August, September and October, and in those months you see no yachts along the Keys. You do not see them because yacht owners know there would be great danger, unescapable danger, to their property if a storm should come. For the same reason, you cannot interest any very wealthy people in fishing off the coast of Cuba in the summer when the biggest fish are there. There is a known danger to property. But veterans, especially the bonus-marching variety of veterans, are not property. They are only human beings, unsuccessful human beings, and all they have to lose is their lives. They are doing coolie labor for a top wage of $45 a month and they have been put down on the Florida Keys where they can't make trouble. It is hurricane months, sure, but if anything comes up, you can always evacuate them, can't you?

This is the way a storm comes. On Saturday evening at Key West, having finished working, you go out to the porch to have a drink and read the evening paper. The first thing you see in the paper is a storm warning. You know that work is off until it is past, and you are angry and upset because you were going well.

The location of the tropical disturbance is given as east of Long Island in the Bahamas, and the direction it is traveling is approximately toward Key West. You get out the September storm chart which gives the tracks and dates of forty storms of hurricane intensity during that month since 1900. And by taking the rate of movement of the storm as given in the Weather Bureau Advisory you calculate that it cannot reach us before Monday noon at the earliest. Sunday you spend making the boat as safe as you can. When they refuse to haul her out on the ways because there are too many boats ahead, you buy $52 worth of new heavy hawser and shift her to what seems the safest part of the submarine base and tie her up there. Monday you nail up the shutters on the house and get everything movable inside. There are northeast storm warnings flying, and at five o'clock the wind is blowing heavily and steadily from the northeast. They have hoisted the big red flags with a black square in the middle, one over the other that means a hurricane. The wind is rising hourly, and the barometer is falling. All the people of the town are nailing up their houses.

You go down to the boat and wrap the lines with canvas where they will chafe when the surge starts, and believe that she has a good chance to ride it out if it comes from any direction but the northwest where the opening of the sub-basin is; provided no other boat smashes into you and sinks you. There is a booze boat seized by the Coast Guard tied next to you and you notice her stern lines are only tied to ringbolts in the stern, and you start belly-aching about that.

"For Christ sake, you know those lousy ringbolts will pull right out of her stern and then she'll come down on us."

"If she does, you can cut her loose or sink her."

"Sure, and maybe we can't get to her too. What's the use of letting a piece of junk like that sink a good boat?"

From the last advisory you figure we will not get it until midnight, and at ten o'clock you leave the Weather Bureau and go home to see if you can get two hours' sleep before it starts, leaving the car in front of the house because you do not trust the rickety garage, putting the barometer and a flashlight by the bed for when the electric lights go. At midnight the wind is howling, the glass is 29.55 and dropping while you watch it, and rain is coming in sheets. You dress, find the car drowned out, make your way to the boat with a flashlight with branches falling and wires going down. The flashlight shorts in the rain, and the wind is now coming in heavy gusts from the northwest. The captured boat has pulled her ringbolts out, and by quick handling by Jose Rodriguez, a Spanish sailor, was swung clear before she hit us. She is now pounding against the dock.

The wind is bad and you have to crouch over to make headway against it. You figure if we get the hurricane from there you will lose the boat and you never will have enough money to get another. You feel like hell. But a little after two o'clock it backs into the west and by the law of circular storms you know the storm has passed over the Keys above us. Now the boat is well-sheltered by the sea wall and the breakwater and at five o'clock, the glass having been steady for an hour, you get back to the house. As you make your way in without a light you find a tree is down across the walk and a strange empty look in the front yard shows the big old sappodillo tree is down too. You turn in.

That's what happens when one misses you. And that is about the minimum of time you have to prepare for a hurricane; two full days. Sometimes you have longer.

But what happened on the Keys?

On Tuesday, as the storm made its way up the Gulf of Mexico, it was so wild not a boat could leave Key West and there was no communication with the Keys beyond the ferry, nor with the mainland. No one knew what the storm had done, where it had passed. No train came in and there was no news by plane. Nobody knew the horror that was on the Keys. It was not until the next day that a boat got through to Matecumbe Key from Key West.

Now, as this is written five days after the storm, nobody knows how many are dead. The Red Cross, which has steadily played down the number, announcing first 46 then 150, finally saying the dead would not pass 300, today lists the dead and missing as 446, but the total of veterans dead and missing alone numbers 442 and there have been 70 bodies of civilians recovered. The total of dead may well pass a thousand as many bodies were swept out to sea and never will be found.

It is not necessary to go into the deaths of the civilians and their families since they were on the Keys of their own free will; they made their living there, had property and knew the hazards involved. But the veterans had been sent there; they had no opportunity to leave, nor any protection against hurricanes; and they never had a chance for their lives.

During the war, troops and sometimes individual soldiers who incurred the displeasure of their superior officers, were sometimes sent into positions of extreme danger and kept there repeatedly until they were no longer problems. I do not believe anyone, knowingly, would send U.S. war veterans into any such positions in time of peace. But the Florida Keys, in hurricane months, in the matter of casualties recorded during the building of the Florida East Coast Railway to Key West, when nearly a thousand men were killed by hurricanes, can be classed as such a position. And ignorance has never been accepted as an excuse for murder or for manslaughter.

Who sent nearly a thousand war veterans, many of them husky, hard-working and simply out of luck, but many of them close to the border of pathological cases, to live in frame shacks on the Florida Keys in hurricane months?

Why were the men not evacuated on Sunday, or, at latest, Monday morning, when it was known there was a possibility of a hurricane striking the Keys *and evacuation was their only possible protection?*

Who advised against sending the train from Miami to evacuate the veterans until four-thirty o'clock on Monday so that it was blown off the tracks before it ever reached the lower camps?

These are questions that someone will have to answer, and answer satisfactorily, unless the clearing of Anacostia Flats is going to seem an act of kindness compared to the clearing of Upper and Lower Matecumbe.

When we reached Lower Matecumbe there were bodies floating in the ferry slip. The brush was all brown as though autumn had come to these islands where there is no autumn but only a more dangerous summer, but that was because the leaves had all been blown away. There was two feet of sand over the highest part of the island where the sea had carried it and all the heavy bridge-building machines were on their sides. The island looked like the abandoned bed of a river where the sea had swept it. The railroad embankment was gone and the men who had cowered behind it and finally, when the water came, clung to the rails, were all gone with it. You could find them face down and face up in the mangroves. The biggest bunch of the dead were in the tangled, always green but now brown, mangroves behind the tank cars and the water towers. They hung on there, in shelter, until the wind and the rising water carried them away. They didn't all let go at once but only when they could hold on no longer. Then further on you found them high in the trees where the water had swept them. You found them everywhere and in the sun all of them were beginning to be too big for their blue jeans and jackets that they could never fill when they were on the bum and hungry.

I'd known a lot of them at Josie Grunt's place and around the town when they would come in for pay day, and some of them were punch drunk and some of them were smart; some had been on the bum since the Argonne almost and some had lost their jobs the year before last Christmas; some had wives and some couldn't remember; some were good guys, and others put their pay checks in the Postal Savings and then came over to cadge in on the drinks when better men were drunk; some liked to fight and others liked to walk around the town; and they were all what you get after a war. But who sent them there to die?

They're better off, I can hear whoever sent them say, explaining to himself. What good were they? You can't account for accidents or acts of God. They were well-fed, well-housed, well-treated and, let us suppose, now they are well dead.

But I would like to make whoever sent them there carry just one out through the mangroves, or turn one over that lay in the sun along the fill, or tie five together so they won't float out, or smell that smell you thought you'd never smell again, with luck when rich bastards make a war. The lack of luck goes on until all who take part in it are gone.

So now you hold your nose, and you, you that put in the literary columns that you were staying in Miami to see a hurricane because you needed it in your next novel and now you were afraid you would not see one, you can go on reading the paper, and you'll get all you need for your next novel; but I would like to lead you by the seat of your well-worn-by-writing-to-the-literary-columns pants up to that bunch of mangroves where there is a woman, bloated big as a balloon and upside down and there's another face down in the brush next to her and explain to you they are two damned nice girls who ran a sandwich place and filling station and that where they are is their hard luck. And you could make a note of it for your next novel and how is your next novel coming, brother writer, comrade shit?

But just then one of eight survivors from that camp of 187 not counting 12 who went to Miami to play ball (how's that for casualties, you guys who remember percentages?) comes along and he says, "That's my old lady. Fat, ain't she?" But that guy is nuts, now, so we can dispense with him, and we have to go back and get in a boat before we can check up on Camp Five.

Camp Five was where eight survived out of 187, but we only find 67 of those plus two more along the fill makes 69. But all the rest are in the mangroves. It doesn't take a bird dog to locate them. On the other hand, there are no buzzards. Absolutely no buzzards. How's that? Would you believe it? The wind killed all the buzzards and all the big winged birds like pelicans too. You can find them in the grass that's washed along the fill. Hey, there's another one. He's got low shoes, put him down, man, looks about sixty, low shoes, copper-riveted overalls, blue percale shirt without collar, storm jacket, by Jesus that's the thing to wear, nothing in his pockets. Turn him over. Face tumefied beyond recognition. Hell, he don't look like a veteran. He's too old. He's got grey hair. You'll have grey hair yourself this time next week. And across his back there was a great big blister as wide as his back and all ready to burst where his storm jacket had slipped down. Turn him over again. Sure he's a veteran. I know him. What's he got low shoes on for then? Maybe he made some money shooting craps and bought them. You don't know that guy. You can't tell him now. I know him, he hasn't got any thumb. That's how I know him. The land crabs ate his thumb. You think you know everybody. Well you waited a long time to get sick brother. Sixty-seven of them and you get sick at the sixty-eighth.

And so you walk the fill, where there is any fill and it's calm and clear and blue and almost the way it is when the millionaires come down in the winter except for the sand-flies, the mosquitoes and the smell of the dead that always smell the same in all countries that you go to—and now they smell like that in your own country. Or is it just that dead soldiers smell the same no matter what their nationality or who sends them to die?

Who sent them down there?

I hope he reads this—and how does he feel?

He will die too, himself, perhaps even without a hurricane warning, but maybe it will be an easy death, that's the best you get, so that you do not have to hang onto something until you can't hang on, until your fingers won't hold on, and it is dark. And the wind makes a noise like a locomotive passing, with a shriek on top of that, because the wind has a scream exactly as it has in books, and then the fill goes and the high wall of water rolls you over and over and then, whatever it is, you get it and we find you now of no importance, stinking in the mangroves.

You're dead now, brother, but who left you there in the hurricane months on the Keys where a thousand men died before you when they were building the road that's now washed out?

Who left you there? And what's the punishment for manslaughter now?

Letter to Maxwell Perkins
7 September, 1935

Dear Max:

I was glad to have your letter and would have answered sooner except for the hurricane which came the same night I received it. We got only the outside edge. It was due for midnight and I went to bed at ten to get a couple of hours sleep if possible having made everything as safe as possible with the boat. Went with the barometer on a chair by the bed and a flashlight to use when the lights should go. At midnight the barometer had fallen to 29.50 and the wind was coming very high and in gusts of great strength tearing down trees, branches etc. Car drowned out and got down to boat afoot and stood by until 5 a.m. when the wind shifting into the west we knew the storm had crossed to the north and was going away. All the next day the winds were too high to get out and there was no communication with the keys. Telephone, cable and telegraph all down, too rough for boats to leave. The next day we got across [to Lower Matecumbe Key] and found things in a terrible shape. Imagine you have read it in the papers but nothing could give an idea of the destruction. Between 700 and 1000 dead. Many, today, still unburied. The foliage absolutely stripped as though by fire for forty miles and the land looking like the abandoned bed of a river. Not a building of any sort standing. Over thirty miles of railway washed and blown away. We were the first in to Camp Five of the veterans who were working on the highway construction. Out of 187 only 8 survived. Saw more dead than I'd seen in one place since the lower Piave in June of 1918.

The veterans in those camps were practically murdered. The Florida East Coast had a train ready for nearly twenty four hours to take them off the Keys. The people in charge are said to have wired Washington for orders. Washington wired Miami Weather Bureau which is said to have replied there was no danger and it would be a useless expense. The train did not start until the storm started. It never got within thirty miles of the two lower camps. The people in charge of the veterans and the weather bureau can split the responsibility between them.

What I know and can swear to is this; that while the storm was at its height on Matecumbe and most of the people already dead the Miami bureau sent a warning of winds of gale strength on the keys from Key Largo to Key West and of hurricane intensity in the Florida straights [straits] below Key West. They lost the storm completely and did not use the most rudimentary good sense in figuring its progress.

Long Key fishing camp is completely destroyed and so are all the settlements on Matecumbe both upper and lower. There is over thirty miles of the R.R. completely gone and there will probably never be another train in to Key West. Highway is not as badly damaged as the R.R. but would take six months to repair. The R.R. may make a bluff that they will rebuild in order to sell the govt their right of way for the highway. Anyway Key West will be isolated for at least six months except for boat service and plane from Miami.

The Marine Corps plane that is flying some of the 1st class mail just brought two sets of page proof going up to page 130. Do you want me to send this back before the other comes?

To get back to your letter.

But first I wish I could have had with me the bloody poop that has been having his publishers put out publicity matter that he has been staying in Miami because he needs a hurricane in the book he is writing and that it looked as though he wasn't going to have one and him so disappointed.

Max, you can't imagine it, two women, naked, tossed up into trees by the water, swollen and stinking, their breasts as big as balloons, flies between their legs. Then, by figuring, you locate where it is and recognize them as the two very nice girls who ran a sandwich place and filling-station three miles from the ferry. We located sixty-nine bodies where no one had been able to get in. Indian Key absolutely swept clean, not a blade of grass, and over the high center of it were scattered live conchs that came in with the sea, craw fish, and dead morays. The whole bottom of the sea blew over it. I would like to have had that little literary bastard that wanted his hurricane along to rub his nose in some of it. Harry Hopkins and Roosevelt who sent those poor bonus march guys down there to get rid of them got rid of them all right. Now they say they should all be buried in arlington and no bodies to be burned or buried on the spot which meant trying to carry stuff that came apart blown so tight that they burst when you lifted them, rotten, running, putrid, decomposed, absolutely impossible to embalm, carry them out six, eight miles to a boat, on the boat for ten to twenty more to put them into boxes and the whole thing stinking to make you vomit—enroute to Arlington. Most of the protests against burning or burying came from the Miami undertakers that get 100 dollars apiece per veteran. Plain pine boxes called coffins at $50 apiece. They could have been quicklimed right in where they are found, identification made from their pay disks and papers and crosses put up. Later dig up the bones and ship them.

Joe Lowe the original of the Rummy in that story of mine "One Trip Across" was drowned at the Ferry Slip.

Had just finished a damned good long story and was on another when this started with the warning on saturday night. They had all day Sunday and all day monday to get those vets out and never did it. If they had taken half the precautions with them that we took with our boat not a one would have been lost.

Feel too lousy now to write. Out rained on, sleeping on the deck of the run boat, nothing to drink through all that business so ought to remember it, but damned if I want it for my novel. We made five trips with provisions for survivors to different places and nothing but dead men to eat the grub...

John Hersey

The Captain

We were on deck making up gear that morning, tied up to Dutcher's Duck opposite Poole's, when the new hand came aboard. Caskie, the skipper, seated on an upended bucket, was stitching some new bait bags, his huge, meaty fingers somehow managing to swoop the sail needle with delicate feminine undulations in and out of the bits of folded net. You could buy bait bags, but would Caskie? He had a closed face, signifying nothing. We knew he must have been hurt by Manuel Cautinho, who had served him as mate 19 long years and had suddenly walked off on him, but there was no reading Caskie's face, any more than you could read the meditations of a rock awash at high tide off Gay Head. His was a tight-sealed set of features, immobile and enigmatic in their weather-cracked hide. His eyes were downcast, the hoods of the lids the color of cobwebs, unblinking as he steadily worked. We never knew what he thought; sometimes we wondered if he ever needed to think.

I had been bowled over with the luck of being given a site as shacker on Caskie Gurr's *Gannet*. I was an apprentice, I got all the dirty work, I was salting stinking remains of pogies and yellowtail for bait with a foul tub between my feet that morning, but it didn't matter. (You could buy frozen bait, but...) Caskie had the best reputation of any of the offshore lobstering skippers out of either Menemsha or New Bedford. Everyone said that he cared, more than most, whether his men got decent shares, and that he knew, better than most, the track of the seasonal marches of the lobbies on the seabed of the shelf out there. *Gannet* was known as a wise boat. Caskie's regulars had been three senior islanders, who had been with him through a great deal of dusty weather—till Cautinho walked off for no apparent reason.

Pawkie Vincent, the engineer, sat far aft rigging a new trawl flag on a high-flyer, —a marker buoy with a radar reflector on it, for one end of a line of pots. Pawkie had only nine fingers, yet he was so deft with them that it sometimes seemed he had three hands. He had lost the index finger of his right hand when it got mashed, one time, while he was shipping the steel-bound doors of a dragging net. Every once in a while, as he worked, he would shake his head slightly from side to side, as if some troublesome doubt had occurred to him. Pawkie was tentative; his pauses to think things out in moments of intricate teamwork were sometimes dangerous to the rest of us.

The cook, Drum Jones, was fastening bricks into some new oak pots that had not yet become waterlogged, to hold them in place on the bottom. He had, beneath a railroad engineer's cap, the gaunt face of someone who has seen a ghost, and he sported an odd little mustache that looked like a misplaced eyebrow and accentuated his habitual look of alarm. This made it all the more surprising that he was always cheerful, always optimistic. When we pulled up a lean trawl of pots, he'd always say the next string would be better. But it seldom had been on recent tips—so Drum's dogged good humor was often annoying.

No one had much to say that morning. Our shares had been slim of late: Pawkie, who had a cranky wife and three wild sons in high school, had said that except for the shame of it, his family would do a damn sight better on welfare. I was an outsider, but I could see that Cautinho's departure had suddenly ruptured a brotherhood of these older men, a closeness rich with memories of many years of risks and scrapes and injuries and quarrels, to say nothing of a never-mentioned pride in the way they had handled together their very hard life under the discipline of their cruel and inscrutable mother, the sea. They were laconic. The only words they used were about tasks. Their tongues could not possibly have given passage to nouns like trust, endurance, courage, loyalty, or God forbid, love. What stood in jeopardy now, with Cautinho gone, leaving a gap like that of a pulled tooth, was the sense of the serene and dependable teamwork *Gannet's* crew had enjoyed, the delicate meshing of Caskie's understated but revered and absolute captaincy with the known capacities—and weaknesses, such as Pawkie's hesitation—of the other three, all working together as parts of an incarnate machine, each one knowing exactly what was expected of him and what the others could and would and wouldn't do in moments of critical stress. One linchpin was gone now out of that smooth-running machine, and I couldn't help wondering if it might fly apart under the strain of breaking in a new man. But of course no one could talk about any of that.

There was another thing we couldn't talk about: The Company. That meant Sandy Persons, the owner of *Gannet*. Persons, a sharp little creature, only about 30 years old, in a snap-brimmed felt hat and a double-breasted suit and what looked like patent-leather shoes, *was* The Company. He reputedly owned six draggers, ours out of Menemsha and the others based in New Bedford. I was aware of the hushed voices with which Pawkie and Drum and Cautinho had always talked about Persons, each time we steamed into New Bedford and tied up and unloaded our catch, after which Caskie walked off with Persons to settle up— our captain shuffling away on the stone pier with a slack pace and a bowed head. The crewmen's voices were muffled then, I inferred, by their sense of Caskie's everlasting humiliation that he couldn't afford to be his own man on his own boat; that he was just another captain on broken-forty shares with a Company embodied in this little peewee, who, we suspected, in our conspiratorial sympathy for Caskie, could not really be the owner but must be some kind of mob underling. We had a sense that vast, unfair and probably crooked forces controlled our lives. You could never read on Caskie's face, when he returned from those conferences, how he felt about this little muskrat of an owner, and you certainly wouldn't dare ask him.

We worked in silence that morning. It was a hot September day, with fog burning away to silvery haze before noon. Our heads were lowered over our jobs. All four of us were startled by a sudden thump, and our downturned eyes swept the deck to see its cause—a backpack thrown down onto it from the dock.

"Cap'n Gurr?" a voice asked.

I looked up and saw a fair imitation of Goliath. That package of beef would certainly have no trouble fetching the pots in over the side as they came up from the deep. This was our new mate. He had a big red beard, full lips, a nose as wide as a fist set in cheerful ruddy cheeks. But it seemed to me that there were empty places where the eyes should have been. You could not tell, looking at those hollows, that he was *there*. There was a flicker of something like a smile—or was it?—tucked in his beard around his mouth. My first thought was: He's on something. This isn't going to work.

But Caskie said, "I'm glad to see you. Come aboard."

His name was Benson, he wanted to be called Ben. He'd heard about the site on *Gannet* from someone at Poole's, and

Caskie, in need of a hand, had accepted him over the phone. This was the first time the skipper had laid eyes on the man. Caskie had told us that Benson said he'd served in the fishery off Nova Scotia—out of Lunenberg, Port Medway, Sidney, Ingonish; rough, cold, sloppy work, the fellow must have liked it. Now Caskie's unreadable eyes searched Benson's vacant ones, and all Caskie said was, "We're shaping up to go out tonight. Bear a hand, would you?" He set Benson to splicing gangions into a new ground line— the short lengths of rope, branching off at intervals from the mile-long line of a trawl, to which individual pots would be tied. Not another word between them. I guess Caskie wanted to see if Benson knew anything. He did. His splices were perfect.

When we'd finished our chores about noontime, Caskie said he'd tune in to the 5:00 p.m. weather forecast, and if it sounded all right he'd telephone to each of us to come aboard. Pawkie and Drum went to their houses, and I to the stark roost I had rented in West Tisbury with a couple of other young adventurers, whose rites of passage involved hammers, Skilsaws, stapling guns. Benson stayed aboard; had no place to go, he said.

At supper time, Caskie phoned and said the weather report was, as he put it, "on the edge of all right," and he guessed we'd better take our chances and go out—the trawls had been set out there for nearly two weeks as it was. That statement had, wrapped in the folds of its succinctness, an unspoken rebuke to the vanished Cautinho for having caused several days' delay while Caskie filled his site. I was young and brash, and before Caskie hung up I asked, "Is the new man going to be O.K.?"

I should have known better. There was a long, long pause—which I took to have a meaning: Mind your own business. "We'll see," he finally said.

When we got to the boat, I heard Pawkie murmur to Drum that he'd listened to the forecast, too, and he said, "Some real dirty stuff's comin' through tomorrer—wind backin' to nawtheast, twenty to thirty."

"It'll be fine," Drum said. "Cask wouldn't do anythin' dumb."

We cast off at 9:00 p.m. sharp, glided out between the jetties, and steamed into the wide bight under a sky that was like a great city of lights. At first, a moderate southwest breeze gently rocked our fatbellied *Gannet* as if she were a cradle. Then we rounded up into those mild airs and made for the open ocean. The big diesel Cat in the boat's guts hummed. I was off watch until midnight, but I stayed out on the afterdeck until we rounded Gay Head and I could know, peering out ahead over the rail, that there was nothing but the vast reach of the sea between our tiny vessel and magical faraway anchorages of my imagination; Bilbao, Lisbon, Casablanca. I felt free out beyond Gay Head and Noman's, on the wide waters of infinity, free from all the considerations ashore that tied one down—telephones, groceries, laundry, parents, the evening news, and, yes, even friends—free to exist without thinking, free to be afraid only of things that were really fearful. That last was a great gift of the sea. I filled my lungs, over and over, with air that I imagined was redolent, thanks to the great sweep of a dying fairweather high, of the sweet flowers of Bermuda. After a while I went below and plunged into sleep in my clothes.

Caskie, who had taken the first watch to set our course solidly for our trawl lines, waked me at eight bells, and I took my turn in the pilothouse. *Gannet* steered herself, on auto, into the void. There was not much to do: check the compass now and then, take a turn on deck every half-hour just to make sure that all was secure—and, well, you couldn't call the gradual emptying of my mind daydreaming: it was dark out.

The skipper had assigned our new mate the dawn watch. I went down at 3:50 a.m. and put a hand on a big round arm, which felt as solid as a great sausage, and shook it. Benson came roaring up out of sleep, looming and pugnacious, his hands fisted, as if he'd had to spend his whole life defending himself. Then he evidently realized where he was and went limp on the bunk for a minute, with his mouth open and working, drinking consciousness until he was full enough to get up. I went back to the pilothouse, and when he turned up, right on time, I showed where things were—Loran, radar, radio, switches, fuses, button for the horn, all the junk. There was a small round seat on a stanchion behind the wheel, like a tall mushroom, and Benson heaved himself up on it and perched there in a massive Buddha's calm. I still couldn't find him in his eyes, but I'd obviously been wrong: he couldn't have been drugged. He understood, he could deal with the electronics, he had handled the marlinspike when he was splicing with an old-time sailmaker's precision.

"What happened with the other mate?" he asked me. His voice was mild and rather high-pitched, as if he housed an inner person who was less assertive, less rough-cut, than the exterior one. He wanted to know how come he had lucked into this site.

"He just up and left," I said.

"I heard a rumor, some guy at Poole's," Ben said. "Somethin' about the guy was fed up with the cap'n hangin' on to lobsterin' when all the rest of 'em give up and switched over to draggin'. Said the cap'n was stubborn as a stone."

"I wouldn't know," I said.

"Said the cap'n was a peddler. Wasn't no lobsters out there."

'We've been getting a few," I said.

Ben gave a resounding snort, deep and haunting, as if he had a conch shell for a nose. I felt uncomfortable hearing such words about the captain behind his back, and I sidled out of there and went below. But I got only an hour's sleep, because Caskie had risen around five and, as usual, had steamed straight to the Loran fix of his first trawl, south of the steamer lanes in 50 fathoms of water, on the shelf about midway between Block Canyon and Atlantis Canyon. He had picked up the radar buoy on the scope in no time, and had sent Ben down to roust the rest of us out.

The wind had freshened from the sou'west, and we were rolling. I pulled on my oilers and my metaltoed boots. *Gannet* had been converted from a 72-foot Gulf shrimper, and her cedar planks clung to oak ribs that had been steam-bent to make a belly as round as a bait tub, unlike the deep-keeled draggers built for northern waters, so to tell the truth she wasn't too sea-kindly. She wallowed in broadside waves. Caskie had gone down to Key West 15 years ago and bought her for The Company for $20,000; she'd be worth 10 times that now. He'd had her hauled and done some work on her, and she was sound, though her white-painted topsides were grimy, chipped and rust-streaked, and her bulwarks were draped with old tires, so she looked like an aging hooker of the sea. Who cared? Inboard she was roomier than the North Atlantic draggers, and we thought we lived in style. Pawkie called her the Georgie's Bank Hilton.

In the gray half-light we were on deck trying to adjust our land legs to the argumentative gravity of the sea. Caskie came out to con the boat and run the hydraulic hauler from the auxiliary controls, abaft the deckhouse on the starboard side. He was cool. He swung the boat into the eye of the wind with his usual skill, as if it were a toy in a tub, and eased up alongside the aluminum staff of the radar buoy marking the western end of the string. We were pitching a bit in the seaway, and Ben, in his first chore as bulwarkman, missed a grab at the flag with a gaff. Pawkie was standing by with a grappling hook in case it was needed, and he made as if to toss it, but Ben waved him off and leaning out over the rail managed to catch the staff. He hoisted it aboard, Drum detached the end line and served it through a block hung from the starboard boom, Pawkie fed the line into the hydraulic lift, Caskie started the winch, and we were in business. The half-inch polypropylene rope snaked and hissed through the sheaves of the hauler and coiled itself on the deck underneath it.

When the anchor of the end line came up—a sturdy bucket full of concrete, a 100-pound weight—Benson lifted it aboard and stowed it as easily as if it were made of styrofoam. Finally the first pot appeared. Not a single lobster. Pawkie groaned. Benson heaved the heavy oaken trap on board with a power in the shoulders and a look of anger in the face that gave me a shiver. He detached the pot from its becket with a snort like the one I had heard from him in the night, when I'd said we were catching "a few." After that we were all herky-jerky, retrieving this first string of pots. Big Ben knew what he was doing, all right, and he had strength to burn, but Pawkie and Drum didn't know his moves, and they kept semi-interfering in efforts to ensure the continuity of rhythms that are a must in hauling pots. Each time they leaned or reached toward Benson to lend a hand, he shook them off with a guttural sound that wasn't quite speech and wasn't quite a growl, whereupon they fell back and got out of sync on what they were supposed to do next themselves.

The harvest was miserable. A good-sized but lonely lobbie now and then, and a few eels and crabs and trash fish—which we would keep and sell in New Bedford. My job was to peg, which in our case meant slipping rubber bands over the claws, and half the time I just stood around and waited. Caskie looked grim. From 30 pots in that first trawl we gleaned only 12 lobsters.

Drum served us breakfast after that trawl. Caskie stayed in the pilothouse. We ate silently. Toward the end of the string I had noticed that a human presence had finally made its appearance in Ben's eyes, and that the persona of that presence was a peckish human being who had decided to hate our captain. It struck me that the eyes had been dead until bad blood infused them with a sparkling life. Between pots those eyes threw laser beams at Caskie. Everyone knows that there is a noble tradition, among seagoing men, of hating the captain. Captain hating, even of good captains, goes very far back; the animals in the ark probably hated Noah, even though he was saving them from drowning. There were two troubles here. One was that Pawkie and Drum had learned over many years, probably not without pain, how not to hate Caskie—who would dare utter the word "love"?—and I could sense that there had been some mute emotional transactions going on out there on the deck between the three crewmen, which were as threatening as the turbulent dark clouds that had begun to loom over the landward horizon. The other was that this guy who had showed up in the hollows of Big Ben's eyes looked like a born spoiler, who didn't belong on a cockleshell of a boat out on the open sea.

The crazy thing was that when we started pulling up the

next trawl, all five of us began working in perfect teamwork, with the marvelous harmonies of a string quintet playing "The Trout." The gang meshed better than it had when Cautinho was aboard. As each pot came up, Caskie stopped the hauler; Big Ben reached out and swung the trap aboard and guided it onto the rail and untied it from its gangion; Caskie re-engaged the hauler to bring up the next trap; Ben and Drum pushed the pot along the rail to the picking station; Pawkie opened it and, first off, stabbed eels that were trapped and dumped them writhing into the eel barrel; he and I dropped the lobbies, if any, in the lobster tank, the trash onto the culling table, and the crabs into the fishbox; Drum re-baited the pot; Ben slid it aft along the rail and stacked it; while Drum, standing at the culling table, threw eggers—females with roe—and shorts—sexually immature ones—overboard; I began banding; Pawkie threw the gurry into the sea and cleaned up; then we'd all be ready to receive the next trap. If anything got the slightest bit out of rhythm, perhaps after one of Pawkie's hesitations, the guys would spontaneously jump to shift jobs without anything said. It was miraculous. It was as if this disdainful muscleman had been on the boat forever, and all of us could see that the smoothness of our work originated in his skill and alacrity—and anger. Whenever a pot would come up empty, the sounds in his throat now shaped themselves as words: "Shit, not again!" or "Jesus, man," or "I can't *believe* this."

Caskie said he had decided not to reset the trawls in that lobster-for-saken area; he said he would wait and set them "inside"—in shallower water north of the ship lanes. "I should hope so," Benson muttered. But as we resumed hauling, in the third and fourth strings, as the stack of empty traps built up on the afterdeck, the catch was a bit better—seemed to be improving as we followed the sets out to the eastward. Meanwhile, the wind had indeed begun to back around, as Pawkie had said it would, and had freshened; it was out of the east at that point. We had to widen our stance on the deck to keep from staggering around. As we got into the fourth trawl, *Gannet* was pitching like a hobbyhorse, the pots swung ominously from the boom when they came up, and the many 100-pound traps tied down in a big stack athwartships strained dangerously at their lashings.

By the time we had shipped all the traps from that trawl, the wind was snarling in from the northeast with its teeth bared, chewing the tops off eight-foot seas. There was a gale brewing. Caskie, with his long habit of consultation with his gang, said, "How about it? Shall we pack it in?"

"Jesus Cripes," Benson shouted into the wind, "just when you're catchin' a few?" His echo of my words in the night gave me the shudders. But now when I think about it, I realize that what really shook me was Benson's challenge to everything that I thought of as valuable in an orderly life. His tone of voice was a threat to the very idea of captaincy. Caskie was a mild island man of a certain age; he consulted out of courtesy but always made his decisions entirely on his own, and the serenity we had enjoyed when Cautinho was aboard, though possibly false, had rested squarely on the dependability of Caskie's gentle authority. He had always got us back safely to Menemsha basin. Now this raw Benson had come down here off Newfoundland's bitter waters to break the contract seamen invariably make, whether they like it or not, with skipperhood. You can hate a captain, but you obey him nevertheless. This wasn't a generational thing; I was far closer to Big Ben's age than to Caskie's, but I had been raised to a reasoned life, and I think I was more frightened of mutiny than I was of drowning.

Caskie, his expressionless face soaked with spray, looked at Benson for a long time. "All right," he finally said, "One more string, then we'll see." I was shocked by his yielding, and I saw Pawkie and Drum both literally step back away from Benson on the deck, as if he had raised a fist against them.

"Maybe it's just a squall," Drum stupidly said, so desirous of peace aboard *Gannet* that he lost all touch with mother wit.

You could hear, over the wind raking the rigging, that conch shell of a nose in a wild snort of derision.

Caskie had gone into the pilot-house, to steam us to the next flag. It seemed to take us forever to get there. And sure enough, after a while, he came out on the careening deck and called out to us over the wind, "Flag ain't there."

"Damn Russians!" Pawkie shouted.

Of all times for this to happen! We always blamed snagged or lost trawls on the Russians, though there were also Japanese, German, Polish, Italian—and maybe Spanish, maybe Bulgarian—and probably other—vessels out there, huge factory ships with satellite boats dragging the bottom with enormous nets, ripping up the ecology of the shelf, slaughtering all God's species with a greed and rapacity that gave no thought to times to come. And ruining puny us, sure enough. Any time we lost a whole string of 40 pots—and it had happened more than once—The Company was out a couple thousand bucks, and we were that much nearer to being out of work.

Caskie shouted that he was going to steam out to look for the tide balls at the other end of the busted line: maybe some of the pots could be salvaged. He went back in the pilothouse.

Pawkie was shaking his head. "How you going to find

those damn floats in this shit?"

"Caskie'll find' em," Drum said, putting his whole heart into his hoping.

And this time Drum was right. Caskie did. The fat hull pounded and shivered and wallowed out to the eastward. I was the first to see the orange spheres playing hide-and-seek in the spume-capped waves, and I called out the bearing at the pilothouse door. Caskie eased up to them. Out on deck Pawkie picked up the grappling iron and its line, but Benson grabbed it away from him and on a single throw caught one of the tide-ball lines and pulled the rope aboard. With all the strength of his anger, Benson got the first ball on deck, and then the second. By this time Caskie was again at the auxiliary controls, and between them Pawkie and Drum fed the end line into the winch sheaves.

"Somethin's wrong," Caskie said right away. The end line was skidding and laboring in the sheaves. It came up slowly. Caskie had brought *Gannet's* bow up into the wind, and she was bucking like a Brahman bull in a rodeo with burrs under its saddle. Each time her fat forefoot crashed down into a trough, a ton of spray flew up over the pilothouse and cascaded down on us, icy and stinging, like a deliberate and repeated rebuke of a sea scandalized by our folly.

When the last 20 feet came up, we saw that the end line had somehow become tangled and twisted with the bottom trawl line, so that the bucket of cement that had anchored the end line and one of the pots had risen together. No sooner had they cleared the waves than those two lethal objects began spinning around each other as the ropes from which they were hanging worked to untwist themselves.

Seeing the danger to his men at once, Caskie braked the lift and, depending on a friend he had worked with through many a hazard, shouted, "Pawk! Get the long gaff and try to hook the pot."

"No!"

It was not a shout, it was a roar. We all froze— or at least, as I look back, I see us immobilized in a still picture of that terrible moment of disobedience. Benson had his hands raised in a stopping gesture, as if to beat back the captain's command. Pawkie already had the gaff, with its murderous hook lifted and aimed out over the bulwarks, in his two hands. Drum was in a kind of crouch, as if to dodge some physical blow against the accepted way of doing things that he could sense but could not believe. Caskie stood with his hands on the conning controls, his face all too readable for the first time I could ever remember. I saw rage there, and I saw knowledge, and I saw defeat—the defeat of a quiet man whose calmness had its footing on a set of old, old rules of the sea, always accepted on *Gannet* until that very instant, the most important of which was that a word from the commanding officer in a tight moment is not to be questioned. The first law of the sea: The captain *is* the ship. He had yielded once, and I saw on his face that he would give in now. In the still picture that hangs on in my mind, *Gannet* herself was poised in a tremble of horror on a high crest, and the concrete weight and the lobster pot, spinning around each other, were making a dreadful blur of the reality to which the big mate had attached his defiance.

Then Ben made his move. With a lunge he snatched the gaff from Pawkie's hands and threw it away on the deck. Next, with breathtaking disregard for the danger, he leaned his body out over the rail and snatched the end line in his left hand, just above the fast-moving handle of the bucket of concrete. He was very nearly pulled overboard by the momentum of that hurtling weight, but he managed to hook himself to the rail with his right hand and a bent knee. The spinning stopped. The deck lurched on the crest of a big wave. Ben took advantage of *Gannet's* plunge and heaved the weight over the rail and onto the deck. The lobster pot came in easily then. It had several big ones in it.

We got in four more pots, and that was all. The trawl had been cut. We headed for home.

In a marvel of balance in the galley as *Gannet* steeply lurched up each wave and then dropped in what seemed a free fall until it hit the rock bottom of the ensuing trough, then rose shuddering again on the next vicious sea, Drum fried four eggs for each of us. Pawkie was on watch. Caskie sat down to his lunch across from Big Ben. I was at the end of the table, and Drum was cleaning up. As if we were floating on a dead calm, Caskie began to speak in a quiet and respectful voice to the man who had countermanded his order and made a success of it, and my heart sank as I listened to his appeasement of Benson. Big Ben gave no answers; eating, he made grunting sounds.

"I don't think you understand," Caskie said. "The Company says, 'Keep on lobsterin',' and you've got no choice. They own you, don't you know. I told Persons, I said, 'It's all over for lobsters out there this year, we ought to go to draggin',' but he says, 'We got to have lobsters, we're gettin' all the yellowtail an' fluke and scup we can handle from the other boats, we need lobsters.' If I say my gang can't make a livin', he says well, it's tough titty, he can get other skippers, he can get other guys for crews. I said I'd been on my boat for nineteen years, I didn't like that kind o' talk, and believe me, Mr. Benson, he blew up, he used language I wouldn't repeat to you. He was extremely definite, you know. Extremely."

It was horrible. The sweet sap of command had been drained right out of Caskie, and now all he had left was his impressive New England decency, which was taking the form of grovelling. Benson didn't even look up at his captain. The brute had egg on his beard. I felt seasick and had to go up on deck.

I don't know what happened after that. I asked Drum, when we got ashore, but he just shook his head. We tied up in New Bedford after midnight, and Benson heaved his backpack up on the dock and climbed ashore and walked off. When we got back to Menemsha, Pawkie quit. I hated to do it after six trips, but I had to tell Caskie that I thought I wasn't going to make it at sea, I didn't have good sealegs, I thought I'd try carpentry.

Caskie said, "Good luck, son. Don't take any wooden nickels." I couldn't for the life of me tell from his face whether he was glad or sorry to have me go.

Judith Kazantzis

Dusk and a
Portuguese Man o'War

We are in the tropics. I'm sorry to say
        what slews round the corner
is no fun: winningly, slidingly
        under its indigo puff sleeve
under its beacon blue eye, its arms
        outspread to me.

The lengthening sea is a sapphire sore.
        Radiant glitter: a bloom
on the face of Gabriel. But this is
        barely healed surface tissue,
reams of plastic recoiled and recoiled
        round diabolisms.

Stir it up with the spoon of the breeze.
        I remember Coleridge's sailor's
jig; the fires pivoting round the hull
        some day or night or not-light,
a stationary process. This is
        to be afraid of the least touch.

Key West Dawn

At once the dogs bark to each other;
but no wandering roosters, buried
by boulevards and carports.
The catbird mews in the pine feathers.

Last evening I drank myself
merrily with pink Seabreezes
into a night of the shivering horrors.
At the end: je ne regret rien.

Like an old lady's gold dress
the dawn embroiders the curtain.

John Leslie

from
Blood on the Keys

A white heron hung around the wide double doors to Pierson's fish house where fish was unloaded, weighed and stored, and later shipped out in trailer trucks. The heron had grown accustomed to receiving handouts over the years and was almost tame.

Pierson's sat on the north side of Key West, the gulf side, on four or five acres of hard marl that contained the fish house, an ice plant, a net-making shop, and enough land to stack and work on the many lobster traps unused during the off-season. There had been three generations of Piersons. Old Tom, now around eighty, still ran the place with the help of his son, Tommy Jr.

Warren was gutting yellowtail on a piece of scarred plywood on top of one of the ice boxes, throwing the guts into the water where a flock of pelicans scrapped over them, when Tom Pierson came down to the dock.

Warren opened the fish with one quick, easy movement of the gutting knife, tore the guts out with his free hand, and, without looking, tossed them to the pelicans; then he scooped the fish into a wire basket at his feet and took another yellowtail from the pile on the ice chest.

"You do any good?" Tom asked.

"Not to speak of," Warren replied. "Two, two hundred fifty pounds."

Tom tapped the ash from his cigar and shook his head.

Times were tough. Warren knew what he was thinking. He still owed the fish house nearly ten thousand dollars for the boat they'd staked him to, not to mention supplies. He was a good fisherman and a hard worker, but he was going to have to do better than that to pay off his debt and still make some money. With lobster season coming up, he was probably going to need new traps. If it was a bad season, he could easily go broke, like any other fisherman around.

Nobody wanted to see that happen. Fishermen were what kept this business going. Tom's son, Tommy Jr., seemed to think it was all over for commercial fishing around here and was advising his old man to get out while he still had some capital.

Pierson's sat on valuable property, a waterfront with a deep harbor perfect for a marina. Developers would have paid top dollar for the property, glad to be rid of the smelly traps and work boats that sat next to their condos and hotels which had sprung up in recent years. Tourism was now Key West's staple industry, and what fishing went on the developers would just as soon see restricted to Stock Island, out of sight and smell of the tourists. Most of the shrimping fleet had already moved out there. Pierson's was the last fish house left in Key West.

But Tom resisted sudden change as if it was some kind of fatal disease. He'd seen the ups and downs of this business, and he didn't like putting a bunch of fishermen out of work and seeing some goddamn condominium thrown up. Warren had heard Tom say more than once that after he was dead, what his son wanted to do was up to him. But as long as he was alive, this place would be a fish house.

"Where were you?" Tom asked Warren.

"Tail End."

"I heard they busted the *Katy Lynn* out there this morning."

News traveled fast over the ship radios. Hard to find anybody in fishing who hadn't heard about the bust, and they hadn't even brought her to the dock yet.

"Yeah," Warren said. "They busted her about daybreak."

Tom wouldn't like learning this way that a boat in his fleet was paying its way by smuggling. Pierson's paid its fishermen a nickel a pound more for their catch than any other fish house around. If Tom had any reason to suspect a boat was smuggling drugs, Warren knew he would tell them to move up to Stock Island to one of the other fish houses.

As they weighed up Warren's fish, he watched Tom go out into the yard and begin working on his long line, the palonga line he liked to get out this time of year. He'd go out at least once a week in his own boat, the *Conch Pearl*, and set out a couple of the lines for snapper and bottom fish.

As much for exercise and fun as anything else, Tom said. God knows, Warren thought, there wasn't much more than that.

"Two hunner twenny-seven an' a ha'f pounds," the Cuban weighing his fish said. "Boy, without bad luck you wouldna have any."

Warren took his slip of paper and shook his head. "You got that right," he said.

He finished cleaning up his boat and moved it into his own slip. He'd go home now, get his first hot shower in four days, have dinner with Maggie tonight, sleep in an unmoving bed, and start all over tomorrow or the next day.

He was about to get in his pickup when Cole and Carter Thompson came up, brothers who'd been fishing out of Pierson's longer than anyone else. "Warren, you hear about the *Katy Lynn*?"

Warren nodded.

"You seen Tommy?" Cole asked.

"No. I just got in. I saw the old man, though. He seems all right."

"He doesn't know shit. They pin this one on Tommy, it'll kill him," Carter said.

"I don't know," Warren said. "Tom's survived a lot." He climbed in the cab, exhausted. He was one of the few who fished alone, without a mate. He figured he made out better without having to cut someone else in on a share, even though he might not catch as many fish. It took a lot out of him.

"Tom's always done right by us," Cole said. "If Tommy took over the business, you know we'd be out of the fishing business in the time it took to sign the papers on this place."

"We don't want the old man to hear it from one of us," Carter added. "If Tommy's involved, he might be able to save his own ass without Tom knowing a damn thing was going on. Tommy's good at that sort of thing."

"Don't worry about me. After I get caught up on sleep, I'll be down at Tail End again. I don't catch some fish pretty soon, I may be out of business myself."

Carter Thompson slapped the side of Warren's pickup. "I know what you mean." The Thompson brothers, a couple of slow-talking, easygoing guys who looked more like beefy New York cops than fishermen, had two boats, a lobster boat and a larger vessel that did double duty as a net boat in kingfish season and a long-line swordfish boat in the spring. They'd made plenty of money over the years. Warren had even worked on their boats as a mate when they were shorthanded. The Thompsons could weather these down times.

"Take it easy," Cole said.

"Any way I can get it," Warren replied.

•••

It was only nine o'clock in the morning, but Warren felt like having a drink. Fishing didn't allow for regular hours. Up most of the night, trying to sleep some during the day on a pitching boat beneath the sun; it took a while to settle into a normal routine once you were back on land. Besides, he liked Sloppy Joe's early in the morning. It was quiet, not many tourists, a few fishermen nursing hangovers, and he could sit at the big horseshoe bar and catch the breeze from the wide-open doors and the overhead fans without being blasted out by the amplified music that would bring people off the streets later in the day.

He'd have a couple of Bloodys, then maybe wander up to Shorty's for breakfast before going to the fish house and getting to work on his traps.

He drove the battered pickup through the rain, the fallen red petals from the big poinciana trees squishing beneath his tires, their roots buckling the sidewalk. It was a damn pretty town, and he had always liked it, but it could wear you down. You had to be strong to survive here, or else you found yourself living on a curb along Caroline Street sharing a bottle of Thunderbird if you didn't know when it was time to get out. Maybe now was the time.

After more than ten years here, he knew that within the next six months he was going to be eyeball to eyeball with his future.

He had boat payments to make, and with an unpredictable lobster season coming up he'd go more in the hole, maybe six or seven thousand dollars in the hole, to pay for trap materials. He could easily lose it all. Go back to running dope? Nobody in his right mind was doing that down here now. The *Katy Lynn* should have proved that. You had a better chance bringing in some cocaine, which was easier to conceal and had a higher profit margin. But when the profit margin went up, so did the risk.

So what was left? Maybe he ought to sell the boat and buy a sleek little Mako and charter it out to the tourists for two or three hundred dollars a day. Stop kidding himself. That's where the money was, in tourists. Or leave.

Or set up house with Maggie. She would sell houses, and he would sell fishing trips, pretend they were doing what they wanted to do and everything was all right. Cinderella stuff. Except Maggie wouldn't be happy, because he wouldn't be happy. So the thing was to just keep going, doing what he was doing, what he knew how to do, and when it ended it ended. Then he could think of something else.

He parked on Greene Street in front of the old unused city hall building and ran into Sloppy's, dodging rain puddles. He ordered a Bloody Mary. There were maybe a dozen people in the bar, some of them the Duval Street riffraff looking to hustle the first beer of the day. Carter Thompson was there, and Warren went over and took the stool next to him.

"Jesus," Carter said. "As soon as I get rid of this hangover, I'll never drink again."

Warren smiled and sipped his Bloody. "I won't bother reminding you of that," he said.

"Don't. You hear the talk?"

"What's up now?"

"Rumors are going 'round the feds may close Pierson's down."

"Jesus Christ," Warren said. "The old man hear that?"

"If he has, he isn't saying anything. But I wouldn't want to be in Tommy's shoes."

Warren shook his head. "I guess not. Jesus, the way things are going, I'd say fishing's about over around here."

Carter agreed it looked bleak. When Warren finished his drink, Carter bought him another one, and they reminisced about the past.

"You remember that boatload of fish we caught, what was it, five years ago?" Carter asked.

Warren nodded.

"One day those fish will be back," Carter said. "And I'm going to be sitting out there waiting on them. Maybe by that time all the asshole high rollers will be gone, the ones come in and fish a season or two, invest in a lot of fancy equipment, and when they haven't made a million, get out. But you and I will still be sitting here."

"Yeah, without a fish house," Warren said.

"We'll work on that," Carter said. "Like you said the other day, the old man's survived a lot in his time. He'll get through this one."

"We better hope so."

Warren finished his drink and got up and left. Hugging the storefronts to keep dry, he walked a few yards up to Shorty's Diner.

The counter was full, most of them eating breakfast or

merchants on a coffee break. Somebody had put a quarter in one of the counter jukeboxes that after several years had been fixed and played some of the original songs, many of them more than thirty years old. Warren found a seat and ordered eggs over easy with home fries, bacon, and a biscuit.

His waitress brought him coffee, poured from a battered and stained aluminum pot. She was tall, skinny, no tits, with a ponytail that hung to her waist. But the remarkable thing about her was the smoothness of her skin and the lack of complexity in her expression. How long, he wondered, before she acquired some dents like those in the coffee pot?

He looked at the people around him, surprised at how many faces he recognized but how few he knew personally. He'd just never been part of this Duval Street scene.

There was something familiar about the guy eating breakfast across the counter from him. A big guy with red hair, his fingernails chewed down to the quick. What the hell was it? He was picking at his food, putting it on the points of his toast, bits of crumbled bacon and grits mixed with his eggs.

● ● ●

Warren moved from one spot to another, looking for fish. He'd started at Western Dry Rocks, worked down to Cosgrove Light, then on to Tail End. In one place the current would be ripping; in another there was no current. After two nights' fishing, he had less than two hundred pounds. Unless something happened tonight, he figured he'd just about pay expenses with the catch he had. Tomorrow he would go in.

When he did go in, he was thinking of things he could say to Maggie. "I'm sorry," was one of them. But he didn't know if he was sorry. You enjoy something that much, how can you be sorry about it? Maybe he should talk to Charlotte first before saying anything to Maggie. He'd told her she was pretty smart, and she'd said, "Not just pretty?" She wasn't being cute. So he'd talk to her, get her advice. Then talk to Maggie. And probably still wind up saying he was sorry. There was something about Charlotte, her attitude toward life, that set her apart.

Life. Sitting here in the dark, one small light burning above his chill barrel, looking across the careless dance of the sea. Life. One dead piece of squid attached to one number-six hook hanging down there ten or fifteen feet below the surface, surrounded by water; some chum sprinkled over the water to attract the fish. Waiting.

He looked at the night sky and watched the sweep of

light from Loggerhead Key near the Dry Tortugas; then he glanced at his watch. Nearly four A.M. Moonlight, waning, spread out from the stern of the vessel in a pie-shaped wedge, sparkling across the water. He sat there in a pair of yellow oilers and a flannel shirt damp with salt water and fish scales. It was cold, with a light breeze coming out of the east. He moved around to the bait container, lifted some crumbled chum, and scattered it over the water as if he were tossing bread to pigeons. Then he paid out a few more hands of the monofilament line.

He felt the peck-peck of a yellowtail. "Take it, sucker," Warren whispered. And the fish did, and he reeled the line in hand over hand, thinking maybe this was it. He could feel that the fish had some shoulder to it. A couple of hours of steady hauling before daylight, and perhaps he could put another hundred pounds of yellowtail on the boat. "Patience, man," Tom Pierson always said. "Patience."

In the moonlight, there was a streak near the surface, and a splash, and Warren felt the weight of the fish gone. "Cuda! The sonsabitches!" he swore. You fought the weather, tides, bad currents, full moons, and just when you thought everything was perfect, in come the barracuda. Whatever school of fish you were working would be gone in minutes; what you did manage to get on your hook they'd eat.

Warren brought the severed head of the yellowtail, bleeding, dripping entrails, onto the boat. He held the fish by its eye sockets with the thumb and forefinger of his left hand; with his right, he removed the hook, picked up a larger hook attached to strong wire leader that had been stuck in the gunwale for the purpose, and threaded the hook through the eyes of the fishhead before tossing it back into the water.

Within seconds, the barracuda struck the fish head, splashing water violently across the surface as it tried to get free of the hook. Warren played it, grunting, leaning his body against the line, feeling the bite of the line against his fingers, which were encased in short sections of old inner tubing that he had cut up and kept on the boat for use when he hand-lined.

He worked the barracuda for a quarter of an hour, keeping the line taut, gaining on it inch by inch. Then he brought the fish up over the stern, nearly four feet in length, silvery, mottled, missile-shaped. Warren let it fall to the deck and quickly put a booted foot on the 'cuda just behind its head, still holding the line taut. He reached with his free hand for the gutting knife that was stuck in the gunwale. He pressed the sharp-pointed tip above the eye of the 'cuda and through its brain. The fish flopped, its mouth opening and closing, the razor-sharp teeth glinting beneath the light from the small yellow bulb over the chill barrel. Blood seeped from the wound.

Death.

He scored the 'cuda's body with the knife, carefully removed the hook from its mouth, and threw it back into the water. "Go and let your buddies have a look at you," Warren said.

He sat down on the gunwale, sweating under the strain, the sweat now drying cold in the breeze. He rested a moment before going back to hand-lining for yellowtail. They were gone, as he was sure they would be. He kept at it for half an hour or more without a bite. Then he slowly packed up his gear, cleaned the boat, and by the time light was showing in the east, began the long trip back to Key West.

Alison Lurie

from
The Truth
About Lorin Jones

In the mauve afterglow of a warm December sunset, Polly Alter stood by the registration desk of a women-only guest house in Key West, dizzy with heat and travel fatigue. This morning in New York everything had been gray and gritty, like a bad mezzotint. She'd woken with such a sick, heavy cold that she called to cancel her flight, but all she could get on the phone was the busy signal. Giving up, she dragged herself and her duffel bag out to the terminal. There, aching and snuffling, she shuffled onto a plane and was blown through the stratosphere from black-and-white to technicolor. Five hours later she climbed out into a steamy, glowing tropical afternoon with coconut palms and blue-green ocean, exactly like a cheap travel poster.

It wasn't only the scenery that was unreal. Most of the people she'd seen, beginning with the taxi driver, were weird. They moved and spoke in slow motion, as if something were a little wrong with the projector. Lee, the manageress of Artemis Lodge, was so slowed down she seemed drugged. It had taken her five minutes to find Polly's reservation, and now she couldn't find the key to Polly's room.

"I know it's here somewhere. I just can't locate it right this moment, is all," Lee drawled, smiling lazily. She was a sturdy, darkly tanned, handsome woman, a middle-aged version of one of Gauguin's Polynesian beauties. She had a bush of shoulder-length black hair streaked with stone gray, a leathery skin flushed to hot magenta on her broad cheekbones, and knobbed bare brown feet.

While Polly waited, Lee shifted papers and slid drawers open and shut. She kept breaking off her search to answer the phone, to find a stamp for another guest, to offer Polly passion-fruit juice and nacho crackers (Polly declined, feeling her stomach rise), and to assure her that if she couldn't get into the room tonight she'd be real comfortable on the porch swing.

Polly slumped against the desk with her duffel bag and her stuffed-up nose and her headache, listening to the irritating tinkle of the colored-glass wind chimes as they swayed in the sultry evening breeze.

The first thing Polly did, after dumping her luggage on a garish orange batik bedspread and going out for a hamburger, was to call Hugh Cameron. She stood in a telephone booth at the front of the coffee shop watching a procession of tourists and weirdos pass along Duval Street, and trying over in her mind the speech she had rehearsed. ("This is Paula Alter from New York, you remember I wrote to you about Lorin Jones. I know you said you were busy, but I've come all the way to Key West to talk to you, it's really important, so . . . please . . . if you could . . .")

As she listened to the ring, she imagined Cameron slowly, impatiently getting up from his chair, crossing the floor. . . He was a difficult, rude person, everyone in New York said so. He might shout at her or curse her—tell her to get lost, to fuck off.

The steady burring of the phone, at first menacing, gradually became mechanical. Either Hugh Cameron wasn't home, or he wasn't answering. Ill, exhausted, she slumped against the side of the booth. She wished she had never come here; she wished she had never heard of Key West, or of Lorin Jones. She was tired of chasing this elusive contradictory woman around the East Coast, tired of trying to sort through the lies and half lies of her former associates. Ultimately, it was Lorin's fault that she was here in this steamy miserable place instead of home in bed.

Polly's nose was running again; her head ached worse. She hung up, paid for the half-eaten hamburger, and staggered back to her room. There she peeled off her once-crisp shirt and slacks, now sweaty and limp. She brushed her teeth with disgustingly lukewarm water that refused to run cold, climbed into the low, creaking rattan platform bed, and more or less passed out.

She woke late the next morning, hot and sweaty in a heavy splash of orange sun from the window whose blind she had forgotten to draw last night—hot and sweaty, too, from the receding clutch of, yes, a wet dream. Well, no wonder; she'd been celibate for nearly a year. Now she was in a place where the very air, blowing from the fishing piers and the tidal flats, smelled of sex. The dream had had a shore and fish in it too, and—she remembered with irritation—a man. She lunged out of bed and went in search of a shower, preferably a cold one.

But as she stood in the cool flood of water Polly noticed something else: her flu was gone. For some goddamn reason, she felt perfectly well. Okay. What she had to do now was finish her research, go back to New York, write the book, and be done with it; through with Lorin Jones forever. She scoured herself dry with a coarse striped beach towel, and put on her Banana Republic jumpsuit, which seemed right for an explorer in dubious tropical territory.

Downstairs, after a late breakfast (sweet, pulpy fresh-squeezed orange juice, decaffeinated tea, and muesli), she tried Cameron's number again from the guest-house phone, while Lee, who had insisted on hearing all about the project, openly listened. When he didn't answer, Lee was optimistic.

"Aw, don't worry. Probably the old guy was out last night; and he could be at work now. What's his job?"

"I don't know. He was teaching at some college in the Midwest about ten years ago, but nobody seems to know which one. But I figure he must have retired by now, since he's back in Key West."

"Well, still. He could be buying groceries at Fausto's or anywhere. Why don't you forget about your research for a while, go out and enjoy yourself? Have a swim; see something of the island."

"I haven't got time for anything like that, I'm afraid," Polly said tightly.

"What's the hurry, hon?" Lee gave her a wide friendly, maybe even more than friendly, grin. "You can stay here as long as you like; I'll put you on the weekly rate. And it's a really pretty day out, you should take advantage of it.

She leaned so far over the cluttered bamboo desk toward Polly that her low-cut oversize tangerine muumuu gaped, revealing full brown breasts with enlarged mushroom-colored nipples. Her flesh had the heavy, inert luster that Gauguin admired, and Polly didn't.

She hesitated only a moment before declining. It was the first offer, or hint of an offer, that'd come her way in a long time, but even if she'd found Lee attractive there was something about her, just as there was about Key West, that put Polly off: something loose and lazily overheated. Besides, even if she stayed longer on this loose, overheated island she had no time to waste: she had to check out all seventeen art galleries in the Yellow Pages, visit the Bureau of Vital Statistics and the library, and keep trying Hugh Cameron's phone number.

Hours later, after leaving yet another gallery where nobody had ever heard of Lorin Jones, Polly headed north and west across the island in the direction of the house where Lorin Jones had once lived. If she was really lucky, its owner would be home and willing to talk. If she was really unlucky, the building would have been torn down and replaced by a motel or a grocery.

The sun had come out again, and the sky was the color of a gas flame, but nothing she passed seemed real. The houses were too small and uniformly white, the sun too large and glaringly luminous, and everything that grew looked as stiff and unnatural as a Rousseau jungle: giant scaly palms like vegetable alligators; scarlet-flowering deciduous trees with enormous writhing roots and varnished leaves and long snaky pale brown creepers hanging down from above. Below them gardens burgeoned with unnatural flowers: oversized pink shrimps, glossy magenta trumpets with obscene red pistils, and foot-long crimson bottle-brushes.

The fauna were just as exotic and unreal as the flora. Huge speckled spiders swayed in six-foot webs between the branches of the tropical trees; little pale gray lizards skittered nervously along whitewashed fences, then suddenly froze into bits of dried leaf. In one yard there were white long-necked birds the size of turkeys; in another a tortoise-shell cat as large as a terrier.

And then, even worse, there were the people. A bearded bum with a foot-long iguana draped around his neck like her grandmother's old fox fur; a woman walking two long-haired dachshunds in plaid boxer shorts; a man in a Karl Marx T-shirt and frayed canvas sandals getting out of a white Cadillac. A half-naked youth waved to Polly from an upstairs window; and in one of the flowering trees overhead a long-haired pirate in a red bandanna and gold earrings, pruning with a wicked-looking chainsaw, grinned and shouted at her to look out below.

As she made her way across town, Polly kept an uneasy watch for Hugh Cameron. She'd never seen a picture of him, but whenever she passed a tall, fair, thin man in his sixties ("pale and weedy" had been one description), she gave him a quick, suspicious stare. In front of the library (which was of shrimp-pink stucco) she almost crossed the street to ask the guy if he was Cameron, and only halted because another elderly man came out of the building at the same time and addressed her suspect as "Frank."

Polly walked slowly back toward her guest house in the increasing afternoon heat, feeling overfed, dazed, and disconnected, as if she were floating through a TV show with the color turned up too high. Maybe she was slightly drunk, or her cold was coming back. Or maybe she was suffering from climate shock;

she had never been in the tropics before, or anywhere south of Washington, D.C. Maybe that was why everything looked so brilliant and nothing seemed real.

Probably I should go back to my room and try to sleep it off, Polly thought. Then I ought to go to the county courthouse and look for the records of Lorin Jones's death—from pneumonia, according to her brother. Before she came to Key West Polly had accepted the diagnosis without question, but now it seemed the most blatant of lies. How the hell could anyone get pneumonia in this climate, let alone die of it?

Partly to delay a possibly futile task, partly because the sun was so hard and bright, Polly turned off onto a shaded side street. Here she had to walk more slowly, for heavy-scented sprays of flowers hung down into her face, and the sidewalks had been crazily heaved and split by twisting reptilian roots.

She checked Lee's map again and saw that she wasn't far from Hugh Cameron's house. Maybe he'd be home now; maybe if she confronted him in person she'd have a chance of getting him to talk. She had to find him and interview him, because nobody else seemed to know what had happened to Lorin Jones after she left Wellfleet, how she got to Key West, what she did there, or how she died. If Polly couldn't talk to Cameron there would be a great awkward gap in her book, and she would look like an incompetent ass. She decided to walk by his house and look for signs of life.

As she approached the low white bungalow overhung with brambly bougainvillea, a man carrying an extension ladder was coming out. It was definitely not Cameron, though, but a tall blond guy about her own age in white painter's overalls, heading for a pickup truck by the curb. But if he'd been working on the house, this guy might know when Cameron would be back. Polly started to run toward him.

At the sound of her feet on the uneven sidewalk the man shoved the ladder into the truck and turned. From a distance of about thirty feet, he gave Polly first a glance of casual curiosity, then a grin of sexual appreciation; finally he held his arms out wide, mockingly, as if to catch her.

Polly stopped short, abashed and angry. The painter grinned, shrugged, climbed into the cab, started the engine, and drove off.

Immobilized, Polly watched the vehicle turn the corner, displaying a legend on its side: REVIVALS CONSTRUCTION. The shiny aluminum ladder winked as it caught the sunlight, and the red rag tied to its end gave her an insulting little wave as it disappeared.

She continued to stand on the sidewalk, breathing hard,

though she'd only gone a few yards—furious at both him and herself. Why hadn't she just run on past, ignoring the bastard? Or, more practically, why hadn't she walked up and spoken to him, asked where Cameron was? She'd lived in New York for years; she was used to being joshed and leered and whistled at by pig construction workers. If this guy imagined she was interested in him, running toward him, she could have turned on the chilly, scornful look that she always directed at those ignorant creeps.

It was this awful climate: the sun, the heat, the humidity: slowing her down, mixing her up. She set her jaw, checked the map again, and started at a steady New York pace for the center of town.

By half-past five Polly had called Hugh Cameron again three times unsuccessfully. She had refused Lee's iced herbal tea and homemade carob cookies. She had discovered that the county courthouse records office was closed for the afternoon, and she had visited two more art galleries and found out nothing. In one of them the walls were covered with overpriced schlock seascapes and posters, and nobody had ever heard of Lorin Jones. The young woman in the other, more sophisticated, gallery had no idea that Lorin Jones had ever lived in Key West.

This gallery was air-conditioned, and her conversation with its owner pleasant; but when Polly emerged onto Duval Street a new blast of depression and hot air engulfed her. Already the shadows of the buildings were lengthening; she had been in Key West for twenty-four hours and accomplished zilch. She had collected no useful information, and she couldn't reach the bastard she'd come to interview. All she had found was a tiny drawing whose authorship could never be proven. As Polly stood on the sidewalk trying to decide what to do next, tourists and hippies and freaks pushed past her, all headed in the same direction. They must be on their way to Mallory Dock, where she had been told throngs gathered every evening to gawk at outdoor performers and the sunset over the Gulf of Mexico. Polly had no interest in either, but the flow of traffic and her own fatigue and lassitude pulled her along with the crowd. And maybe that wasn't such a bad thing. After all, sunset on Mallory Dock was an established local ritual, one that Lorin Jones must have known of—probably witnessed.

At the dock, a raised cement jetty on the far side of a large parking lot, the tourists were already thick. The pale, light-speckled sea was dotted with boats of all sizes from dinghy to trawler: sailboats plunged and turned, motor launches idled raucously, and in the middle distance a cream-sailed schooner rocked at anchor. Farther out, low gray-green mangrove islands floated on the horizon like vegetable whales.

A few members of the crowd sat on the low wall at the outer edge of the pier, gazing across the water. Others loitered at the stalls on the inland side, buying cheap shell jewelry, palm-frond hats, slices of red watermelon, bad watercolors, clumsy woven leatherwork, hand-painted T-shirts, and crumbly homemade cookies. But the press was greatest around the street performers: two clowns, one on a unicycle; a skinny contortionist; a huge sweating giant who juggled with flaming torches; a Caribbean steel band; and a pair of white-faced mimes accompanied by a performing poodle.

Could any of them have been here in Lorin Jones's time? Not likely; in the late sixties most of these people would have been toddlers; only the mimes looked even middle-aged.

As the hazy sun slid toward the pale crumpled water, she headed back up the pier, idly scanning the stalls. Then, less idly, she halted near a table heaped with batik-print shirts that looked as if someone had thrown up on them in Technicolor. Behind it stood someone she thought she'd seen before: the workman with the ladder who'd been at Cameron's house earlier that afternoon. At least, this guy had the same golden tan, long narrow features, and streaked light hair. And, look, his faded green T-shirt, with the sleeves rolled to the muscled shoulders, was printed with the words REVIVALS CONSTRUCTION. Maybe her luck had turned; at least she'd been given another chance to find out where Cameron was.

She moved toward the stall, then hesitated.

"Hey, lady!" Revivals Construction called to her. "Don't go away. I've got just the thing for you." Up close he looked more worn than he had at a distance: his tan was leathery and tattooed with lines, especially around the eyes, and his hair wasn't blond, but a bleached and faded brown.

Polly halted, prepared to give him a freezing look. But the guy's tone was anonymous; probably he didn't remember seeing her before. Very likely he routinely stared and whistled at any female that came within range. She moved forward again through the crowd.

"Here. This'll look real good on you." From the pile of T-shirts he pulled out a rose-red one speckled in a white paint-drip design like an early Pollock.

"I don't know—"Actually the shirt wasn't half-bad. "How much is it?"

Revivals Construction gave her a sidelong smile. "For you, four dollars."

Polly studied the cloth for flaws.

"Sure it's washable." (This was to another customer) "You

can put it into the machine if you want. It's up to you."

"All right," Polly decided, digging into her tote bag.

"I saw you before this afternoon," she added as she paid. "Over on Frances Street."

"Yeah." He half smiled. "I saw you too."

"I wanted to ask you something," Polly persisted, a little discomfited.

"Sure . . . All right, ask me."

"You were working on a house."

"I was . . . What? Six-fifty each, like the sign says, two for twelve." Three oversize teenagers in shorts had shoved their way through the crowd. "Extra-large, right over here. . . . Listen," he added to Polly. "This is a madhouse. Why don't you meet me for a drink after sunset? Say in half an hour. . . . Sure, we've got children's sizes, wait a sec. They're in a box underneath here somewhere . . . Okay?"

"Okay," Polly agreed.

"Billie's on Front Street. Out back in the garden, it's quieter. You got that? . . . Right. Here you are, don't grab, please: kiddie sizes two, four, six, eight. If you don't want that one, don't throw it at me, just put it back on the table, okay? Jesus . . . So I'll see you later."

Around Polly as she turned to go there was a change in the crowd; a rise and focusing of sound, a movement away from the stalls and the performers toward the sea. Caught in a layer of smoky vapor, the sticky raspberry sun balanced on the shimmering horizon, then began to flatten and dissolve. There was a hush, then an increasing patter of applause; finally even a few cheers. Polly didn't join in. The ceremony seemed to her not, as Phil had put it, "kind of cute," but phony and self-indulgent. Even before the applause had slackened she had begun to make her way back through the crowd toward Duval Street.

The garden of Billie's bar was hedged and overhung by lush, loose-leaved tropical plants, and by strings of colored Christmas-tree bulbs just beginning to spark the lilac twilight. On a low platform under a shredding palm a man in a cowboy shirt was strumming a guitar and wailing a sad country-Western song into a microphone.

Polly chose one of the scabby white-painted metal tables near the shrubbery and far enough from the music to make conversation possible, and waited.

Soon the tables were beginning to fill; it was nearly half-past six. Maybe Revivals Construction wasn't coming; maybe he'd decided he didn't want to see her again after all. Polly felt cross, restless, and—very irrationally, because why should she give a damn—rejected. She picked at the blistered white paint of the table, and stared at the laughing and drinking tourists around her.

"Hi!" Revivals called, waving from the entrance to the garden.

"Hi," Polly called back. As she watched him dodge, with considerable speed and grace, between the crowded tables, she admitted to herself that he was what most women would consider a very attractive man; tall, broad-shouldered and narrow-hipped, with a lot of light hair and a face almost cubist in its assemblage of elegant angles and planes.

"Sorry I'm late." He yanked out the chair next to hers, smiling unapologetically.

"That's all right," Polly said.

"Never again. I'm through with those damn T-shirts."

"You're quitting your business?"

"Huh? Oh, no. That's not my business; I was just minding the stall for a friend. This place okay by you?"

"Oh, sure." Polly sat back a little. It was clear from Revivals Construction's easy triangular smile and the way he had dragged his chair closer to hers across the gravel that he thought he'd picked her up—or, worse, that she'd picked him up. She could disabuse him of this idea, but then he might get huffy and uncooperative.

"Like the music?"

"Oh, sure," Polly repeated, though she hadn't been paying attention.

"That guy used to be a star up in Nashville."

"Really?"

"Had three record albums. He's damn good. But nobody here's even listening to him, if you notice." He shook his head. "Stupid bastards."

"That's too bad."

"Yeah. But that's tourists for you." Revivals Construction shrugged, then half smiled. "Present company excepted, of course." He set his elbow on the table and leaned toward Polly. His arm, bare almost to the shoulder under the rolled sleeve of his dark green T-shirt, was also cubist in design, its blocks of muscle and bone outlined in veined ridges. "So how'd you like the sunset?"

"Well." Polly hesitated, but there was no point in not saying what she thought. Revivals, thank God, wasn't somebody she had to interview, and had no connection with the New York art world or with Lorin Jones. "It really wasn't all that great, you know. I was surprised anybody applauded."

"Yes. But they always do. The tourists assume it's a show put on for their benefit."

"That's what I thought too," she said, surprised.

"They believe that the sun bows down before them. Literally." He grinned and touched her wrist. "So what're you drinking?"

"I guess I'll have a beer," Polly said, aware of an instinctive reaction in her arm and thinking that she'd better clarify the situation fast. "What I wanted to ask you—" she began.

"Just a sec." He waved to the waitress. "Two Millers. Okay?"

"Sure." But maybe what she ought to do was play along until she found out what the hell had happened to Hugh Cameron, who still didn't answer his phone.

"By the way, the name's Mac."

"I'm Polly," she responded, thinking that in her childhood first names had been a sign of intimacy. Now, when waiters and flight attendants introduced themselves as Jack and Jill, their meaning was reversed.

"Nice to meet you." Mac held out his hand. The strength and duration of his grip clearly suggested that he had designs on her person. "So, how long are you in Key West for?"

"I'm not certain. Three or four days, maybe."

"Aw, too bad. I was hoping you were down for the whole season." He grinned.

"No." Polly smiled back almost against her will, feeling a once-familiar rush of consciousness. Five years ago she would have enjoyed sitting in a tropical garden, flirting with a good-looking guy; she knew better now.

"Having a good time so far?"

"So-so." Polly told the truth automatically, then realized that it sounded like a line; and that was how Mac responded to it:

"Maybe you haven't been to the right places. You like to dance?"

"Yes . . . no." She felt as if her feet were sinking into quicksand. "It depends."

"Depends on what?"

"Well—" Polly was rescued by the arrival of their beers.

"Thanks, Susie. . . . So, here's to your stay in the last resort."

"The last resort?"

"That's what we call it." He lifted his sloppily foaming glass and knocked it against hers. Polly heard herself laugh awkwardly. "So what've you seen up to now?"

"Nothing much. The ocean, a lot of art galleries. I mean, one resort town is much like the next, isn't it?"

"Not always," Mac grinned.

"Say, what did you want to ask me?" The question was put almost mockingly; Mac clearly thought it had been just an excuse to meet him.

"I wanted to know—" Polly took a breath. "That house you were working on this afternoon—"

"Mm?" He sat back, smiling lazily. The colored bulbs in the bush beside him cast a hot red-and-blue half light on the flat weathered planes of his cheek and jaw.

"On Frances Street, near the cemetery." Polly plowed ahead. "You were there with a pickup truck."

"Right: I was cleaning out the gutters. They always get jammed up with leaves this time of year." He frowned, as if suspecting Polly for the first time of an ulterior, nonsexual motive, then smiled slowly. "You want something revived, maybe, or constructed?" His tone hovered equivocally between contractor and seducer.

"No, what I want—" Polly remembered to smile back. "See, I was trying to find the man who lives there, Hugh Cameron—"

"Yeah?" Now Mac looked wary, displeased: the progress of his pickup had been interrupted.

"I came down here to Key West to interview him, actually." Polly leaned toward Mac, smiling, but his manner and tone remained cool.

"Oh, yes? What did you want to interview him for?"

"Well, it's for this book I'm writing. It's a biography of a painter he used to know. I've been phoning him ever since I got here Tuesday night, but nobody answers. I was wondering if he was out of town."

"Yes, he might be." Mac leaned back even farther now, and looked away.

"You haven't seen him lately?" she persisted, knowing as the words sounded out that this was a strategic mistake.

"What? No." Mac took a swig of beer, staring into the foam-crusted glass. "The house is rented out from this weekend, anyhow."

"Rented?"

"Oh, yeah. A lot of local people rent their places in the winter. A house like that, three bedrooms, a pool, you can get twenty-five hundred a month for it, easy." He still wasn't looking at her.

"Really?" Polly smiled hard, and tried to reestablish a friendly conversational tone. "I had no idea of that. No wonder there's so many yuppie types around."

Mac did not reply, only shifted in his chair and stared off sideways. She followed the direction of his gaze to three pretty girls at a table on the other side of the garden. He's caught on that I'm not interested in him, she thought, so he's turned off. She felt a researcher's anxiety—and a stupid, automatic pang of loss. "You think Mr. Cameron's left town already?"

"Could be." Mac shrugged.

"Do you have his new address?"

He shook his head slowly.

"But you must know how to get in touch with him," Polly persisted. "He has to pay you for cleaning his gutters, doesn't he, for instance?"

"I've been paid already." Mac surveyed the garden again, drained his beer, checked his watch. "Listen, I've got to go. Got to have dinner with some friends."

"Okay," Polly said in a falling tone of frustration and disappointment. Her bad luck had returned with a vengeance.

"Well," Mac stood up. "See you around." He produced a meaningless, empty smile.

"Thanks for the beer."

"No problem." Mac started to lope away; then he stopped and turned, looking hard at her. "Say." He took a step nearer, paused for what seemed to Polly a long while, then added, "How about you meeting me later on tonight? We could go dancing."

A reprieve, Polly thought. "Sure, why not?" she heard herself answer. It's not that I care anything for him, she told herself, but I've got to get that address.

"I could pick you up about nine. If you're not too fancy to ride in a truck." He grinned.

"Of course I'm not." Polly tried to make this casual rather than either indignant or suggestive.

"Okay then. Just say where."

•••••

Back at the guest house Lee, in a tropical-flowered red muumuu, set two plates of steamed fish on the table and refilled both their balloon wineglasses. She'd insisted on cooking supper, though she'd allowed Polly to contribute a bottle of Soave.

While Lee busied herself in the kitchen Polly sat frowning at the hand-loomed tablecloth, displeased with herself. Because of her impatience, she had nearly messed up at Billie's. She should have let Mac think she was here on vacation, and later just casually asked him about Hugh Cameron.

Now, though, she had to spend a whole evening with him in some local dive. Well, it could be worth it. He must know how to reach Hugh Cameron, or at least be able to find out. And he might have other information too. If he'd worked for Cameron before, for instance, he could have been inside the old bastard's house and seen if he'd still got any of Lorin's paintings. Until Polly found out all Mac knew, she'd better go on pretending she was interested in him.

You are interested in him, a voice said inside her, not in her head but considerably lower down.

I am not, Polly said.

"Here you are." Lee returned bearing a rough-hewn wooden bowl heaped with brilliantly colored tropical fruit, and looking even more like a Gauguin painting. "I wish I could take you out myself, show you some of the town," she said. "There's really good piano bar down on Duval Street. Trouble is, I have to stay in tonight, I've got guests driving from Miami, and God knows when they'll turn up."

She placed the bowl in the center of the table and, standing so close that her broad hip brushed Polly's shoulder, ran one sinewy brown hand through her curls. "You've got really nice hair, you know that?"

That was all she said, but Polly was as sure as if it were spelled out in the complicated hand-weave of the tablecloth that Lee was attracted to her and, having just heard that Polly didn't care for men, wanted to make something of it.

But since women were more subtle and tactful about these matters, if Polly didn't respond Lee would make no further approaches, or certainly no overt ones. Lee would never grab her, or blurt, "Hey, let's go to bed." No one would be embarrassed, and no one's feelings would be hurt. But it would be easy now for Polly, just by touching or complimenting Lee in return, to silently reply, *Yes, let's.*

"Are those real mangoes?" she asked instead.

"That's right." Lee smiled as easily as if nothing had happened or been decided. And maybe it hadn't, not yet. "Why don't you try one? I should warn you, though, they're kind of messy to eat."

"Wow," Polly said, gasping with surprise and also with relief as the door of the Sagebrush Lounge swung to behind her and Mac, shutting them into a warehouselike space hung with animal horns and antlers and vibrating with noisy air conditioning and amplified country-rock music. On their left was a crowded dance floor, on their right a long bar against which men in work clothes and cowboy gear were leaning. Mac's costume matched theirs; he had traded his Revivals Construction jersey for a blue Western-cut shirt with pearl snaps. Polly still wore her rumpled Banana Republic jumpsuit; she wasn't going to change as if for a date, especially not with Lee around.

"Didn't expect anything like this in Key West, huh?" Mac shouted against the music. Waving to two men at the bar, he led her to a table.

"You can say that again," Polly shouted back, taking another deep breath. The Sagebrush Lounge was on an ill-lit back street somewhere out near the airport, next to a swamp and across from a trailer camp. On the way there, though she had kept up a sort of conversation, most of her mind had been occupied by Lee's remark about dark alleys, and the possibility, increasing as Mac drove farther and farther from the center of town, that he would turn out to be a psychopathic rapist. Her instinct told her he wasn't; but how many women had been raped or even murdered because they trusted their stupid instincts?

"Like a beer?"

"Sure."

Polly thought that in this clamor it wasn't going to be easy to bring up the subject of Hugh Cameron's present whereabouts.

She resolved to drink it as slowly as possible: she'd need to keep her head in case Mac did turn out to be a psychopathic rapist. Maybe what she should do right now was make some excuse to leave the table, call Lee, and tell her she was in the Sagebrush Lounge with Mac—Mac who?

"Say." Polly made an effort to breathe normally. "What's your name, besides Mac?"

"Huh?" Under the pounding beat of the music she heard a fractional hesitation, which she put down to Mac's reluctance to, as he would probably put it, get involved. "MacFlecknoe. Richard MacFlecknoe. Like the poet. But we're not related, far as I know. And you?"

"Polly Alter." The music had crashed to a romping halt, and her name sounded out abashingly loud. "Well, Paula really," she said, moderating her voice. "Only nobody I can stand ever calls me that."

"Then I'll make sure not to." Mac smiled slowly. "Hey. You know that guy you wanted to interview?"

"Hugh Cameron. Yes, of course."

"I found out he's in Italy for the winter."

"Italy?" It came out almost as a wail.

"Yep. In Florence. I've got the address for you, right here." He held out a scrap of folded paper.

"Oh, thanks." Polly tried to look grateful, but it wasn't easy. She had neither the time nor the money to follow Hugh Cameron to Italy, and even if she did there was no guarantee he'd agree to talk to her. All she could do now was get whatever information she could from Mac. Maybe he could give her the names of some of Cameron's friends in Key West, people who, if she was lucky, had been here when Lorin Jones was alive.

"Like to dance?" The music had started again, just as loud but to a slower beat.

"All right," she agreed.

But as Mac led the way onto the floor, Polly realized that the other couples had stopped jigging and shaking *en face*, and were now clasped together in swaying pairs. Uneasily, she allowed him to put his arms around her, and placed her hand on his shoulder. It was years since she'd danced the two-step with anyone—by the time she got to college it was already out of fashion.

The tune was simple, soupy, a childlike whine of lost love spun over a slow pounding beat. Mac held her at a polite distance at first, but soon he began to gather her closer. Annoying, presumptuous, but it was easier to move in sync this way, swaying together, almost soothing. She only liked it because it had been so long since she'd held anyone. . . . But this was a man, and a complete stranger. She should pull back, so as not to give him any ideas.

But she didn't pull back. You can't afford to get him miffed, you've got to remember your research, she told herself, easing her arm farther along Mac's shoulder, feeling his muscles move under the cloth. First things first.

"That man whose address you gave me," she murmured. "Hugh Cameron."

"Mh." Mac looked down at her.

"D'you know him well?"

He swung her around, then spoke. "Not all that well, no."

"I understand he's a real basta—, I mean, kind of a difficult person."

"Oh yeah? He hasn't treated me too badly." Mac took a firmer grip on Polly, bending their joined hands behind her back and pulling her so close that the whole length of his body was pressed against hers.

Taking a long breath, trying not to notice this, Polly plowed on. "You've been working for him quite a while?"

"Huh?"

"Cameron, I mean."

"Mh"

She waited, but he said no more. But the beat of the lowbrow music continued, they moved smoothly together. Polly felt herself blurring, loosening, becoming sensually addled, as if she'd been soaking too long in a hot bath. She gave herself a hard mental shake and tried again, speaking now in a sleepy murmur that matched the music. "So have you been in Key West a long time?"

"Yeah, I guess you'd say so."

"Really—how long?"

"I d'know. Nineteen, twenty years, off and on."

"Then you could have met Lorin Jones yourself." Mac, swinging Polly deftly around, did not reply. "The artist I'm writing about."

"Mh?"

"Did you ever know her?"

"Nope." Mac was resting his head against Polly's now; as he spoke his hot breath fluttered her hair. "Can't say I did."

Bad luck again, Polly thought; but another part of her, which was sick to death of Lorin Jones, breathed *thank God*. What it wanted now, what it needed, was to forget Jones for a while, to stop questioning and prying, to move to the simple thump and twang of the country band and murmur almost meaningless remarks.

"I always liked this old tune."

"Yes, it's nice."

But she could not disguise from herself that all the time, under their slow, banal exchange, another far more lively conversation was going on. Mac's body and hers, like two good-looking oversexed morons, were speaking to each other; and she could hear clearly what they were saying, over and over again:

—*Hey, you want to?*

—*Aw, sure.*

—*When?*

—*Anytime.*

I don't do that anymore, she said to the moron that was her body; but it didn't hear her.

The band repeated the last chorus and went into a crescendo. Holding her close, Mac did an expert dip, and came up again as the song ended.

"I like the way you dance," he said, moving back but keeping one arm around her.

"Thanks." Polly didn't return the compliment. What she had to do now, she thought fuzzily, was get out of here before anything else could happen.

The band paused for breath, then started another slow number, a wailing song about lost love.

"Let's dance," Mac said.

This time Polly didn't try to make conversation. She allowed herself to fall at once into a warm drifting blur, to lean against Mac, move with him. Because it didn't matter, as soon as the music ended she'd go home. But now—now—

"Hey," Mac whispered presently, his mouth against her

face. "You know that place you're staying? That Artemis Lodge."

"Mm."

"Artemis, you know who she was?"

"I think she was some kind of Greek goddess," Polly said.

"Right. A jealous virgin. She turned her best friend into a bear on account of she'd slept with Zeus."

"Really?"

"I'm not as illiterate as you might think."

"Mm." Polly recalled something someone had said, that many of the permanent residents of Key West were middle-class dropouts, ex-hippies now managing restaurants or galleries, or running charter boats—or, why not, repairing houses for a living.

"Anyhow," Mac said. "That place of yours. It's a lesbian guest house; at least that's what I hear."

Polly swallowed; then, damning herself for her hesitation, said, "Yes, I know. I'm a lesbian."

"Yeah?" Mac laughed. "You could have fooled me." He circled with the music, holding her even closer. It was clear that he didn't believe her; or if he did believe her, didn't care.

"So how's it going, your research?" he asked as they returned to the table.

"Oh, okay. Well, not all that great lately. Coming down here wasn't much use."

"Not much use, huh? Mac said, with a grin. "Sorry to hear that."

"I didn't mean—It's just—" What is the matter with me, the beer, Polly thought. "I mean, I came all the way to Key West, and spent all that money, and now I can't locate Hugh Cameron or anybody who knew him or Lorin Jones, and I can't even get into his house."

"Get into the house? What good would that do, if he's not there?"

"I want to see if he still has any of Lorin Jones's paintings. The museum where I work put on a show a couple of years ago in New York, and I wrote to ask if he had anything we could borrow, but he never answered."

"Ah." Mac rotated his empty glass.

"Maybe you've noticed, if you've ever been in the house."

"Noticed what?"

"If there were any pictures. Oil paintings, they'd be, or maybe watercolors."

"Pictures." Mac appeared to be thinking. "I don't remember, really. I guess I never paid much attention. Like another beer?"

"Oh no, no thanks. I've got to get back." Polly looked at her watch. "The manager at the guest house said she was going to call the police if I wasn't home by twelve."

"She did?"

"She's afraid you might be a psychotic rapist," Polly heard herself say, or rather lie.

"She never even saw me," Mac protested.

"I know."

"She probably thinks all men are rapists." He laughed.

"I guess she might." Polly mentally kicked herself for playing along, for misquoting and misrepresenting Lee.

"Personally, I've always liked cooperation when I make love." Mac turned toward Polly. Something looked at her out of his eyes; she tried to look away, didn't quite make it. "Okay, shall we go?"

Abruptly the smoky, pulsing sensual blur of the Sagebrush Lounge was replaced by the warm, silent night outside. Polly felt a tense, twanging apprehension—or was it expectancy?—as Mac drove along a dark side street, taking her—where?

"So you're gay, huh?" he said abruptly. "Since when?"

"I've been living with a woman for two months," Polly told him. That is, I was living with her," she added, unwilling to suggest that she was two-timing someone.

"You mean you aren't anymore" he said, or asked.

"No, not exactly," she admitted.

"Ah." They had turned onto a street that Polly recognized as not far from Artemis Lodge. There seemed to be nothing more to say, so she said nothing. It's over, I'm safe; I won't see him again, she thought, and was furious at herself for not being relieved.

"Listen, I've got an idea," Mac said as he pulled up outside the guest house. "What if I was to get—I mean, I think maybe I could get the key to Hugh Cameron's house, from the rental agent."

"Oh, could you?" Polly gasped.

"Sure. Well, probably. I could tell them I had to check the bathroom pipes or something. Then you could meet me there tomorrow after I finish work and look for those paintings."

"That'd be really great." In her enthusiasm, Polly put a hand on his arm. "If it's not too much trouble—"

"No. A pleasure." Mac covered her hand with his. "So I'll see you over there, say about four?"

"Great," Polly repeated. She started to slide away across the seat of the truck, but he didn't remove his hand; instead, he tightened his grip. "Well, hey, thanks for the drink."

"Hey, you're welcome." Mac turned full toward her. He kissed her hard but very briefly, releasing her before she had time to react. "See you at four tomorrow," he repeated as she scrambled down out of the cab.

The pickup truck roared off, and Polly, in what her mother would have called a State, stood on the porch of Artemis Lodge. The door was locked, and only one ruby-chambered electric lantern burned in the hall. Either Lee was out, or she'd already gone to bed. Polly let herself in and climbed the stairs to her room.

What are you so upset about? she asked herself. Your luck's turned. Tomorrow you're going to see Cameron's place, and who knows what you might find there? Pictures, drawings—letters and notes even, if Mac doesn't stop you—

Or, let's put it this way, another voice said. You're going to meet a man you hardly know in a town you hardly know, in an empty house, where there probably aren't any paintings anyhow, because probably that was just his way of getting you there, and doing what he wants to you.

And what you want, said another treacherous voice.

The room felt hot and close and crowded; Polly shoved up the sash of the window, but the breeze that blundered in, sticky with the odors of tropical flowers and auto exhaust and tidewrack, was even more insidious and oppressive. Sex, it whispered.

All right, you feel something, the first voice shrilled in Polly's ear as she paced the narrow strip of straw matting between the bed and the open window. But that's just because you haven't made it with anyone in nearly a month; naturally you're susceptible. It doesn't mean you have to fall into bed with whoever comes along, especially not with a man.

All right, you'll be alone with Mac. But if he makes what your mother would call an indecent suggestion, all you have to do is say no; he's not going to jump you. If you can't control yourself, if you have to sleep with someone, Polly told herself, it doesn't have to be Mac. There's Lee, for instance—a generous and warmhearted (if rather scatty) woman who likes you and is right downstairs in the guest house.

Polly fixed the image of Lee in her mind: mentally she removed Lee's flowered muumuu and contemplated her low full leathery breasts, her thick waist, her sturdy brown Polynesian hips; her bushy black armpits, the probable black bush below. . . . But she felt less than nothing. Lee wasn't what she wanted; what she wanted—

It was her old ignorant desire for the Romantic Hero, recurring like some persistent tropical weed. Over the last two years this rank growth had been, she'd thought, thoroughly rooted up, and the earth where it once flourished raked hard, trampled down. But now, in the steamy, unnatural climate of Key West, the weed had sprouted again.

•••••

At a quarter to four the following afternoon Polly sat on the wide leaf-littered steps of Hugh Cameron's house, under heavy bulging clouds that had done nothing to lower the temperature. It seemed if anything warmer than yesterday; the light had a diffuse, oppressive purplish tint. Mac's not coming, she thought for the fourth or fifth time. You should be glad; now you can't do anything you'll be sorry for afterward. But she didn't feel glad; she felt ashamed and angrily disappointed, like a recovered alcoholic who'd tried to fall off the wagon in front of a package store that turned out to be shut. Probably most people in Key West slept with anybody they fancied who came along, regardless of their sex, occupation, age, marital status, or political party. Sexual alcoholics.

The whole trip to Key West had been a waste of time and money, a useless expense of spirit. Today, for instance, she had spent hours in the newspaper files at the county library without finding a single reference to Lorin Jones. She had also gone to the county courthouse and, after an interminable delay, seen a certificate that listed the cause of Lorin's death as "pneumonia." Polly still has her doubts.

She would give Mac five more minutes, Polly decided; then she'd leave. There was probably nothing here anyhow.

Two minutes. One minute. Okay, the hell with it. But as Polly started down the walk, the Revivals Construction pickup turned the corner.

"Sorry!" Mac called, parking on the wrong side of the street with a screech of brakes and leaping onto the curb. "Been waiting long?"

"It's okay." Late three times out of three, she thought; it must be a character trait. No point in complaining, though; she'd probably never see him again after today.

Mac gave her the warm, uneasy smile of someone who deserves and expects to be scolded. "Had a good day?"

"So-so." Polly shrugged.

"Sorry to hear that." He grinned; it was clear that he wasn't particularly sorry—or, to be fair, particularly glad. "Shall we go in?"

Behind its closed shutters and drawn bamboo blinds the interior of Hugh Cameron's house was silent, shadowy and almost cool. At first Polly could see nothing; then she began to make out, floating halfway between the floor and ceiling, a very large painting. It might be—it was, surely—

"That what you were looking for?" Mac asked.

"I—I think so," she said in a strangled, panting voice.

"Wait a second." There was the rattling sound of a blind being raised. A slotted golden light widened across the tiles; the huge canvas glowed out, white and umber and peach, patched with vermilion and scribbled with black writing. Yes: it had to be one of Lorin Jones's late graffiti paintings, but looser and more brilliant than any she'd ever seen. What might be an M or an H had been scrubbed in thick pale color down one side of the canvas, in the manner of a pastel Franz Kline; and a line of fine writing ran diagonally up from the opposite corner.

"Yes. It's Lorin's, it's got to be!"

"Really," Mac said indifferently.

"I don't understand it. Lorin Jones's brother was supposed to have come here after she died and collected all her work, and he never even mentioned this picture."

"Mh?"

"I don't see how he could have missed it."

"Maybe it wasn't in the house," Mac suggested, gazing idly through a sliding glass door at a pool surrounded by unnaturally white plastic furniture and unnaturally green shrubs. He doesn't care, he's not interested, Polly thought. And he's not interested in me either, not anymore. She should feel relieved, but instead she felt hurt and miserable.

"You mean Cameron could have hidden it?" she said.

Mac shrugged, not turning around.

"You couldn't hide something like this; it's too big."

"Sure you could," he said. "Put it out back against the fence, cover it with an old drop cloth or something."

"Maybe. I suppose that would have been like him, the creep."

"What makes you think he's such a creep?" Mac strolled back into the center of the room.

"Everybody says so. For one thing, he walked out on Lorin Jones when she was dying. He didn't even try to help her."

"That's what they say?"

"Mm."

"And that's what you're going to put in your book, huh?"

"Yes, why not? I'm planning to tell the truth." Polly turned back to the picture; holding her head sideways, she tried to decipher the line of writing. "*What is . . . what is the meaning,*" she read out. "It looks like *meaning,* or maybe it's *morning—of wind.* What do you think?"

"Lemme look." Mac came up close behind her. "Memory, I think," he said after a pause. "What is the memory of wind under the sea?"

"It sounds like verse. Lorin Jones's dealer—, he thinks the words in these late paintings mostly came from Hugh Cameron's poems."

"Could be," Mac said.

He's bored with me, he's waiting for me to leave, she thought. All right, forget about him. Concentrate on your job. "I'll have to check," she said. "The trouble is, I haven't tracked down much of Cameron's work, though I know—"

Polly started; Mac had just rested his hands on her shoulders."—there were at least two volumes of poems, but I haven't—" She turned and opened her mouth to finish the sentence; he closed it with a long kiss.

I'm not ready for this, Polly thought, feeling herself sinking; I didn't expect—Her eyes focused on a wall of book-shelves behind his head. Cameron's books. And Cameron's poems must be here somewhere—"Wait," she whispered when Mac paused for breath. "Not now—not yet—"

"I know." Mac grinned. "You want to see the other picture."

"There's another one?"

"I think so. In there." He gestured with his head toward an open door.

The second room, which also opened onto the deck, was mainly occupied by a low queen-sized bed. Over it hung what was surely, even in the dim light from the shuttered window, Lorin Jones's lost painting, *Aftershocks*. Polly recognized it from the blurred black-and-white photo in the files of the Apollo Gallery, but only by the semiabstract seaweed shapes along the lower edge, for this painting had been terribly damaged. There was a raw, jagged-toothed hole in the center, as if something large and violent had burst through the canvas from behind.

"Oh, shit," she choked.

"What's the matter?"

"You can see." Polly was in better control of her voice now, but her head was still full of angry buzzing. "It's Lorin Jones's picture, the one that disappeared after her last show, but it's been all ripped up." By Hugh Cameron, of course. He was the sort of man who might destroy his lover's painting and hang the evidence of the crime over his own bed for nearly twenty years.

"Yeah?" Mac came closer. "Looks to me like it was done on purpose," he said.

"I suppose it was," Polly said tightly. "By that bastard who lives here."

"No, I meant by Lor—your artist. Look at the way the words are written."

It was true; a line of script, not present in Jacky's

photograph, began in the upper left of the picture and continued below the hole, curving out and up toward the right. To make it out Polly had to lean forward over the platform bed—Mac must be farsighted.

"*You never saw it coming . . . till it was gone,*" she read slowly. "I don't know—I suppose it's possible she did it herself," she conceded, realizing as she spoke that, if this were so, the importance of the work hadn't been reduced; it might even have been enhanced. "But there's no way of proving that. I wonder—"

"Wonder about it later, okay?" Mac had moved much closer. He ran his hand slowly down her back; all the way down.

"No, wait. I have to—"Breathing hard, Polly took a step away.

"Come on." He pulled her to him. "That thing won't fly off."

No, it won't, she thought. But I will, my ticket is for the day after tomorrow. I've got to plan. What I need is evidence that the paintings are here. Photographs, I need color photographs. It's too late today, but I could rent a camera tomorrow, or borrow one—maybe from Lee? Then when I get back to New York—

But she couldn't think clearly now. Now she was in a bedroom in Key West with a man who was kissing the back of her neck. His mouth was hot, his tongue insinuating. She was leaning toward him, against him.

"Oh, Polly," Mac whispered, pulling her toward the bed.

Stop, wait, she told herself. But another part of her replied, Why not? It's what you want. And besides, it's what Mac wants; even what he deserves for letting you into this house, helping you to find Lorin's paintings. She swayed and fell slowly onto the rough off-white cotton bedspread.

All right, go ahead, a voice said in her mind. But keep some control of yourself. All right, kiss him, it panted. All right, let him pull open your shirt and lick your breast. But for God's sake don't let yourself care about him, or you'll be hurt and betrayed again.

He rolled toward her; with one warm, work-roughened hand, he pulled her Banana Republic safari shirt fully open. "Shhh."

Half an hour later the squares of the straw rug were littered with cast clothes, and their owners lay dizzy and entangled on the rumpled bedspread. Above them, Lorin Jones's lost painting floated, mysterious and—in spite of the gaping hole in its center—serene. If it hadn't been for you, Polly thought blurrily, slipping toward sleep, I wouldn't be here in Hugh Cameron's bed. I would never have known—

It was weird what she felt. t was as if she had magically become Lorin Jones, and the man who lay beside her, with his work-roughened hand loose on her breast and one leg across hers, was Hugh Cameron.

But of course that wasn't even right magically, because this had never been Lorin's house. It was only another backwash of all these months of immersion in Jones's history: a sign of her obsession, her confusion of her own life and Lorin's.

Half-awake now, Polly unwound herself from Mac and raised herself on one elbow to look at him. Naked, he was a worn and flawed umber above the waist, but smoothly pale below to the ankles. His body, like his face, was long and spare, all steep planes, narrow ridges, and clearly outlined muscles.

Well, you did it, didn't you, she told herself, and waited to feel shame and embarrassment, but felt only pleasure, joy, and a rush of affection. I like him, it said: I don't want to leave Key West, I want to stay here with him. . . . She shook her head angrily: how stupid and greedy the body is, how careless of the good of its tenant!

She ought to be angry, though; if not at herself, then at the world. Why should it be arranged so badly? Why should it be so much better with a man she hardly knew than with a woman she loved?

A warm shudder of wind bent the branches outside and gushed into the bedroom. Mac stretched, yawned, opened his eyes, and smiled lazily at the ceiling. Then he turned toward Polly, and his expression changed.

"Oh, Christ," he whispered, and sat up.

"What's the matter?"

"Nothing." He smiled again, but briefly and uneasily. "That was lovely, lovely," he said, not looking at her.

Yes, Polly thought. Now he wishes he hadn't. That's how men are, remember? He wants to get away as soon as he can. She began to rise.

"Wait. Don't get up yet." Mac put out one hand to stop her. "You're so beautiful lying there." He stroked her near breast with one finger, as if it were a sculpture made of some rare, exotic material, then leaned over to kiss it.

"Shouldn't we—"

"Shh."

"Jesus, look at the time," Mac said after a considerable interval. "Maybe we should get some clothes on."

"All right," Polly agreed. This isn't his house, she suddenly remembered, it's a rental property. He's not supposed to be here, not like this. She imagined Hugh Cameron walking in; or, much more likely, the rental agent. Shameful for her; disastrous for Mac. Rapidly, she bent to retrieve her red cotton bra and panties from the floor.

"Listen, I've got to go back to the job, check with my crew," Mac said, dragging on his jeans. "But that shouldn't take long. How about supper?"

"All right," Polly heard herself agree, too eagerly.

"It's nearly five now. I can pick you up in about an hour at the guest house, okay?" he smiled as if sure of her answer.

"Well . . . Okay," Polly said.

• • • • •

Now Mac sat next to her at the outdoor bar of an oceanside restaurant called Louie's Backyard. The wind, stronger here, shook the trees overhead, sending down a scatter of tiny leaves; it flung a succession of spotlit creamy green waves against the sea wall. Most of the other customers had retreated to a higher and more sheltered deck or gone inside.

"What would you like?" he asked.

"I'll have a spritzer."

Mac waved and ordered. "Listen, I don't want you to give up on Key West. Tomorrow we'll go to the Full Moon Saloon; it's a kind of funky place, but they have good conch chowder and real Key Lime pie."

"You think I'm having supper with you tomorrow," Polly said, trying not to smile.

"What's the matter, can't you make it?"

"I'm not sure."

"Do you really have to go back to New York Sunday morning?"

"Well, I was planning to."

"Why don't you stay a while? There's a lot here I'd like to show you. And I've got the whole day off Sunday. We could go out to the reef, if this storm blows over." Mac glanced again at the waves, now spotlit to a milky aqua.

"You ever been snorkeling?"

"No," Polly admitted.

"It's beautiful under the water. Literally out of this world." He leaned toward her, stroke her arm. "I bet you could change your ticket."

Don't do it, her guardian angel remarked, appearing suddenly in Polly's mind; she was a tall stern marble figure like a Greek statue, probably the Artemis of Artemis Lodge. *You've had your fling, if you don't watch out you could become emotionally involved with this unsuitable person.*

"Well, I could try," Polly said, stubbornly refusing to listen to this inner voice. "But I've got to be back by Wednesday, I have an interview scheduled then." What does it matter, she argued; it's only three more days. I just want to get him out of my system. *Yes*, Artemis remarked. *That's what addicts always say. One more fix. Get it out of my system.*

"Great." Mac leaned farther toward Polly; he touched the side of her face.

"I said I'd try, that's all." In spite of her resolved, she smiled. Okay, she admitted. I like him. I could love him, even. What's the matter with that? *It's stupid and dangerous; you'll get hurt*, Artemis replied, but her voice was shrill and faint.

"Great," Mac repeated, putting his hand on her arm. The wind blew harder; the thick pale green lace-trimmed waves churned under the deck. He and Polly gazed at each other, half smiling.

"Hey," he said finally. "There's something I have to tell you."

"Okay." She laughed.

"It's, uh. This bastard that you're looking for, Hugh Cameron. . . . That's me. I mean I'm him." In the gathering dark his expression was impossible to read.

"What?"

"I'm Hugh Cameron."

He's kidding, Polly thought. "Oh, you are not," she said. "You already told me he's in Italy. Besides, you're not anywhere old enough to be him."

"I'm forty-eight."

"Yes, well." She smiled, though it was a few years more than she'd assumed. "If Lorin Jones were alive now she'd be nearly sixty. When she left Wellfleet with Cameron she was thirty-seven; that's twenty-two years ago, and you would've been only—"

"Twenty-six." Mac nodded solemnly, keeping up the joke.

"Right." Polly smiled. "Besides, Hugh Cameron is a poet—he was a college professor."

"Yeah. He was a professor, but he didn't get tenure, so now he's a contractor in Key West." Mac still did not smile; his expression could almost be called grim.

Polly started at him. "Prove it," she said.

"Okay." Mac sighed; then he reached into the back pocket of his jeans and took out a worn pigskin wallet stitched with thongs. "Here. Driver's license, library card, food co-op, Visa—" He fanned them out on the damp wooden bar.

Cameron, Hugh Richard. H.R. Cameron. Hugh Cameron.

"Oh, my God," Polly said slowly. Then a crazy laugh came out of her. She shoved her stool toward the ocean, away from him.

"I tried to tell you before, back in the house. Only I couldn't. I knew you'd start asking a lot of questions, and I don't like talking about those years now. It was a bad time in my life."

"Yes?" Polly said half-consciously. I was right this afternoon, she thought, feeling disoriented, as if she had made it happen.

"And besides, I figured you wouldn't sleep with me if you knew. You were so down on Cameron, that bastard, that creep, that shit, you kept saying."

"Jesus."

"Y'know, after I saw you on Frances Street, I kept kicking myself for losing my chance. When you turned up again on Mallory Dock, I thought somebody up there loved me." He pointed at the sooty lowering clouds. "Then when I got to Billie's I found out you were the woman from New York that'd been hounding me, so I decided to get out of there fast. And I started to leave, right?"

"Right," Polly echoed, dazed.

"But the thing was, you looked so great, sitting there. I couldn't let you go. I thought, what the hell, it's karma. You've got to play it out."

"You're Hugh Cameron," Polly said, finally taking this in. Mac nodded.

"So that was your house."

"Yes."

"And it's not for rent; you live there."

"Yes—no. It's rented all right, from tomorrow."

"But nothing else you told me is true." Now she was trembling, furious.

"Most of it's true. And Mac is what everybody calls me down here. I never liked the name Hugh, I don't know why I stood it for so long. Back in Nebraska, where I come from, it was a sissy name. I had to take all these jokes at school. 'Who? Who Cameron? You, Cameron.'"

"You lied to me," Polly said, paying no attention to this story.

"Well, yes. But it was in a good cause." Mac grinned, but nervously. "Anyhow, you lied to me too."

"I did not."

"Sure you did. You told me you were a lesbian." Mac was smiling now. "Last night when I took you back to the Artemis Lodge I was almost scared to kiss you. I let go real fast, in case maybe you'd hit me."

"I should have hit you," Polly said, with a short

hysterical laugh.

"Come on. It's not as bad as all that. I'm the same guy I was this afternoon."

"No, you aren't." *You see,* the tall winged goddess said in her mind. *You rushed into this like a greedy, sensual fool. Now you are punished.*

"I didn't have to tell you," Mac protested. "I could have kept quiet. Only I thought we should start out straight." He grinned awkwardly.

"It's a little late for that," she said, with an angry tremor in her speech.

"Better late than never."

Polly did not trust herself to answer. She turned away from Mac, staring out over the ocean, milky green near the deck, but dark and shaky beyond the lights, like some kind of poisonous Jell-O.

"Hey, baby." Mac leaned toward Polly and put a strong hand on her arm. "Let's give this a chance. You don't know anything about me really."

"I know enough," she replied, casting a miserable glance at him and then looking away over the churning Jell-O toward other countries full of folly and deception.

"Hell, what do you want? Do you want me to take you back to the guest house?"

"I don't know." Polly's voice shook. "Maybe you'd better."

"Okay." Mac stood up.

"I have to think."

"Okay. You want me to call you tomorrow morning?"

"Yes—no. All right."

Thomas McGuane

from
Panama

This is the first time I've worked without a net. I want to tell the truth. At the same time, I don't want to start a feeding frenzy. You stick your neck out and you know what happens. It's obvious.

The newspaper said that the arrests were made by thirty agents in coordinated raids "early in the a.m." and that when the suspects were booked, a crowd of three hundred gathered at the Monroe County Courthouse and applauded. The rest of the page had to do with the charges against the men, which were neither here nor there. Most people I heard talking thought it was just too Cuban for words.

I stepped out onto the patio as the city commissioner was taken to the unmarked car in handcuffs. He was in his bathrobe and lottery tickets were blowing all over the place. Last week they picked up my dog and it cost me a five. The phone number was on her collar and they could have called. I knew how badly they had wanted to use the gas. But then, they're tired of everything. The wind blows all winter and gets on your nerves. It just does. They have nothing but their uniforms and the hopes of using the gas.

Out on the patio, I could see the horizon. The dog slept in the wedge of sun. There were no boats, the sea was flat, and from here, there was not a bit of evidence of the coordinated raids, the unmarked cars. The lottery—the bolita—was silent; it was always silent. And behind the wooden shutters, there was as much cocaine as ever. I had a pile of scandal magazines to see what had hit friends and loved ones. There was not one boat between me and an unemphatic horizon. I was home from the field of agony or whatever you want to call it; I was home from it. I was dead.

I went up to the Casa Marina to see my stepmother. The cats were on the screen above the enclosed pool and the grapefruits were rotting in the little grove. Ruiz the gardener was crawfishing on the Cay Sal bank and the bent grass was thick and spongy and neglected. I was there five minutes when she said, "You were an overnight sensation." And I said, "Gotta hit it, I left the motor running." And she said, "You left the motor running?" and I said, "That's it for me, I'm going." And she tottered after me with the palmetto bugs scattering in the foyer and screamed at me as I pulled out: "You left the motor running! You don't have a car!" I actually don't know how smart she is. What could she have meant by that? I believe that she was attacking my memory.

She is a special case, Roxy; she is related to me three different ways and in some sense collects all that is dreary, sinister, or in any way glorious about my family. Roxy is one of those who have technically died; was in fact pronounced dead, then accidentally discovered still living by an alert nurse. She makes the most of this terrible event. She sometimes has need of tranquilizers half the size of Easter Eggs. She drinks brandy and soda with them; and her face hollows out everywhere, her eyes sink, and you think of her earlier death. Sometimes she raises her hand to her face thinking the drink is in it. Roxy can behave with great charm. But then, just at the wrong time, pulls up her dress or throws something. I time my visits with extreme caution. I watch the house or see if her car has been properly parked. I used to spy but then I saw things which I perhaps never should have; and so I stopped that. When she thinks of me as an overnight sensation, she can be quite ruthless, flinging food at me or, without justification, calling the police and making false reports. I tolerate that because, under certain circumstances, I myself will stop at nothing. Fundamentally though, my step-mother is a problem because she is disgusting.

I guess it came to me, or maybe I just knew, that I have not been remembering things as clearly as I could have. For instance, Roxy is right, I don't have a car. I have a memory problem. The first question—look, you can ask me this—is exactly how much evasive editing is part of my loss of memory. I've been up against that one before. My position with respect to anyone else's claims for actuality has always been: it's you against me and may the best man win.

I'm not as stupid as I look. Are you? For instance, I'm no golfer. I did have a burst, and this is the ghastly thing which awaits each of us, of creating the world in my own image. I removed all resistance until I floated in my own invention. I creamed the opposition. Who in the history of ideas has prepared us for creaming the opposition? This has to be understood because otherwise . . . well, there is no otherwise; it really doesn't matter.

The first time I ran into Catherine, coming from the new wing of the county library, I watched from across the street noting that her Rhonda Fleming, shall we say, *grandeur* had not diminished. It seemed a little early in the present voyage to reveal myself. I sat on the wall under the beauty parlor, just a tenant in my self, or a bystander, eyes flooded, pushing my fingers into my sleeves like a nun. I thought, *When I find the right crooked doctor, I'm going to laugh in your face.*

I followed her for two blocks and watched her turn up the blind lane off Caroline where the sapodilla tree towers up from the interior of the block as though a piece of the original forest were imprisoned there. This spring they dug up the parking lot behind some clip joint on lower Duval and found an Indian grave, the huge skull of a Calusa seagoing Indian staring up through four inches of blacktop at the whores, junkies, and Southern lawyers.

So I sent her flowers without a note and two days later a note without flowers; and got this in return, addressed "Chester Hunnicutt Pomeroy, General Delivery": "Yes Chet I know you're home. But don't call me now, you flop you. —Catherine." I went into the garden and opened the toolshed, bug life running out among the rake tines. I got the big English stainless-steel pruning shears and came, you take it from me, *that* close to sending Catherine the finger I'd lost in her darkness so many thousand of times. The palmetto bugs are translucent as spar varnish and run over your feet in the shed. The sea has hollowed the patio into resonant chambers and when the wind has piped up like today you hear its moiling, even standing in the shed with the rakes and rust and bugs.

I felt better and lost all interest in mutilating myself, even for Catherine. Tobacco doves settled in the crown-of-thorns and some remote airplane changed harmonics overhead with a soft pop like champagne, leaving a pure white seam on the sky. I was feeling better and better and better. On stationery from my uncle's shipyard, I wrote, "There is no call for that. I'm just here with respect of healing certain injuries. Catherine, you only hurt hurt hurt when you lash out like that. I don't believe you try to picture what harm you do. —Chet." I traced my finger on the back of the sheet with a dotted line where the shears would have gone through. I said nothing as to the dotted line. It seemed to me with some embarrassment that it might have looked like a request for a ring.

I dialed information and asked for Catherine Clay. The operator said it was unpublished. I told her it was a matter of life or death; and the operator said, I know who you are, and clicked off. They wouldn't treat Jesse James like that.

When they build a shopping center over an old salt marsh, the seabirds sometimes circle the same place for a year or more, coming back to check daily, to see if there isn't some little chance those department stores and pharmacies and cinemas won't go as quickly as they'd come. Similarly, I come back and keep looking into myself, and it's always steel, concrete, fan magazines, machinery, bubble gum; nothing as sweet as the original marsh. Catherine knows this without looking, knows that the loving child who seems lost behind the reflector Ray-Bans, perhaps or probably really is lost. And the teeth that were broken in schoolyards or spoiled with Cuban ice cream have been resurrected and I am in all respects the replica of an effective bright-mouthed coastal omnivore, as happy with spinach salads as human flesh; and who snoozing in the sun of his patio, inert as any rummy, Rolex Oyster Chronometer imbedding slightly in softened flesh, teeth glittering with ocean light like minerals, could be dead; could be the kind of corpse that is sometimes described as "fresh."

"I am a congestion of storage batteries. I'm wired in series. I've left some fundamental components on the beach, and await recharging, bombardment, implanting, *something*, shall we say, very close to the bone. I do want to go on; but having given up, I can't be expected to be very sympathetic."

"That's all very pretty," Catherine Clay said. "But I don't care. Now may I go?"

"There's more."

"I don't care. And above all, I don't want you stalking me like this in the supermarket. I can't have you lurking in the aisles."

"It's still the same."

"It's not, you liar, you flop!"

Slapping me, crying yelling, oh God, clerks peering. I said, "You're prettiest like this." She chunks a good one into my jaw. The groceries were on the floor. Someone was saying, "Ma'am? Ma'am?" My tortoiseshell glasses from Optique Boutique were askew and some blood was in evidence. My lust for escape was complete. Palm fronds beat against the air-conditioned thermopane windows like my own hands.

Two clerks were helping Catherine to the door. I think they knew. Mrs. Fernandez, the store manager, stood by me.

"Can I use the crapper?" I asked.

She stared at me coolly and said, "First aisle past poultry."

I stood on the toilet and looked out at my nation through the ventilator fan. Any minute now, and Catherine Clay, the beautiful South Carolina wild child, would appear shortcutting her way home with her groceries.

I heard her before I could see her. She wasn't breathing right. That scene in the aisles had been too much for her and her esophagus was constricted. She came into my view and in a very deep and penetrating voice I told her that I still loved her, terrifying myself that it might not be a sham, that quite apart from my ability to abandon myself to any given moment, I might in fact still be in love with this crafty, amazing woman who looked up in astonishment. I let her catch no more than a glimpse of me in the ventilator hole before pulling the bead chain so that I vanished behind the dusty accelerating blades, a very effective slow dissolve.

I put my sunglasses back on and stood in front of the sink, staring at my blank reflection, scrutinizing it futilely for any expression at all and committing self-abuse. The sunglasses looked silvery and pure in the mirror, showing twins of me, and I watched them until everything was silvery and I turned off the fan, tidied up with a paper towel, and went back out through poultry toward the electric doors. Mrs. Fernandez, the store manager, smiled weakly and I said, "Bigger even than I had feared." The heat hit me in the street and I started . . . I think I started home. It was to feed the dog but I was thinking of Catherine and I had heartaches by the million.

My father was a store detective who was killed in the Boston subway fire, having gone to that city in connection with the Bicentennial. He had just left Boston Common, where we have kin buried. Everything I say about my father is disputed by everyone. My family have been shipwrights and ship's chandlers, except for him and me. I have been as you know in the Svengali business; I saw a few things and raved for money. I had a very successful show called *The Dog Ate The Part We Didn't Like.* I have from time to time scared myself. Even at the height of my powers, I was not in good health. But a furious metabolism preserves my physique and I am considered a tribute to evil living.

Those who have cared for me, friends, uncles, lovers, think I'm a lost soul or a lost cause. When I'm tired and harmless, I pack a gun, a five-shot Smith and Wesson .38. It's the only .38 not in six-shot configuration I know of. How the sacrifice of that one last shot makes the gun so flat and concealable, so deadlier than the others. Just by giving up a little!

As to my mother, she was a flash act of the early fifties, a bankrolled B-girl who caught cancer like a bug that was going around; and died at fifty-six pounds. There you have it. The long and the short of it. And I had a brother Jim.

The money began in a modest way in the 1840's. A grandfather of minor social bearing, who had fought a successful duel, married a beautiful girl from the Canary Islands with two brothers who were ship's carpenters. They built coasters, trading smacks, sharpie mailboats, and a pioneer lightship for the St. Lucie inlet. The Civil War came and they built two blockade runners for the rebellion, the *Red Dog* and the *Rattlesnake*; went broke, jumped the line to Key West again while Stephen Mallory left town to become Secretary of the Confederate Navy. At what is now the foot of Ann Street, they built a series of deadly blockade boats, light, fast, and armed. They were rich by then, had houses with pecan wood dining-room tables, crazy chandeliers, and dogwood joists pinned like the ribs of ships. Soon they were all dead; but the next gang were solid and functional and some of them I remember. Before our shipyard went broke in the Depression, they had built every kind of seagoing conveyance that could run to Cuba and home; the prettiest, a turtle schooner, the *Hillary B. Cates*, was seen last winter off Cap Haitien with a black crew, no masts, and a tractor engine for power, afloat for a century. She had been a yacht and a blockade runner, and her first master, a child Confederate officer from the Virginia Military Institute, was stabbed to death by her engineer, Noah Card, who defected to the North and raised oranges at Zephyrhills, Florida, until 1931. He owed my grandfather money; but I forget why.

My grandfather was a dull, stupid drunk; and the white oak and cedar and longleaf pine rotted and the floor fell out of the mold loft while he filed patents on automobiles and comic cigarette utensils. I recall only his rheumy stupor and his routine adoration of children.

Let me try Catherine again.

"One more and I go to the police for a restraining order."

No sense pursuing that for the moment.

My stepmother had a suitor. He was an attorney-at-law and affected argyle socks and low blue automobiles. He screamed when he laughed. What I think he knew was that the shipyard was a world of waterfront property and that when the Holiday Inn moved in where the blockade boats and coasters had been built, Roxy got all the money. His name was Curtis Peavey and he was on her case like a man possessed, running at the house morning noon and night with clouds of cheap flowers. Roxy had been known to fuck anything; and I couldn't say she ever so much as formed an opinion of Peavey. I noticed though that she didn't *throw* the flowers away, she pushed them into the trash, blossoms forward, as if they'd been involved in an accident. In this, I pretended to see disgust. I myself didn't like Peavey. His eyes were full of clocks, machinery, and numbers. The curly head of hair tightened around his scalp when he talked to me and his lips stuck on his teeth. But he had a devoted practice. He represented Catherine. No sense concealing that. If Peavey could, he'd throw the book at me. He said I was depraved and licentious; he said that to Roxy. Whenever I saw him, he was always about to motivate in one of the low blue cars. Certain people thought of him as a higher type; he donated Sandburg's life of Lincoln to the county library with his cornball bookplate in every volume, a horrific woodcut of a sturdy New England tree; with those dismal words: Curtis G. Peavey. As disgusting as Roxy was, I didn't like to see her gypped; which is what Peavey clearly meant to do. I didn't care about the money at all. I have put that shipyard up my nose ten times over.

I don't think Peavey was glad to see me hunker next to him on the red stool. The fanaticism with which he slurped down the bargain quantities of ropa vieja, black beans, and yellow rice suggested a speedy exit.

I said, "Hello, Curtis."

"How long are you back for—"

"Got a bit of it on your chin there, didn't you."

"Here, yes, pass me one of those."

"How's Roxy holding up?" I asked.

"She's more than holding up. A regular iron woman."

"A regular what?"

"Iron woman."

"You want another napkin?"

"Get out of here you depraved pervert."

I said, "You'll never get her money."

"I'd teach you a lesson," said Curtis Peavey, rising to his feet and deftly thumbing acrylic pleats from his belt line, "but you're carrying a gun, aren't you?"

"Yes," I said, "to perforate your duodenum."

"You have threatened me," he said softly. "Did you hear that, shit-for-brains? It won't do." Peavey strolled into the heat and wind. I stopped at the cash register and paid for his slop.

I went for a walk.

Something started the night I rode the six-hundred-pound Yorkshire hog into the Oakland auditorium; I was double-billed with four screaming soul monsters and I shut everything down as though I'd burned the building. I had dressed myself in Revolutionary War throwaways and a top hat, much like an Iroquois going to Washington to ask the Great White Father to stop sauteeing his babies. When they came over the lights, I pulled a dagger they knew I'd use. I had still not replaced my upper front teeth and I helplessly drooled. I was a hundred and eighty-five pounds of strangely articulate shrieking misfit and I would go too god damn far.

At the foot of Seminary I stopped to look at a Czech marine diesel being lowered into a homemade trap boat on a chain fall. It was stolen from Cuban nationals, who get nice engines from the Reds. The police four-wheel drifted around the corner aiming riot guns my way. Getting decency these days is like pulling teeth. Once the car was under control and stopped, two familiar officers, Nylon Pinder and Platt, put me up against the work shed for search.

"Drive much?" I asked.

"Alla damn time," said Platt.

"Why work for Peavey?" I asked.

Platt said, "He's a pillar of our society. When are you gonna learn the ropes?"

Nylon Pinder said, "He don't have the gun on him."

Platt wanted to know, "What you want with the .38 Smith?"

"It's for Peavey's brain pan. I want him to see the light. He's a bad man."

"Never register a gun you mean to use. Get a cold piece. Peavey's a pillar of our society."

"Platt said that."

"Shut up, you. He's a pillar of our society and you're a depraved pervert."

"Peavey said that."

"Nylon said for you to shut your hole, misfit."

"I said that, I said 'misfit.'"

Platt did something sudden to my face. There was blood. I pulled out my bridge so if I got trounced I wouldn't swallow it. Platt said, "Look at that, will you."

I worked my way around the Czech diesel. They were going to leave me alone now. "Platt," I said, "when you off?"

"Saturdays. You can find me at Rest Beach."

"Depraved pervert," said Nylon, moving only his lips in

that vast face. "Get some teeth," he said. "You look like an asshole."

The two of them sauntered away. I toyed with the notion of filling their mouths with a couple of handfuls of bees, splitting their noses, pushing small live barracudas up their asses. The mechanic on the chain fall said, "What did they want with you? Your nose is bleeding."

"I'm notorious," I said. "I'm cheating society and many of my teeth are gone. Five minutes ago I was young. You saw me! What is this? I've given my all and this is the thanks I get. If Jesse James had been here, he wouldn't have let them do that."

The mechanic stared at me and said, *"Right."*

I hiked to my stepmother's, to Roxy's. I stood like a druid in her doorway and refused to enter. "You and your Peavey," I said. "I can't touch my face."

"Throbs?"

"You and your god damn Peavey."

"He won't see me any more. He says you've made it impossible. I ought to kill you. But your father will be here soon and he'll straighten you out."

"Peavey buckled, did he? I don't believe that. He'll be back.—And my father is dead."

"Won't see me any more. Peavey meant something and now he's gone. He called me his tulip."

"His . . .?"

"You heard me."

I gazed at Roxy. She looked like a circus performer who had been shot from the cannon one too many times.

In family arguments, things are said which are so heated and so immediate as to seem injuries which could never last; but which in fact are never forgotten. Now nothing is left of my family except two uncles and this tattered stepmother who technically died; nevertheless, I can trace myself through her to those ghosts, those soaring, idiot forebears with their accusations, and their steady signal that, whatever I thought I was, I was not the real thing. We had all said terrible things to each other, added insult to injury. My father had very carefully taken me apart and thrown the pieces away. And now his representatives expected me to acknowledge his continued existence.

So, you might ask, why have anything to do with Roxy? I don't know. It could be that after the anonymity of my fields of glory, coming back had to be something better than a lot of numinous locations, the house, the convent school, Catherine. Maybe not Catherine. Apart from my own compulsions, which have applied to as little as the open road, I don't know what she

has to do with the price of beans . . . I thought I'd try it anyway.
Catherine. Roxy looked inside me.

"Well, you be a good boy and butt out. Somehow, occupy
yourself. We can't endlessly excuse you because you're
recuperating. I *died* and got less attention. Then, I was never an
overnight sensation."

I went home and fed the dog, this loving speckled friend
who after seven trying years in my life has never been named. The
dog. She eats very little and stares at the waves. She kills a
lizard; then, overcome with remorse, tips over in the palm
shadows for a troubled snooze.

Catherine stuck it out for a while. She stayed with me at
the Sherry-Netherland and was in the audience when I crawled
out of the ass of a frozen elephant and fought a duel in my
underwear with a baseball batting practice machine. She looked
after my wounds. She didn't quit until late. There was no third
party in question.

I could throw a portion of my body under a passing
automobile in front of Catherine's house. A rescue would be
necessary. Catherine running toward me resting on my elbows, my
crushed legs on the pavement between us. All is forgiven. I'll be
okay. I'll learn to remember. We'll be happy together.

I had a small sharpie sailboat which I built with my own
hands in an earlier life and which I kept behind the A&B Lobster
House next to the old cable schooner. I did a handsome job on this
boat if I do say so; and she has survived both my intermediate
career and neglect. I put her together like a fiddle, with longleaf
pine and white-oak frames, fastened with bronze. She has a
rabbeted chine and I let the centerboard trunk directly into the
keel, which was tapered at both ends. Cutting those changing
bevels in hard pine and oak took enormous concentration and drugs;
not the least problem was in knowing ahead of time that it would
be handy to have something I had made still floating when my
life fell apart years later.

She had no engine and I had to row her in and out of the
basin. When the wind dropped, I'd just let the canvas slat around
while I hung over the transom staring down the light shafts into
the depths. Then when it piped up, she'd trim herself and I'd slip
around to the tiller and take things in hand. Sailboats were never
used in the Missouri border fighting.

I went out today because my nose hurt from Peavey's goons
and because I was up against my collapse; and because Catherine

wouldn't see me. My hopes were that the last was the pain of vanity. It would be reassuring to think that my ego was sufficiently intact as to sustain injury; but I couldn't bank that yet.

The wind was coming right out of the southeast fresh, maybe eight or ten knots, and I rowed just clear of the jetty and ran up the sails, cleated off the jib, sat back next to the tiller, pointed her up as good as I could, and jammed it right in close to the shrimp boats before I came about and tacked out of the basin. I stayed on that tack until I passed two iron wrecks and came about again. The sharpie is so shoal I could take off cross-country toward the Bay Keys without fear of going aground. I trimmed her with the sail, hands off the tiller, cleated the main sheet, and turned on some Cuban radio. I put my feet up and went half asleep and let the faces parade past.

Immediately east of the Pearl Basin, I found a couple shivering on a sailboard they had rented at the beach. He was wearing a football jersey over long nylon surfing trunks; and she wore a homemade bikini knotted on her brown, rectilineal hips. What healthy people! They had formed a couple and rented a sailboard. They had clean shy smiles, and though they may not have known their asses from a hole in the ground in terms of a personal philosophy, they seemed better off for it, happier, even readier for life and death than me with my ceremonious hours of thought and unparalleled acceleration of experience.

I rigged the board so that it could be sailed again, standing expertly to the lee of them with my sail luffing. I told them they were ready to continue their voyage and she said to the boy, "Hal, it's a bummer, I'm freezing." And Hal asked me if she could ride back in my boat because it was drier. I told them I'd be sailing for a while, that I had come out to think, that I was bad company, and that my father had died in the subways of Boston. They said that was okay, that she would be quiet and not bother me. I let her come aboard, politely concealing my disappointment; then shoved Hal off astern. He was soon underway, with his plastic sailboard spanking on the chop, the bright cigarette advertisement on his sail rippling against the blue sky.

I continued toward the Bay Keys while the girl watched me with cold gray eyes, the shadow of the sail crossing her slowly at each tack. Then she went forward and took the sun with her hands behind her head.

"Your boyfriend a football player?" I asked.

"No, he deals coke."

"I see."

"Do you like coke?"

"Yes, quite a lot."

"Well, Hal has some Bolivian rock you can read your fortune in, I'll tell you that."

"Oh, gee, I—"

"Anybody ever tell you the difference between acid and coke?"

"Nobody ever did."

"Well, with acid you think you see God. With coke you think you *are* God. I'll tell you the honest truth, this rock Hal's got looks like the main exhibit at the Arizona Rock and Gem Show. Did you ever hear a drawl like mine?"

"No, where's it from?"

"It's not from anywhere. I made the god damn thing up out of magazines."

"How much of that rock is left?"

"One o.z. No more, no less. At a grand, it's the last nickel bargain in Florida."

"I'll take it all."

"We'll drop it off. Hey, can you tell me one thing, how come you got hospitalized? The papers said exhaustion but I don't believe everything I read. You don't look exhausted."

"It was exhaustion."

That night, after I had paid them, I asked if the business in the boats that afternoon had been a setup. She said that it had. "Don't tell him that!" giggled the boyfriend. "You coo-coo brain!"

My eyes were out on wires and I was grinding my teeth. When I chopped that shit, it fell apart like a dog biscuit. Bolivian rock. I didn't care. I just made the rails about eight feet and blew myself a daydream with a McDonald's straw. Let them try and stop me now!

By the time I got to Reynolds Street I was in tears. I went down to the park and crossed over to Astro City. The ground was beaten gray and flat and the tin rocketships were unoccupied. I climbed high enough on the monkey bars that no one could look into my eyes and wept until I choked.

I considered changing my name and cutting my throat. I considered taking measures. I decided to walk to Catherine's house again and if necessary nail myself to her door. I was up for the whole shooting match.

I walked over to Simonton, past the old cigar factory, and the schoolyard and synagogue, and stopped at the lumber company. I bought a hammer and four nails. Then I continued on my way. On Eaton Street, trying to sneak, I dropped about a gram on the sidewalk. I knelt with my red and white straw and snorted it off the concrete while horrified pedestrians filed around me. *"It takes toot to tango,"* I explained. Nylon and Platt would love to catch me at this, a real chance to throw the book. I walked on, rubbing a little freeze on my gums and waiting for the drip to start down my throat and signal the advent of white-line fever or renewed confidence.

The wind floated gently into my hair, full of the ocean and maritime sundries from the shipyard. A seagull rocketed all the way from William Street close to the wooden houses, unseen, mind you, by any eyes but mine. A huge old tamarind dropped scented moisture into the evening in trailing veils. Mad fuck-ups running to their newspapers and greasy dinners surged around my cut-rate beneficence. I felt my angel wings unfold. More than that you can't ask for.

Catherine's house with her bicycle on the porch was in a row of wooden cigarmakers' houses grown about with untended vegetation, on a street full of huge mahoganies. I thought to offer her a number of things—silence, love, friendship, departure, a hot beef injection, shining secrets, a tit for a tat, courtesy, a sensible house pet, a raison d'etre, or a cup of coffee. And I was open to suggestion, short of "get outa here," in which case I had the hammer and nails and would nail myself to her door like a summons.

I crossed the street to her house, crept Indian style onto the porch, and looked through the front window. Catherine was asleep on the couch in her shorts and I thought my heart would stop. I studied her from this luxurious point, staring at the wildly curly hair on her bare back; her arm hung down and her fingertips just rested on the floor next to a crammed ashtray. I had the nails in my shirt pocket, the hammer in the top of my pants like Jesse James's Colt.

"Catherine," I said "you let me in." This handsome woman, whom Peavey had once had the nerve to call my common-law wife, was suddenly on her feet, walking toward me with jiggling breasts, to ram down the front window and bolt the door. Then she went upstairs and out of sight. I called her name a couple of more times, got no answer, and nailed my left hand to the door with Jesse's Colt.

James Merrill

Clearing the Title
for DJ

Because the wind has changed, because I guess
My poem (what to call it though?) is finished,
Because the golden genie chafes within
His smudged-glass bottle and, god help us, you
Have chosen, sight unseen, this tropic rendezvous
Where tourist, outcast and in-groupie gather
Island by island, linked together,
Causeways bridging the vast shallowness—

Through the low ceiling motors rip.
Below me twisting in the asphalt grip
Of mall and pancake house, boatel and bank,
What's left of Nature here? Those trees five thousand tin
Roofs, like little mirrors in distress,
Would flash up from if the sun were out. . .
Oh for the lucid icebound book of winter
I gave up my rapt place in for this trip!

Such a mistake—past fifty and behaving
As if hope sprang eternal. At the baggage claim
Armed with *The Power and the Glory* (Greene),
I notice, finger-drawn in a soaped pane,
One black sun only, spokes in air
Like legs of a big bug flipped on its back,
Above a clumsy WELLCOME TO THE KEYS
—Then see the open car. You in it, waving.

Couldn't one have gone into the matter
Before succumbing? Easier said than done,
What with this tough white coral skeleton
Beneath a crop of shanties built on rocks,

On air, on edge for, any day,
Water and wind to sweep them clean away—
Ill-braced like me, capricious chatterbox,
Against your blasts of horn and floods of casual patter.

Sales patter? The appalling truth now bores
Into my brain: you've *bought* a house
And pass, en route to it, the peeling white
Five-story skyscraper in which "our" title
Is being cleared!—activity no more
Thinkable (you park, fling a green-painted door
Open onto a fresh white hall)
Than what the termites do, look! to those floors

Between the muddy varnish of whose lines
(But can you picture *living* here? Expect
Me to swelter, year by sunset year,
Beneath these ceilings?—which at least aren't low.
What about houses elsewhere, rooms already packed
With memories? That chiffonier
Would have to go, or else be painted white. . .)
More brightly with each word the daylight shines.

And fresh as paint the bare rooms, if you please,
Having consumed whatever came before,
Look up unblinking: will *we* bring
Their next meal—table, mirror, bed, lamp, chair?
Serve the ravenous interior
With real-life victuals, voices, vanities
Until it lolls back purring?—like our slum
Garden zonked by milk-bombs from two old bent trees.

Presuming, then, tripod and pendulum
Tell truly, and the freckled county clerk
Completes, adds to the master file
A Gothic-lettered "title" with your name—
What happens next? Behind a latticework
Of deeds no one has time or patience to undo
We cultivate our little lot, meanwhile
Waiting companionably for kingdom come?

Close-ups: hibiscus broad as garden hats.
Large winged but nameless insect excavated
By slaves; the abdomen's deep strata
Primitive-intricate, like macramé.
Then from beneath the house, fee fi fo fum!
Caller the color of good smoke blown through the years

Into this dumb scarred mug he lifts to say:
"Huh? Not want *me*. Man, the whole world wants *cats*!"

No. No, no, no. We can't just cast
Three decades, friendships and possessions out.
Who're our friends here? (In fact I recognize
Old ones everywhere I turn my eyes—
Trumpet-vine, cracked pavement, that faint sulphur smell
Those see-through lizards, quick as a heartbeat . . .)
But people? (Well, the Wilburs live downstreet . . .)
Of course, if shutting doors onto the past

Could damage *it* . . . Wherever that thought led,
Turning the loose knob onto better-late-
Than-never light, we breast its deepening stream
Along with others who've a date
With sunset. Each day's unspent zinc or red brass penny
—Here at land's end not deposited
In winter palisades crowned by antennae,
Fuel for the all-night talk shows of the dead—

Inflates to moidore, melts toward an oblivion
Alone, its gravity unspecified,
The far-off mangrove islet saves
From being wholly formed of air and waves,
Of light and birdcry, as with each step less
Divides the passer-through from, what to call
Such radiance—creative? terminal?
Day's flush of pleasure, knowing its poem done?

Our poem now. It's signed JM, but grew
From life together, grain by coral grain.
Building on it, we let the life cloud over . . .
Time to break through those clouds, for heaven's sake,
And look round. Any place will do
(Remember, later at the discothèque)
And what at first appall precisely are the changes
That everybody is entitled to.

Here at the end's a landing stage swept clean
Of surplus "properties" and "characters".
Gone the thick banyan, the opaque old queen.
Only some flimsiest human veil
Woven of trickster and revivalist,
Musician and snake-charmer (and, yes, us as well)
Pot- and patchouli-scented floats between
The immense warm pink spotlight and the scene.

Here's the Iguana Man, from lands
"Beneath the world." Dragons, withered like him,
Unwinking drape his fishnet singlet; Here
Balloons are straining for release; we pick
A headstrong silver one. And here a clown
Cat-limber, white-lipped with a bright cerulean tear
On one rouged cheek, rides unicycle, hands
Nonchalantly juggling firebrands.

Circles round every act form, or to groans
Disperse. This portion of the dock's been cleared
By the Salvation Army. (They're
Nine strong, a family; beneath the same
Grim visor glowers, babe to grandmother,
The same grim love.) "Ya'll give!" our deadpan clown
Tells brandishing a hammer fit for Thor,
"Give or Ah'll clobber yew!" and *grunt* go the trombones.

Though no one does, no thunder strikes. Because—
Say, because a black girl with shaved skull
Sways on the brink: flexed knee and ankle-bell
And eyes that burn back at the fiery ball
Till it relenting tests with one big toe
Its bath, and Archimedean splendors overflow.
As the sun sets, "Let's hear it for the sun!"
Cry voices. Laughter. Bells. Applause

(Think of the dead here, sleeping above ground
—Simpler than to hack a tomb from coral—
In whitewashed hope chests under the palm fronds.
Or think of waking, whether to the quarrel
Of white cat and black crow, those unchanged friends,
Or to dazzle from below:
Earth visible through floor-cracks, miles—or inches—down,
And spun by a gold key-chain round and round . . .)

Whereupon on high, where all is bright
Day still, blue turning to key lime, to steel
A clear flame-dusted crimson bars,
Sky puts on the face of the young clown
As the balloons, mere hueless dots now, stars
Or periods—although tonight we trust no real
Conclusions will be reached—float higher yet,
Juggled slowly by the changing light.

Monday Morning

Hot sun on Duval Street.
Bicycling very slowly
I see, by all that's holy,
An acute blur of fleet

Parrot-green plumage coast
Onto the bus-stop bench:
Less bird, after all, than mensch
"Free as a bird"—its ghost

Face cocked. Now Daddy Kaiser
Of Angelo's Cut 'n Comb
Waddles forth, spry gnome
Waving his atomizer,

Diamonding with spray
One instant hedonist!
Pure whim? Fair-weather tryst?
Already a block away,

I keep risking collision
(In each year's crazier traffic)
To fix that unseraphic
Duo within my vision.

George Murphy

Rounding Ballast Key

Beyond Man Key, rounding Ballast in the sink-mud,
when Woman Key loomed, an impossible swim
from the mangrove bank we could not walk through,
I stood waist-deep in your wake, sinking,
our erratic trail erased behind us and ahead,
a soup-like, sucking bottom of worm holes where spider crabs
scuttled past my legs, and me in some small panic with a camera bag
which would not float were we to give in, start kicking,
and ride the current back past the southwest bank
toward the shipping channel or the thin sandy spit
which jutted to the north. Knowing we might get back or might not,
and either Key, this one we were sinking in
or the other across the channel, was likely to keep our gear,
suck down our shoes, and humble us:
we kept walking.

I'd been stalling my heart by studying your back,
the muscled twist of shoulder blades
as you hauled first the left, then right foot,
porting a satchel on your head and calling back to me,
"Just pull your foot out and take another step."
As the sun was scorching us doubly off the flat rushing water
of the channel, I stood in your wake, sinking
in that mud, its surface webbed with turtle grass
and calcareous algae rising on my calves.
About us the conchs crawled from green to brighter green,

the sea turtles lolled the miles across the keys from Tortuga,
and tarpon and porpoise broke the surface at the edge
of the shallows, when you turned toward my growing panic
and, over your shoulder, as unexpected as each turn
in this life now given over to accident, there burst
from its perch in the mangroves a great snowy heron
which you never saw tilt and glide ahead as I did
around the windward curve of the coast
toward the house which you would call home,
and hold a moment there, like some angel's kite.

And tonight, in this coastal house, in Massachusetts,
in Humarock, in the utter quiet of the night,
a great hush of snow has been thrown over the saltmarsh
while these seashells and chips of coral, these pinks and yellows
on an oak table, lie before me in the light of this fire.
And having come in to wrestle off these wet boots
and lift my feet against the lip of the hearth,
I pause to wonder what all this portends.
Into what worm holes scuttle our hearts?
What is it that bursts from us and disappears?
And what of light and its failure to hold all colors apart,
that gathers them like a feast into things we call white
and are airborne: clouds, a heron,
the snow, our breath in the frigid night?

How like the damaged heart is it, which sees in everything
something else, which gathers memory toward anesthesia?

I don't know. But, tonight, I can say this: in memory at least,
that sinking feeling is again, I thank you, gone:
once more a foot pulled out of whatever uncertain waters
and another step taken.

Thomas Sanchez

From
Mile Zero

As Justo slowly made his way down narrow Olivia Street old times called to him from wood-covered porches so close to his car he could reach out and touch them. Justo could not help but recall the spicy scent of Cuban cooking that drifted from these humble houses when he was a boy. Olivia was the street he grew up on. Sizzling garlic and shrimp once permeated the air, drifting on a jasmine-scented breeze. Flaming red bougainvillea grew in haughty arches over kitchen doors then, brilliant yellow allamanda blossoms spilled along the sills of open bedroom windows. Olivia was a street crowded with small houses and big childhood memories. The now vanished Cuban *grocería* on the corner once sold *productos Latinos, buches* to blast your brain back to Guantanamo Bay and curvacious loaves of womanly thin Cuban bread. *Cervezas* kept the men animated in the store's back room crowded with cider barrels, stacked blocks of jellied mango paste, and sacks of black-eyed pea flour. The men argued endlessly about what caused the blight of '39, when the sea went slack, spit up dead lobsters, sponges and conchs, then glittered bright and pristine, as if spread with a veneer of shark oil, the shallow bottom standing out in vibrant relief. Tall glasses of cool *vinos* kept the men betting on *boleta* or sweating through wednesday afternoons around the radio, waiting for the high-pitched voice of an orphan boy in Havana to arrive with a static hum across ninety miles of ocean from Cuba, singsonging the winning numbers of the

Lotería Nacional drawing. After the sweltering wait for the numbers a roar or a moan would go up from the men, depending on whether or not Lady Luck had also made the ninety-mile trip across the Florida Straits from Cuba that afternoon. Then the static hum of the radio stretched into a languid Latin rhythm, a distant faraway throb of rhumbas and saltwater breakers striking sandy shores. The music from Cuba filled the backroom of the *grocería* with the swish of swaying palm trees. *Bang!* Justo's grandfather's cane would strike the pine-plank floor *"Niño!"* Justo's *Abuelo* called to him. *"Mas marquitas y bollos!"* Off Justo went running with the single-minded intensity of a bird dog about to jump a covey of quail, returning to Abuelo and the men with bags of fried green plantain bananas and boxes of sweet *bollo* penny cakes. Abuelo then poured out shots of *compuestô*. The fiery sugarcane liquor fueled talk of cockfights and revolutions past and future. The urgency of passions stirred the hair on the back of young Justo's neck with reckless excitement, as if the men in the back room were the center of a dangerous universe propelled by big ideals of political gambling. Justo felt he was perched at the edge of this universe, a boy among men, a mouse in a bull pen, unobserved, privileged to be present at the continual rebirth of cultural pride generated by wild talk and selective memories. Nailed high to the back room wall were two fading posters. One bore the fierce-eyed and mustached face of José Martí, the martyred George Washington of Cuba. The colorful poster opposite was the image of the Russian dancer Pavlova. Pavlova once catapulted across the stage of the formidable Instituto de San Carlos, which dominated Duval Street with its towering pillared arches and glittering Cuban tiles. Pavlova pirouetted on the very stage where Martí once preached eagerly to crowds about the seeds of rebellion growing in Cuba to a forest of *Los Pinos Nuevos*, the new pines of independence. Pavlova's thighs swelled from the back room's wall in white dancer's tights hugging a forceful thrust of buttocks, where her daring blade of black hair came to rest in a moment of tense repose. Pavlova threatened to explode from the poster in an energetic hurl through the colossal hoop of implacable male desire surrounding her in the room, to land squarely on the heart of the matter. Young Justo was lulled into a deep swim of desire over Pavlova, but so were all the men, none more than Abuelo. For Abuelo such was not adulterous desire pricked by lust. Abuelo had all the lust he could fathom in the cherry-dark crevices of his African bride of forty years. No, this was desire of another order. Desire for an object to end disorderly thoughts. Thoughts dwelling on the mystery of that alien race, woman. Pavlova in her dance of eternal delirium was a desired object to be understood by men primitive in their intentions and clumsy in their methods. All were such in the back room, except Abuelo. Abuelo was a man of *Letters*, looked up to with respect. Abuelo was a man gifted with the delicious wine of sweet-sounding metaphors and laced with knowledge spun from books. Abuelo in his youth had ascended to the altar of respect attained by only a chosen few. At the precocious age of nineteen Abuelo had become a Lector, a reader in the cigar factories that once hummed at the heart of the small island's body of enormous productivity.

Abuelo had arrived in Key West from Havana filled with good nature, cocky promise, and a generous portion of luck, for he was born in 1878 at the end of the failed Ten Years' War, when the Spaniards swung their sword of terrorism with dictatorial precision, cutting the throats crying "Cuba Libre," releasing a flood of martyrs' blood to fertilize the seeds of *Pinos Nuevos*. The seeds of *Pinos Nuevos* lay fallow through a desert of oppression, which would not show growth until 1895, when Martí called for all men to rise as one, and final revolt began. The revolution began without Abuelo. The Spaniards tried to conscript him into an army of brothers preparing to fight brothers. It was then Abuelo's family was smuggled aboard a schooner to make passage across the Florida Straits to Cayo Hueso, Star of the Sea shining with bright promise of two hundred cigar factories producing one hundred million cigars a year, and a powerful cigarmakers' union, La Liga, organizing among the six-thousand-man work force. Abuelo's father was a true artist, who had risen rapidly through the rigid caste system of the cigar factories of Havana, from a lowly Stripper, who prepared the fan-shaped spread of thin-veined tobacco leaves for wrappers and filler, to become a Cigarmaker. His fingers knew the perfect airy weight of the cigar to be born, then rolled and glued it with natural gum, all in a deft motion of such rapid fluidity only a mere trace of moisture escaped his skin to permeate the impressionable product, taint its natural perfume. The newborn cigar was in and out of his hands in less than a minute. Abuelo's father was one of the few capable of constructing the difficult Cuban Bances Aristocrato. The Aristocrato was filled with the finest Vuelta tobacco, its pliant leaf wrapper tapered the shape of a delicate glass-blown bottle, its svelte end pinched to a flat pucker to meet the flame of a match with the ease of a kiss, releasing a smoky reminiscence of freshly turned humus on a deeply jungled mountainside. The muscles in Abuelo's father's arms grew and his fingers flew as he sat year after year in the center of the two-tiered cigarmaker's table creating the finely balanced rolled contours of everything from cheap Cheroot Pinas to lordly Bances Aristocratos. Finally he was elevated to the position of Picker. Surrounded by the grand sweep of a crescent-shaped table where bundles of finished cigars were delivered to him, Abuelo's father mastered the art of Spanish Picking. From the untied bundles he picked through thirty-two shades of leaf-wrapper colors, carefully matching the correct colorations required to pack four layers of cigars in a proper order demanded by tradition. Cedar box after cedar box he filled. The cedar wood guaranteed no worms or bugs would feast off the aromatic bounty. Only the most appreciative lips would suck on Cuban's finest. All of this Abuelo's father mastered and taught his son before the schooner they escaped on arrived in Key West.

Abuelo, like his father, worked his way up quickly in the cigar factories of his newly adopted country. As a youth he was a Stripper in a *Chinchalito*, a small, independent factory with only ten workers, men from villages around Havana, Spanish mountain towns and West Indies fishing ports, all working together in the confines of a plankwood shack barged over from the Bahamas. The shacks had been shotgunned closely next to one another by the hundreds, along newly created streets inching across the island to house ever-growing numbers of cigar workers. The intimate working conditions of the *Chinchalito* was soon to give way to grander fortunes for Abuelo. His father had become one of the Jefes in La Liga, believing only the union could prevent the Spaniards from once again stealing what was rightfully Cuban. Too many Spaniards were being hired to work against the brotherhood of La Liga, so Abuelo's father took his son from the independent *Chinchalito* and fixed a job for him as Cigarmaker in one of the block-long, three-storied limestone factories off Duval Street. It was there Abuelo's life was given two fortuitous twists to seal the fate of his manhood emerging at age seventeen.

The first twist came in the form of a female body taking every dangerous curve along the course of its supple frame to stop a man's heart dead in its tracks. Her name was Pearl, the jewel in a family of nine brothers and one daughter. Pearl's father was an Ibu, brought to the Bahamas as a boy in chains from West Africa and freed fifteen years later in 1838 by the British. Freed by the very ones who had enslaved him, given a dowry of no money and a new name in a white man's world, John Coe. John Coe worked flat-land crops of Bahamian plantations, but his eyes always went to the vast ocean's reach, where wealth was held beyond the voracious grasp of slave masters. The sea surging between the thousands of islets woven through the great chain of Bahamian islands was a place where a man could fish, and sponge, and turtle. A place where an industrious man could dip his pole beneath the pristine water's surface and stir up an honest meal or a lifetime's fortune.

John Coe became a student of the sea when freed. The sea became John's new master. Turtles attracted him first, their gliding nonchalance, so few flipper strokes needed to navigate through a watery universe, an economy of effort worth emulating, which bespoke ancient liberation from the here and now. John felt kinship with this marine creature's abiding sense of ease, its deep breadth of freedom. John was a simple man who knew not the turtle's source of symbolic power, he understood only the animal's daily inspiration. John learned the ways of thousand-pound leatherback and loggerhead turtles, cruising and blowing water stacks like sporting baby whales. He studied eight-hundred-fifty-pound gentle greens, which fed solely on vegetarian fare, content to snap through carpets of sea grass. He gained respect for the small fifty-pound hawksbill, whose fast bite could gash a man's hand swift as a machete blow and bleed him to death on flat water in hot sun.

John followed the turtles down the length of the Bahamas, through the Windward Passage between Haiti and Cuba, around the Caymans and across the Caribbean Sea to the Lesser Antilles, then back up the South and Central American coasts, riding the warm current of the Gulf Stream. John mastered the harpoon, taking a turtle coming up for a blow with his first thrust, driving the harpoon's sharpened steel peg cleanly into the precious shell. John never lost a turtle as it dove deep after the pegging, its weight strong against the whirring line, pulling for freedom. John went wherever the turtles went. He could con his canoe-shaped longboat by eye through razor-sharp walls of coral, reading the deep-water blue surging with currents of urgency between the yellow-shadowed reefs. John could net turtles, harpoon them or take them by hand. He began to think like a turtle, the taste of ghost crab in his mouth, the brine of shipworms in his nostrils, turtle grass between his toes. In the polar pull of a late winter warming moon John could intuit the male turtle's fervor of romance. It was during this mating season he would capture a she-turtle and heft her aboard his longboat, then wait patiently with his glistening prisoner of passion, until a trailing male thrust suddenly from water, attempting in a heroic leap of faith to hurl his amorous hulk over the edge of the longboat to be forever joined with his mate, not feeling the bite of John's harpoon until it was too late. John knew where turtles roosted at night, deep in sleep beneath a float of soft kelp, wreathed in seaweed. John Coe had their dreams.

John migrated with loggerheads and greens in late winter down the Florida Keys. During nights of spring moonlight he stalked crescent-shaped trails left in damp sand where females stabbed flippers, heaving hard-shelled bodies beyond the tideline to nest their eggs safely. John turned the she-turtles in the vulnerable moment when their tidal surge of eggs flowed, flipping them over on their backs, where they remained helpless and immobile as he carved his initials, JC, into their soft undershells, the crude brand a warning to other Turtlers that these turtles were his. The flipped females were left stranded on the beach, the fresh cut of JC on their bellies glowed in moonlight as John worked quickly through the lengthening night on other beaches, turning as many females as he could before the moon disappeared from the heavens. In the dawn's early light John returned exhausted and exhilarated to his females on the sandy beaches, laying claim to his prized catch of eggs, meat and shells. This was how John Coe came to Key West, to sell his skiffload of prizes from the sea of plenty, fresh brimming baskets of turtle eggs and live she-turtles, their pierced front and back flippers tied through with palm thatch.

Along the Key West docking wharves of the big turtle canning factory in 1855 talk among the Turtlers was of Sponger money and nurse sharks. Spongers were many in Key West, and many were from the Bahamas, both white and black Conchs, equal in their pursuit to take a livelihood from the sea. John knew their language, the clipped sounds of men given to few words and patient actions as they poled skiffs across shallows. Through glass-bottom buckets dropped over the skiffs' sides the Spongers searched briny depths during the long day's tidal rise and fall for flowering black-skinned sheepswool sponges hiding deep in coral crevices and the wavering underwater flow of grassy flats. More than a thousand men in hundreds of boats left the Key West wharves before dawn each day to harvest the vast sponge beds of the back-country flats. Sharp three-pronged hooks at the tip of eighteen-foot poles brought up tons of yellow sponge, grass sponge, and thick sheepswool. There was plenty of Sponger money for all, but John Coe did not settle in Key West because he became a Sponger. John Coe became a Sharker.

Talk on the docks when John Coe arrived with his she-turtles in Key West was of how a man who knew his way with sharks could make as much or more than a Sponger. On those days when the bottom of the flats were kicked up by distant stormy weather, sending chops and swells against the Keys for days on end, the Sponge Hookers couldn't spy their catch in the murk. Mistakenly they would strike at bulging coral heads, dancing sea fans and shadowy jellyfish, anything and everything but the desired object of their deft aim. They could not fill their skiffs. A Sponger who could not fill his skiff could not fill his children's bellies and his glass with rum, so the Sharker became the Sponger's friend fair and true. The Sharker possessed magic to clear storm-befouled waters. The Sharker had oil of the young nurse sharks. A Sponger could swish nurse shark oil a hundred feet across the water on both sides of his skiff, then the murk of the flats would part quick as an underwater stage curtain, the marine heaven shimmer clear beneath the gaze of the Sponge-Hooker standing tall at the bow. A Sponger needed a Sharker on a gray day when promise is dim and the skiff empty. John Coe knew the ways of the shark. To know the ways of the turtle is to know the ways of the shark.

The sea taught John Coe it's a horseshoe conch-eats-shipworm world. John baited his hooks with mackerel heads and feathered chicken wings and searched the shallows of the Keys for the pale brown shadows of nurse sharks nosing across the sandy bottom. John dragged hundreds of six-foot nurses ashore, their mouths hooked, the noose of a rope cinched around their dangerously thrashing tails. Over an open fire John boiled gallons of oil from the freshly cut poundage of shark livers. John sold the skins to leather brokers from Texas, the dried fins to Chinese seamen to make a nourishing soup while on the long clippership passage around Cape Horn back to China; there shark fin powder was such a fabled aphrodisiac it bestowed upon man required properties to prowl through a woman's sea with the stand-up certitude of a bull walrus. John Coe earned his money from sharks, Spongers, Chinese seamen and Texas bootmakers. From the sea of plenty John earned himself enough money to buy a wife.

John Coe was a man of superstitious faith. John believed the natural world exposed signs along the road of life for a man to obey. If the high cirrus clouds deserted the heavens by noon, and a curtain of rolling dark clouds descended on the western horizon, then John did not voyage out to shark on the following morn. When the moon grew full, spilled its silver illumination on a shimmering sea, John felt the shrimp move in his veins and set out on a path of light across the strong current of the Gulf Stream to find a schooling swarm of giant loggerheads. John had faith in the gods of men and animals in the old African world. He believed in the power of those gods to instruct him daily in a godless new world. That is why when the Slaver-schooner *Wildwind* sailed into Key West, its vast open deck crowded by unclothed shadow-dark African bodies thinned to the bone by hunger and fear, John Coe was there to take a wife.

John Coe did not know he was going to take a wife that fateful day. John knew only that the day before the thin wispy cirrus clouds pulled out of the heavens by noon, replaced by brooding thunderheads descending in the west, so instead of sharking he ambled down to the docks where he could hear the Bahamian accent so dear to his ears being bantered back and forth among Turtlers and Spongers. Talk was among the black Bahamians that a Slaver had sailed in from the West Coast of

Africa; Mandingo, Ijo and Ibu were aboard. Rich cotton growers from Natchez and New Orleans had come to buy them. Talk was that war was going to be fought in America, war over slaves. No one on the docks knew if this meant there were to be more slaves or none. All they knew for certain was sure as good weather follows bad a war was coming. John Coe decided to go among the crowd watching the human cargo from the Slaver being auctioned. This was something unnatural to him. The sea had made John free inside, yet some part of him still felt captured. An indentured piece of John's soul lingered uncomfortably on the meathook of his recent history. John cared not to be around purveyors of human flesh. His eyes could not take the sad old sight, smells of desperation, wide lost look of Africa in the people's eyes. All of this drummed on his heart with the force of a hammer beating nails into a coffin. John had turned away from this dark corner of his life, closed the door on his own origins. Whatever compelled John to be standing among the crowd at the auction was not something to be questioned, it was instead a prayer about to be answered. The answer came when John heard the white auctioneer shout: "Brenda Bee! One Ibu wench age nineteen!"

Brenda Bee stood perched on a pickle barrel with skinny hands crossed over the center of her sex, cast off and alone, separated forever from her former self. Brenda looked not nineteen, but sixteen, naked and vulnerable atop an up-ended wooden barrel, shivering in the glare of male eyes crowded around her on the dock. Brenda was not sound of body. She had narrowly escaped becoming one of the two hundred who died on board the Slaver as days without food slipped by on a sea growing wide as a continent. On this new continent Brenda would have little value in the cotton rows up south. The well-dressed gentlemen in the crowd from Charleston and Mobile didn't see anything of value in Brenda worth bidding the hard metal of dollars for, they weren't even interested in purchasing Brenda for their breeding sheds.

"Come now, gentlemen!" The auctioneer waved his cane toward Brenda, as if it were a magic wand which could disperse the white crawl of lice in the matted braids of her hair. "What is offered the Company for this good wench?"

"My dog!" A laughing answer came from the crowd.

"My dog's fleas!"

"The blood of my dog's fleas!"

John Coe knew Brenda could not understand any of this, but it seemed her exposed skin shaded a deeper color of black from a spreading blush of shame, a black almost obliterating jagged red cuts and purple bruises spotted over her body. John Coe's hand flew up of its own will. John was a tall man made taller by pulling the weight of sharks and turtles from the sea, he was two heads above every man in the crowd. When John's hand went up a silence fell as if something evil had tumbled from great height into the midst of civilized society. The silence was broken by John's voice, thundering deep as a stormy sound slamming down from a brood of inky clouds roiling in a summer sky. "Suh, be mah offah! Two hunna dollah!"

So it was John Coe bought himself a wife in a town where a man of dark skin was not allowed to walk the streets after the nine-thirty ringing of the night bell, unless he bore a pass from his owner or employer, or was accompanied by a white person. Nor could a dark-skinned man play the fiddle or beat a drum, unless he desired thirty-nine whiplashes for violating the public peace. John Coe took this woman, called by her captors Brenda Bee, to his one-room shack on Crawfish Alley in the section of town called La Africana. That shack was John Coe's palace, owned and built with hands calloused from pulling turtles and sharks from the sea. Now all the plenty given John by the sea he was about to return. What John and Brenda Bee had in common was an ocean of hardships. As John bathed Brenda's bony body with the humped softness of his favorite sheepswool sponge he vowed to treat this woman with kindness, drive the unspeakable terror from her eyes. John spoke to Brenda in a tongue she could understand, touched her only in a healing way. John brought Brenda red cotton dresses, strolled with her hand in hand on saturday eves down the rutted dirt length of Crawfish Alley, stopping to tip his cap to folks cooling themselves on the front wooden steps of their shacks. John planted a papaya tree behind his shack and a mango in front, for on Sundays the preacher man swayed in the stone church before the congregation tall as an eleuthera palm in a high wind, shouting his clear message that the Bible teaches to plant the fruiting tree. A man must sow seeds to harvest. John watched Brenda grow out of her bag of bones into a prideful woman with a strong gaze and firm lips. John measured his prosperity by the image of Brenda's flesh. Tracing the girth of Brenda's strong buttocks and thighs with his fingertips late at night in the shack filled him with contentment. John Coe was man enough to keep his woman solid. When the children came, Brenda's hips and breasts swelled and John overflowed with a newfound joy. The ever-increasing size of Brenda's body became a living monument to a niggardly past so narrowly escaped.

Brenda Bee Coe had no envy for the Ship Captain's wife she scrubbed and cooked for in the sooted kitchen shed behind the three-storied house with a widow's walk perched atop its steep tin roof from which tall-masted ships could be spied tacking inside the reef toward the island. Brenda felt gratitude she was living life after death, swept up from the ocean of hardship in the net of John Coe's kindness. Envy did not gnaw at Brenda's soul, only a bitter sense buried deep and hidden from the world that one day the Evil Eye would be upon her, carry her away from the strong arms of John back onto the Slaver into a whale belly of white misery. For this reason Brenda always wore a clove of garlic around her neck on a thinly braided rope, to hold off the Eye of the Evil One lest he come upon her unawares to carry her away from her sea of plenty. Brenda insisted her nine sons each wear a garlic necklace, even though she knew they discarded them when they left the crowded little shack on Crawfish Alley. But Brenda's only daughter, the jewel in her sea of plenty, Pearl, never discarded her garlic necklace. Pearl obeyed her mama. Pearl knew the Evil Eye could snatch her away quick as a pox can worm the life out of a child's heart.

When Pearl turned sixteen and went off to work in the cigar factories, she still wore the garlic necklace. That is what first attracted young Abuelo to Pearl, the creamy colored garlic against a black skin shining brilliant with vibrance of life. Years after they were married Abuelo suspected Pearl had not so much worn the garlic necklace to keep off the Evil Eye, but to beguile him with her voluptuous charms and deeply contented nature. Perhaps, Abuelo thought with a laugh which always sent a bright image of Pearl's lovely face to mind, she tricked him with that jungle religion her mother brought across the seas on the Slaver from Africa.

Pearl became the gem setting which closed the ring of Abuelo's young life. Pearl was the first of two fortuitous twists to seal Abuelo's fate forever. Abuelo believed when his father abruptly took him at the age of seventeen from the *Chinchalito*, it had less to do with his father's desire to have his son become part of the emerging La Liga, more to do with an African plot of love planned by Pearl's mother to put one more ocean between her only daughter and slavery, marry Pearl off to a Cuban man, into the sea of a different society where the Evil One would never find her. Such is what Abuelo thought, that he was ensnared by jungle conspiracy. Like many men who are convinced they have fallen prey to a charmed woman highly coveted by others, Abuelo accepted a preordained fate guiding larger passions which made him victim of an inescapable coup d'état of the heart. Abuelo's love for Pearl came up so big and unexpectedly it overpowered his sense of self, left him trembling with the blind faith of newfound religion. *No te agites qué el corazón no opera*, that is what Abuelo's father counseled at the turn of the century when his untried son first started with Pearl. *Take it easy, the heart can't be operated on.*

No. In those days the heart could not be operated on, but if it could it would have been to no avail. Abuelo lost his heart the morning he saw Pearl his first day of work in the large cigar factory. He did not yet know she had stolen his heart. Abuelo thought he still had a choice in the matter. Pearl was one of the few women who worked in the cigar factory, the only woman on the third floor where Abuelo began his new job of Cigarmaker. Abuelo was not so much struck by Pearl's beauty, rather by the position she held in the factory. Most women labored in the lowly roll of Stripper, who each day untied hundreds of *tercios*, bundled tobacco leaves barged from Havana. The women carefully stripped precious leaves from spiny stems, then pressed them between two boards to be sent on as wrappers to the Selectors. Never had Abuelo seen a female Selector. A Selector was an exalted position held by men with a keen sense of vision to distinguish the air-cured tobacco leaves by true color value. Perhaps Pearl inherited her extraordinary eyesight from her father, who could read the bottom of a storm-tossed sea. To watch Pearl's hands work quickly through stacks of tobacco leaves, eyes searching between colors ranging from golden papaya to ripe mahogany shading called *maduro*, was like witnessing a cat in a dark granary go about its stealthy nocturnal business of separating mice from mountains of wheat. Pearl did not work like a machine, rather as an adroit athlete laughing at a task made simple by exertion of inbred attributes. The creamy clove of garlic on Pearl's braided rope necklace rose and fell where her breasts began their full swell beneath a thin cotton dress. Pearl's skin glistened in the heat, her fingers flew, her eyes did not miss a trick. Blue clouds from the narrow cigars she continuously smoked swirled around her. Pearl appeared to exist in a haloed mist, struck by steady light cascading through lofty north-facing windows blocking fickle sea breezes which could disturb the cigarmaking so carefully laid out on the rowed tables of the great hall. Pearl's body exuded aromas fueling every man's desire high up in the third story of the cigar factory. The perfume of Pearl was a heady mixture of succulent reminiscences, of green dreams and urgent yearnings, of growing tobacco leaves hidden in slippery shade of muddied hillsides, of the pungent burnt scent of garlic rooted from firm earth. In a sea of heat the men of the great hall watched Pearl from afar and on the sly as she selected among tobacco leaves for those of the chosen colors. Perspiration of honest work ran coolly along the back of Pearl's arched neck, then out of sight beneath her white dress, traveling the length of her strong female spine. To the men of the great hall Pearl was a sweeter dish than *boniatello*, the sugary preserve boiled from pulpy flesh of sweet potato. The men of the great hall desired someone they could sniff, lick and eat up, a great gorgeous feast of female. Pearl became the fantasy entrée on the menu of every self-respecting Latin male in the great hall. The problem was Pearl was born with an appetite greater than that of all the sniffing males combined.

Pearl's appetite could be quenched by only one man, the young Abuelo, whose arms had the steel muscles of one born to roll perfect cigars. Pearl's appetite for Abuelo would never be satisfied in a lifetime. She wasted no precious moments letting her desire be known. The job of Selector was to bundle twenty-five carefully chosen leaf wrappers into an earthenware crock, then call for a boy to run the crock to the Cigarmakers' benches. Each time Pearl sent a crock she knew was headed for Abuelo's bench it contained among the perfectly matched leaves a small, star-shaped pink blossom. The flower emitted no scent to distract from the natural aroma of the tobacco, but bore the meaning of not so hidden intentions to be acted upon beneath the eye of future moons. When the future arrived the moon winked time and time again as the hot skin of Pearl's and Abuelo's bodies came together crushing the clove of garlic between them in a fateful sea of plenty.

As La Liga grew among cigar workers so too did the family of Pearl and Abuelo grow. By the end of the century, Key West was the cigar-producing capital of the world and Pearl and Abuelo had five children. Abuelo's voice had also grown, deep and mellow from free smokers, the imperfect cigars inhaled continuously from dawn till dusk by workers in the great hall. The vowels of Abuelo's voice came strong as notes from a bass cello being played in the depths of a well. It was Abuelo's voice which gave his life its second fortuitous twist, elevated him to unrivaled status among the workers. Abuelo became a Reader. Through the long, tedious days in the great halls of the cigar factories, amidst the flat fall of light from high windows sealed against fickle winds of the outside world, there was one voice above all in the void of passing time. This voice filled ears and minds, becoming familiar as one's own conscience, cajoling like a crony, spiteful as a spurned lover, thunderous as a bull in a spring meadow. The owner of this voice earned more than the lordly cigar Pickers and Packers at the pinnacle of their careers. This man was the Reader, elevated on a platform in the center of the great halls, seated purposefully on a stool, straw hat cocked at advantageous angle. When the Reader spoke, no other talking was allowed, in English, Spanish or Bahamian. The Reader's voice made the day jump with thoughts, translating into Spanish the island's English newspapers, reading newspapers fresh off the ferry from Havana bearing news of Cuba, Barcelona, Buenos Aires. The Reader read from the classics, becoming every character in *Don Quixote, The Count of Monte Cristo, A Tale of Two Cities*. As he read he

educated himself and the others. He became a one-man school for
the cigar workers. They paid him a handsome profit from their
own pockets, voted upon favorites from his readings, to hear them
time and again. Among the glories of literature Abuelo brought to
life his personal favorite was the great Góngora, the Spaniard
who emerged cloaked in a glowing mantle of lyricism, magically
inventing his poetic self from the crusty seventeenth century with
a sudden awesome "melancholy yawn of the earth." The great
Góngora was a favorite of Abuelo's father. The leather-bound
book of Góngora's poems was the only possession his father
brought on the smuggled night voyage of the schooner from
Havana so long ago. More and more the workers wanted to hear
from the great Góngora. Not because Góngora was the favorite of
Abuelo's father, who had become the iron-fisted *jefe* of La Liga.
Not because Abuelo's father placed his son at center stage of the
vast hall to read to the workers. The workers wanted that which
could not be faked or bought. The singular fact was, more than at
any other time, when Abuelo recited the great Góngora his voice
rose from the well of the printed page tinged with mystery of
infinity, surged with an inner beat of lyricism on the wing:

> *The bee as queen who shines with wandering gold;*
> *Either the sap she drinks from the pure air,*
> *Or else the exudation of the skies*
> *That sip the spittle from each silent star.*

Years later, as young Justo stood at Abuelo's side in the
back room of the Cuban *grocería*, there was still respect for the
retired Reader. Ears pricked up at the sound of Abuelo's voice still
steady and strong through an ever-present cigar smoke swirling
about his craggy face. The cigar factories had long since been
boarded up against modern times, when cigars are made by
machines in air-conditioned rooms. A generation had passed since
La Liga grew so strong among the workers the owners started
nonunion factories three hundred miles north of the glitter and
culture of Key West. The factories had been transplanted to the
swampy palmetto lands around Tampa, where malaria waited,
and insects swarmed in rain barrels of precious drinking water
drained from roofs of hastily constructed houses. Such was not a
place for Abuelo. No. Abuelo's family stayed in Stella Maris, Star
of the Sea, where Pavlova once danced at old San Carlos. Even
though bright important times had faded to Depression-era gray,
the star of cultural pride still burned bright in hearts and
memories of men who put the coral-capped island on the map,
rolling out one hundred million cigars a year. *Bang!* Justo could
still hear Abuelo's tamarind cane striking the floor in the back

room of the *grocería*. *Bang!* The metal tip of the cane struck again, all the men coming to attention as Abuelo elevated the cane haughtily as a teacher with a pointer in a classroom of thick-headed boys destined to grow to men forever ignorant of the ways of women, unless they heeded the words of great Góngora. Abuelo raised the cane higher, until the metal tip nudged the white dancer tights banded around the forceful thrust of Pavlova's thighs, her body trapped forever in an eternal leap from the poster nailed to the wall. Never taking his eyes from the curved spirit of Pavlova's leap Abuelo's voice swelled with wisdom of great Góngora, filling every square inch of the small room as if it were the vast hall of a ghostly cigar factory:

> *That fixed armada in the eastern sea*
> *Of islands firm I cannot well describe,*
> *Whose number though for no lasciviousness*
> *But for their sweetness and variety,*
> *The beautiful confusion emulate*
> *When in the white pools of Eurotas Rose*
> *The virginal and naked hunting tribe...*

Great Góngora's words echoed in Justo's ears as if spoken only moments before by Abuelo in the backroom of the *grocería*. Justo last heard Góngora's poetry twenty years ago, in a time of "beautiful confusion." All gone now, gone the way of handmade cigars and natural sponges. The turtles were endangered, and sport fishermen let their less than prize catches from the sea off the hook. What would Abuelo think of it all now? This time of rich rock and roll crooners of drug tunes and hot dogs in alligator loafers blowing away slow greyhounds. A time of conspicuous corruption which had less to do with simple survival and more to do with spiritual greed. Stella Maris had lost more than her virginity and glitter. The Góngorian time of "sweetness and variety," which Abuelo once hailed in the now deserted great halls of the cigar factories, gone forever, along with sponges in the sea and arias soaring to the chandeliered ceiling of the San Carlos.

Wallace Stevens

The Idea of Order
at Key West

She sang beyond the genius of the sea.
The water never formed to mind or voice,
Like a body wholly body, fluttering
Its empty sleeves; and yet its mimic motion
Made constant cry, caused constantly a cry,
That was not ours although we understood,
Inhuman, of the veritable ocean.

The sea was not a mask. No more was she.
The song and water were not medleyed sound
Even if what she sang was what she heard,
Since what she sang was uttered word by word.
It may be that in all her phrases stirred
The grinding water and the gasping wind;
But it was she and not the sea we heard.

For she was the maker of the song she sang.
The ever-hooded, tragic gestured sea
Was merely a place by which she walked to sing.
Whose spirit is this? we said, because we knew
It was the spirit that we sought and knew
That we should ask this often as she sang.

If it was only the dark voice of the sea
That rose, or even colored by many waves;

If it was only the outer voice of sky
And cloud, of the sunken coral water-walled,
However clear, it would have been deep air,
The heaving speech of air, a summer sound
Repeated in a summer without end
And sound alone. But it was more than that,
More even than her voice, and ours, among
The meaningless plungings of water and the wind,
Theatrical distances, bronze shadows heaped
On high horizons, mountainous atmospheres
Of sky and sea.

                    It was her voice that made
The sky acutest at its vanishing.
She measured to the hour its solitude.
She was the single artificer of the world
In which she sang. And when she sang, the sea
Whatever self it had, became the self
That was her song, for she was the maker. Then we,
As we beheld her striding there alone,
Knew that there never was a world for her
Except the one she sang and, singing, made.

Ramon Fernandez, tell me, if you know,
Why, when the singing ended and we turned
Toward the town, tell why the glassy lights,
The lights in the fishing boats at anchor there,
As the night descended, tilting in the air,
Mastered the night and portioned out the sea,
Fixing emblazoned zones and fiery poles,
Arranging, deepening, enchanting night.

Oh! Blessed rage for order, pale Ramon,
The maker's rage to order words of the sea,
Words of the fragrant portals, dimly-starred,
And of ourselves and of our origins,
In ghostlier demarcations, keener sounds.

O Florida, Venereal Soil

A few things for themselves,
Convolvulus and coral,
Buzzards and live-moss,
Tiestas from the keys,
A few things for themselves,
Florida, venereal soil,
(Disclose to the lover.)

The dreadful sundry of this world,
The Cuban, Polodowsky,
The Mexican women,
The negro undertaker
Killing the time between corpses
Fishing for crayfish . . .
Virgin of boorish births,

Swiftly in the nights,
In the porches of Key West,
Behind the bougainvilleas,
After the guitar is asleep,
Lasciviously as the wind,
You come tormenting,
Insatiable,

When you might sit,
A scholar of darkness,
Sequestered over the sea,
Wearing a clear tiara
Of red and blue and red,
Sparkling, solitary, still,
In the high sea-shadow.

Donna, donna, dark,
(Stooping in indigo gown)
And cloudy constellations,
Conceal yourself or disclose
Fewest things to the lover—
A hand that bears a thick-leaved fruit,
A pungent bloom against your shade.

Hunter S. Thompson

The
Gonzo Salvage Company

The TV is out tonight. The set went black about halfway through "Miami Vice," just as Don Johnson dropped a KGB thug with a single 200-yard shot from his high-tech belly gun.

The storm got serious after that, and the mood in The Keys turned mean. Junk cars crashed in the mango swamps and fishheads whipped on each other with sharkhooks in all-night bars and roadhouses along Highway A1A. These people will tolerate almost anything except being cut off in the middle of "Miami Vice."

On nights like these it is better not to answer the telephone. It can only mean trouble: Some friend has been crushed on the highway by a falling power pole, or it might be the Coast Guard calling to say that your boat was stolen by dope fiends who just called on the radio to say they are sinking somewhere off Sand Key and they've given you as their local credit reference, to pay for the rescue operation.

In my case it was a just-reported shipwreck involving total strangers. An 88-foot tramp motor-sailor called *The Tampa Bay Queen* had gone on the reef in Hawk Channel, and all hands had abandoned ship.

There were only three of them, as it turned out. They had all washed ashore on a ice chest, raving incoherently about green sharks and coral heads and their ship breaking up like a matchbox while they screamed for help on a dead radio.

"Why not?" I thought. We are, after all, in The

Business—and besides, I had never covered a shipwreck, not even a small one . . . and there was also talk about "losing the cargo" and the cruel imperatives of "salvage rights."

None of this talk seemed worth going out in a storm to investigate at the time, but that is not how The Business works. I went out, and not long after midnight I found myself huddled with these people in a local motel where they'd been given shelter for the night . . . and by dawn I was so deep in the story that I'd hired a 36-foot Cigarette boat to take me and the captain out to his doomed wreck, at first light, so he could recover whatever was left of it.

"We'll have to move quick," he said, "before the cannibals get there. They'll strip her naked by noon."

The sun came up hot and bright that morning. The storm was over and the chop in the channel was down to 3 feet, which means nothing to a fast Cigarette boat. We were running 40 mph by the time we got out of the bay, and about 40 minutes later we were tying up to the wreck of *The Tampa Bay Queen*. It was lying on the bottom, tilted over at a 45-degree angle, and the sea had already broken it open.

There was no hope of saving anything except the new nylon sails and the V-8 engine and six nickel-plated brass winches, which the distraught captain said were worth $5,000 each--and maybe the 80-foot teakwood mast, which would fetch about $100 a foot in Key West, and looked like a thing of beauty.

We climbed up the steep rotted deck and the captain set about slashing down the sails with a butcher knife and ordering the first mate to take a hatchet to the winches. "Never mind a screwdriver," he shouted. "Just rip'em out by the stumps."

The first mate was in no mood to take orders. He had not been paid in three weeks, he said, and he was wearing fancy black leather pilot's boots with elevator heels and slick leather soles, which caused him to constantly lose his footing and go sliding down the deck. We would hear him scream as he went off, and then there would be a splash. I spent most of my time pulling him back up the deck, and finally we lashed him to the mast with a steel safety cable, which allowed him to tend to his work.

By this time I had worked up a serious sweat, and the mystique of this filthy shipwreck had long since worn off. The captain was clearly a swine and the first mate was a middle-aged bellboy from New Jersey and the ship was probably stolen . . . But here I was out on the high sea with these people, doing manual labor in the morning and bleeding from every knuckle. It was time, I felt, for a beer.

I was moving crabwise along the deck, homing in on the cooler we'd left in the Cigarette boat, when I saw the scavengers coming in. They had been circling the wreck for a while, two half-naked thugs in a small skiff, and the captain had recognized them instantly.

"God help us now," he muttered. "Here they come. These are the ones I was worried about." He looked nervously out at the two burly brutes in the cannibal boat, and he said he could see in their eyes that they were getting ready to board us and claim the whole wreck for themselves.

"It won't be much longer," he said. "These bastards are worse than pirates. We may have to fight for it."

I shrugged and moved off toward the beer cooler, at the other end of the wreck. The captain was obviously crazy, and I had lost my feel for The Story. All I wanted was a cold can of beer.

By the time I got to the Cigarette boat, however, the thugs had made their move and were tying up alongside us, grinning like wolves as they crouched between me and the cooler. I stared down at them and swore never again to answer my phone after midnight.

"Was this your boat?" one of them asked. "We heard you whimpering all night on the radio. It was a shame."

The next few minutes were tense, and by the end of that time I had two new partners and my own marine salvage business. The terms of the deal were not complex, and the spirit was deeply humane.

The captain refused to cooperate at first, screeching hoarsely from the other end of the wreck that he had silent partners in Tampa who would soon come back and kill all of us . . .

But you hear a lot of talk like that in The Keys, so we ignored him and drank all the beer and hammered out a three-way agreement that would give the captain until sundown to take anything he wanted, and after that the wreck would be ours.

It was the Law of the Sea, they said. Civilization ends at the waterline. Beyond that, we all enter the food chain, and not always right at the top.

The captain seemed to understand, and so did I. He would be lucky to get back to shore with anything at all, and I had come close to getting my throat slit.

It was almost dark when we dropped him off on the dock, where he quickly sold out to a Cuban for $5,000 in cash. Mother ocean had prevailed once again, and I was now in the marine salvage business.

Salvage Is Not Looting

"The crew took a vote, and she lost, so we traded her for two cases of beer to the first boat we ran into, about 100 miles north of Aruba. It was a gang of shrimpers from Savannah. They were headed back to port . . . That was four years ago, and the girl is still in a state mental hospital somewhere out West."
                    -Boat Captain from Key West

The sea is nervous tonight. Another cold front is coming in, a north wind is putting whitecaps on the waves. The Mako is tied up to a sea-grape tree just in front of my door, whipping frantically around at the end of its rope like a wild beast caught in a trap. I go out every once in a while to adjust the docking knots, but the line is still rubbing bark off the tree and my new Japanese wind sock has been ripped to shreds by the gusts.

The neighbors complain about my screaming, but their noise is like the barking of dumb dogs. It means nothing. They are not seafaring people. The only boats that concern them are the ones they might want to rent, and when a storm comes they hide in their rooms like house cats.

My own situation is different. I am now in the Marine Salvage Business, and cruel storms are the lifeblood of our profession. It is the nature of salvage to feed on doom and disaster.

My new partners moved quickly to consolidate our position. We formed a shrewd corporate umbrella and expanded at once into the reef-diving and deep-water game fishing business, in order to crank up the revenue stream while we plundered the odd wreck here and there, and searched for sunken treasure.

Capt. Elgin took charge of all fishing and diving operations, Crazy Mean Brian would handle plundering, and I was in charge of salvaging sunken treasure.

Our fortunes took an immediate turn for the worse less than 24 hours after we seized our first wreck, when the elegant teakwood mast on the doomed *Tampa Bay Queen* turned out to be split from top to bottom with a long spiral fracture filled with termites, black putty and sea worms. It was utterly worthless, and the rest of the ship was stripped overnight by what my partners called "filthy cowboys from Big Coppitt Key," a gang of seagoing Hell's Angels who have terrorized these waters for years.

"They stripped out a whole submarine one night," Capt. Elgin told me. "The Navy left it open so the local school kids could take tours through it, but a storm came up and the Navy guys went ashore for the night, and by morning it was totally looted. They even took the torpedoes."

Our only other asset was an ancient cannonball that Crazy Mean Brian had plundered from a site that he refused to disclose, because he said we would have serious problems "establishing jurisdiction."

"There are a lot more of them down there," he said, "along with at least two brass cannons, but we would have to drag them at least three miles underwater before we could file for salvage rights."

They weighed about 1,600 pounds each, and they would not be easy to sell on the open market, due to the maze of conflicting claims already filed by other thieves, looters and competing treasure salvagers.

"Nobody took this stuff seriously until Mel Fisher came along," Capt. Elgin explained, "but the way it is now you can't come in with anything older than one of those green glass Coca-Cola bottles without having the whole federal court system on your neck." He laughed bitterly. "If we try to sell this cannonball in town, Mel Fisher would have us in jail for piracy."

"Nonsense," I said. "I've known Mel for years. He'd be happy to help us out."

They both hooted at me. "We'd be better off trying to rip souvenir teeth out of living sharks," said Crazy Mean Brian. "You *have no friends* in the marine salvage business."

I called Mel Fisher at once and arranged to tour his facilities on the Navy base in downtown Key West.

I met him at the Two Friends Patio, a chic hangout on Front Street, where the whole Fisher operation goes after work because, they say, they drank there for free before the Mother Lode came in.

Fisher, of course, is wallowing these days in gold bars and emeralds. He has discovered more wrecks than the Triple A in a New York blizzard, and he appeared on "Good Morning America" the other day to trumpet his recent finds.

The wreck of the fabled *Atocha*, a Spanish galleon that

went down in a storm off Key West in 1622, was located by Fisher's divers a few years ago and estimated to be worth about $400 million, mainly in gold and silver—but Mel said all that was chicken feed, now that he'd found emeralds.

"It's into the billions and billions now," he said.

Mel started out with a dive shop in the back of his parents' chicken farm in Redondo Beach in the late '50s. He'd moved from Indiana to California where his destiny was almost certainly to become heir to a poultry empire. In retrospect, and only recently so, Mel seems to have chosen the wiser path.

There are 12 boats in the harbor tonight, and four of them are ours. My 17-foot Mako is the smallest of the lot, but it is extremely fast and agile and it will go anywhere, day or night.

Crazy Mean Brian's new boat is tied up just behind mine. The local charter fishermen are not comfortable with the sight of it, because it reminds them of the "old days," when everybody was crazy. It is 27-foot custom-built hull, with no name, mounted with twin 200-horse-power Johnsons, and it will run to Cuba and back on one load of gas.

Opposite Brian's is Capt. Elgin's 23-foot Roballo, the *Bobbi Lynn*—the reef diving boat--next to the gas pumps, shrouded in fog, and bounding around in the sea like some kind of rooted ghost out of Key Largo.

The kid came back and took the battery out of the boat again. It happened late in the afternoon, the second time in three days.

The first time he took it for money—which was dumb, but at least I understood it. The man was a fishhead, a creature without many cells. He was like one of those big lizards that never feels any pain when you rip off its tail, or one of its legs—or even its head, as they do down in Chile—because it will all grow back by dawn, and nobody will know the difference.

Dawn at the Boca Chica

The Boca Chica Lounge is distinguished in many ways, but mainly it is a savage all-night biker bar where you go at your own risk and here many ugly things have occurred.

Key West is the last stop in this weird chain of islands that runs south of Miami like a national coccyx bone on the swollen spine of Florida, and the Boca Chica is the only place in town where real men are still whooping it up at 5 o'clock in the morning.

We got there around 5:03—after a failed visitation with the Halley's comet crowd on the beach in Key West—and took the only two seats at the big horseshoe-shaped bar. I ordered a Bud and a Coke, and Maria became instantly involved with a wild-eyed Cuban gentleman standing next to her, who was feeling crazed by loneliness.

"I'd like to talk to somebody someday," he said. "I'm not that bad. I'm a nice guy."

The bartender reached over and smacked the guy in the neck. "So what?" he said. "Keep your weepy bull---- to yourself."

The Cuban cringed, but the bartender was obviously in a mood for personal action. "You dirty little animal," he said. "Why don't you get on the floor and dance for a while?"

Across the bar, behind a chain-link hurricane fence that separated the whole place into quadrants, I could see a crowd of 20 or 30 swarthy bikers milling around the pool tables in a haze of rancid smoke. A smell of beer was heavy on the place, and the sharp click of pool balls cut through the dense thumping of the music.

The DJ in his smoked-glass booth above us was cranking the music out to a serious full disco frenzy. The terrible flashing of the strobe lights made us all seem like ghosts, and the music was like the amplified sound of a Studebaker throwing a rod.

The weepy Cuban was still refusing to dance, but the floor was filling up with other players. A tall transvestite wearing a black corset and a red garter belt was sandwiched between two boys from the Boca Chica U.S. Naval Air Station, just down the road—and a bearded man wearing short pants and flipflops had put aside the ball point pens and the fat spiral notebook he'd been laboring over all night, and suddenly gone wild on the dance floor.

He was graceful, in his own way, and he seemed to feel in his heart that at any moment he would take off and soar with wild sea birds. He flapped his arms like wings and tried to leap high off the floor.

He was wrong—but I understood the spirit of the dance, and I sensed what he was trying to say. He had been observing the action in the Boca Chica, making copious notes, for about as long as he felt he could handle it—and now he was expressing himself.

His girlfriend, a plump blonde wearing wet cutoffs and a T-shirt that said, "Drink whiskey or die," had been admiring his antics with starry-eyed affection for a while, but when he appeared to be getting away from himself she jumped out on the dance floor and seized him from behind in a spoon grip.

Maria was weeping from the pain in her legs and dawn was coming up outside. I turned to the man sitting next to me—who looked like Sting, the rock singer—and asked him if Tennessee Williams was buried anywhere nearby.

He quickly palmed the small bottle of RUSH he'd been snorting from and eyed me nervously. "I don't think so," he said. "Why do you ask?"

"I thought I just saw his name on TV," I replied. "And I drove past the graveyard tonight while we were looking for Halley's comet." I offered him a Salem from a pack I'd found on the sidewalk outside. "I had a terrible experience today," I said. "My boat went up on the rocks and I had to swim ashore naked with an oar."

He shrugged. "Mister Williams is not buried here," he muttered. "The highest point on the island is only two feet above sea level. You can't dig down more than two feet without hitting water."

"So what?" I said. "You go down three feet and you hit rocks. I destroyed my whole lower unit today, and they mocked me when I climbed up on shore. I had to carry my clothes and my cigarettes above my head in a plastic bag wrapped with duct tape."

I offered him a Budweiser, but he said he was drinking gin and was going home soon. "This place never closes," he said. "But it gets pretty dull after sunrise."

We left shortly after that, and I taped a note on the gate at Boog Powell's marina, saying my boat had run into a storm and would be needing serious repairs. The windshield was shattered and the battery had jumped out of its moorings, filling the hull with sulfuric acid and paralyzing the solenoid. Many wires shorted out and the power tilt jammed at low tide while I drifted onto the rocks in Niles Channel.

My bullhorn was broken, my flares were all wet, and my VHF marine radio blew a fuse every time I squeezed on the talk button . . . But luckily we had gone aground at the mouth of a sleazy canal that led down to Capt. Elgin's dock, just beyond the Summerland Key Marina.

That was when I came to grips with the humiliation of having to strip naked, abandon ship and wallow ashore in full view of the local lobster-fishing community, which was a sad and crazy experience.

I left Maria on board, badly crippled from the storm, with a bottle of gin and a new Buffet tape and the big Mercury engine rumbling helplessly in neutral to maintain the electrical flow.

Capt. Elgin was sick with swine flu, but his neighbors were keeping him company and they had a good laugh when I showed up at sundown with my clothes in a bag and a broken oar in my hand. One of them, who wore the many gold chains and sharks' teeth of a successful free-lance boater, had just been told that his landlord was arrested last night on the Pennsylvania Turnpike with 16 pounds of cocaine, and that life as he had known it was coming to a fork in the road.

But I had my own problems. The sun was going down and my boat was still out on the rocks, and no rising tide until midnight.

"Never mind," shouted the captain. "The boys will go out and get her. We've never lost one yet."

Which was true. We got back at the dock in time for the evening news. I cashed a huge check and flew out to Miami the next day. When I got to Denver I made a few calls and ended up selling my boat to Gary Hart for use in the '88 Florida primary.

Richard Wilbur

The Pelican

Pellicanus is the word
    For a certain breed of bird
Who truly is a crane;
    Egypt is his domain.
There are two kinds thereof;
    Near to the Nile they live;
One of them dwells in the flood,
    The fishes are his food;
The other lives in the isles
    On lizards, crocodiles,
Serpents, and stinking creatures,
    And beasts of evil nature.
In Greek his title was
    Onocrotalos,
Which is *longum rostrum,* said
    In the Latin tongue instead,
Or *long-beak* in our own.
    Of this bird it is known
That when he comes to his young,
    They being grown and strong,
And does them kindly things,
    And covers them with his wings,
The little birds begin
    Fiercely to peck at him;
They tear at him and try
    To blind their father's eye.

He falls upon them then
　　And slays them with great pain,
Then goes away for a spell,
　　Leaving them where they fell.
On the third day he returns
　　And thereupon he mourns,
Feeling so strong a woe
　　To see the small birds so
That he strikes his breast with his beak
　　Until the blood shall leak.
And when the coursing blood
　　Spatters his lifeless brood,
Such virtue does it have
　　That once again they live.

Know that this pelican
　　Signifies Mary's Son;
The little birds are men
　　Restored to life again
From death, by that dear blood
　　Shed for us by our God.
Now learn one meaning more,
　　Revealed by holy lore:
Know why the small birds try
　　To peck their father's eye,
Who turns on them in wrath
　　And puts them all to death.
Men who deny the light
　　Would blind God's blazing sight,
But on such people all
　　His punishment will fall.
This is the meaning I find;
　　Now bear it well in mind.

Trolling for Blues
for John and Barbara

As with the dapper terns, or that sole cloud
Which like a slow-evolving embryo
Moils in the sky, we make of this keen fish
Whom fight and beauty have endeared to us
A mirror of our kind. Setting aside

His unreflectiveness, his flings in air,
The aberration of his flocking swerve
To spawning-grounds a hundred miles at sea,
How clearly, musing to the engine's thrum,
Do we conceive him as he waits below:

Blue in the water's blue, which is the shade
Of thought, and in that scintillating flux
Poised weightless, all attention, yet on edge
To lunge and seize with sure incisiveness,
He is a type of coolest intellect,

Or is so to the mind's blue eye until
He strikes and runs unseen beneath the rip,
Yanking imagination back and down
Past recognition to the unlit deep
Of the glass sponges, of chiasmodon,

Of the old darkness of Devonian dream,
Phase of a meditation not our own,
That long mêlée where selves were not, that life
Merciless, painless, sleepless, unaware,
From which, in time, unthinkably we rose.

Joy Williams

The Route

Ballston Spa, New York

We had the car so we went. We left as soon as possible for our marriage was not doing well. I am just a youngster and attractive. He is middle-aged.

I am hoping for the best from this trip. He is a chemist. We have many problems. He is working at present on a theory that shark size is dependent upon fin diameter and liver weight. Of course there are no sharks in Ballston Spa. That is one of the problems. We have never had a meeting of minds but we wed because we had good bodies.

Every day I used to wait for him to come home from the laboratory. I would make up big glasses of chocolate milk and pop-up waffles in the morning and then he would go off and I would stay in our rented bungalow by the sulphur springs and watch the old fools totter up and down the hills with their jugs and jars and paper cups. I couldn't stand to even wash my hands in that water. It turned my earrings black. But everybody was crazy about it. It made rotten coffee. The whole town smelled like a bathroom. But they were mad for it. And then at 2:00 on the dot they'd all plug in their rock tumblers and scramble my television for the rest of the afternoon.

That was the point where I would go to The Office and buy myself a bottle of Jack Daniels giftly boxed. The liquor store was

conveniently located. That was one thing about the place—
nothing was anywhere if it wasn't right on top of you. I always
bought my product boxed for then I could give the plastic insert of
that Tennessee fellow to those various bands of children that
roamed the streets of Ballston Spa. Those babies didn't have a
thing, though I would bet if you went through that town today you
would find them playing with those little plastic heads at least.

I would be drinking in the breakfast nook.

And just when I believed I couldn't stand it for another
moment, the man who I married would rush up the walk, still in
his smock, rubber-soled shoes and safety goggles and we would
make frantic love.

But the zing was out of it.

Actually I didn't know him very well. He had a long dun-
blond head and an absent manner.

So we were both wanting something nice to occur to us
again. And Herbie at the corner Humble who's the same age as me
and doesn't have a tooth in his head kindly planned the trip and
made suggestions and reservations. All we had to have was the
destination.

When we went we didn't leave a thing behind.

East Windsor Hill, Connecticut

My first memory as a child was of a moth in my milk.

He can't recollect what his was. Nothing stands out. He
had four brothers and one weird sister. Of the brood she was the
only one I had the displeasure to meet, and she indirectly. We
honeymooned at her cabin on Lake George. She was unmarried
herself. I never even saw her photograph but I became acquainted
with her washcloth full of pubic hairs—sort of hidden on a
special little rod beneath the lip of the tub. Leave it to me to find
it, of course. *Covered* with them as though she were going to make
an afghan. Saving them like decent people would Green Stamps.

I remind him of this when I am annoyed with him. His
sister. And he believes himself to be so sophisticated. What can
he say? I have him there. We gobbled at each other all day. So
far the trip has been dreadful. I tease his lap but he is unmoved.
He dislikes attendants at toll booths. I think he would like to
hurt them. He looks at them out of his heavy-lidded eyes. He has
eyes like Jean-Paul Belmondo. There, I believe, similarity ends.
The attendants smile at me. Their tongues protrude a little. I am
really a knockout. I could have been in films but I lack the
ambition. So this first day is not a good one. We are mumbled like
bunnies in the cold. We stop at a tourist home. The owner is an

ancient soul. I don't know whether a little old man or a little old lady. It wore Hush-Puppies and an overcoat.

Our room is warm, however, and very modern. All done in Colonial with eagles everywhere—even on the toilet tissue holder. I prepare myself and snuggle into bed, darling as a cupcake. For supper we had martinis and a soufflé but he is not happy. He sits and writes something out in a notebook. I think it is about me but when I look I realize that it concerns his goddamn sharks which he has never seen. He has never showed the slightest desire to be different. When we first met I thought he knew a lot about love but now it's clear he knows only as much as I do.

Spotsylvania, Virginia

We stop for gas and the boy says, "Right over there is where Dr. Mudd was at." My husband refutes this. They glare at each other. I can't imagine what they're talking about. "He thinks we're tourists," my husband says. The boy doesn't put the gas cap back on. We remove some of our clothes because it is getting hot and we have some ice cream. The car is old and has old scratchy seats. Everywhere are trees and arsenals. He begins to talk about fishes. If I could get one starved shark, he says, just one, I could prove a lot. We are swerving along and I am having a cup of gin and tonic from our thermos. He talks and talks. I notice a clutch of freckles on his forearm that I have not seen before. They resemble a banana. A little later they bring to mind two parachutists. I am fascinated. I swear it's like going to the movies.

He is driving. This car takes a lot out of one. It is exhausting and seems to have intentions of its own. It is a Buick with big fins. I do not think about cars one way or the other but I have an opinion about this one. It has a strange odor about the right hubcap. Now I have heard that pranksters do this for a prank. They remove the hubcap and put dead fish or something awful there. Items that ladies use for their personal hygiene are popular. These same creeps will replace a perfectly good car engine with a broken-down one while you are in a restaurant or enjoying yourself somewhere. I have a suspicion that we might be victims, but I am not going to examine this further. We are traveling in a straight line but he is struggling with the wheel. His forearm bulges and sweats. He is so sorrowful. He sighs and tips the thermos to his mouth, getting the sliver of lime which is all that's left. He doesn't mind. He says chewing it keeps him awake. He is very polite and selfless. I used to be nuts for him.

That night at the La Crème de la Crème, which was clean

but unexceptional, I am after him as always but he is sleeping and later when he wakes up, we take advantage of it, but he is so blue. He says, I have no dreams. I can hardly make him out in the darkness of this room but I say, Oh sweet potato, you dreamed up me. But he said Kehule dreamt about a snake swallowing its own tail which illumined for him the structure of the benzene ring.

He talks like this. How was I to know? I was only a baby when we met. My momma was still buying my brassieres.

Otto Loewe derived the whole neurohumoral concept from a dream, he says.

I am so disgusted.

Alert, North Carolina

This is the saddest day of my life. He was bitten by a bat. We were coming out of a restaurant after a very nice dinner and the little bugger staggered out from under a bush and fastened onto his sock. I beat it to a paste with my handbag but the act was done. I have never seen my husband under stress before. He is very calm. We went back to the motel and drank a little gin. I bought some crackers from a machine. He spoke about *N. brevirostris* and *C. milberti*, looking occasionally at his ankle where nothing could be seen. Now I am not a cerebral person if you know what I mean. I was made for better things. For example, I simply cannot be topped. Now last night I was enraged. I said to myself that never again would I have anything to do with him. We were through! And I would leave him for good in Miami. For what is in Key West? I can't imagine. Key West is merely the end of the country is all. He can go down on the sea with a fish it's all the same to me was my attitude of the night before. But life is very funny. Now he is going to die. It's very sexual. I kiss him, deeply traveling. The fillings of his teeth are like ice. There's a hint of chive and ketchup. He says, lightly, I thought, under the circumstances, I need the fluid from the brain of a suckling mouse. He knows everything and makes it all sound difficult. I am willing to go out and get it I say. He says, Or a duck embryo would do just as well. We have some more gin and he says that he's decided not to do anything about it. He goes out and around the pool of the Sun Tan Motel where we are and buys a bag of fried pork rinds from the machine. The pool has an algae problem. No one is in it. It's green as a Christmas tree. I am waiting on the bed and he comes back in all dressed up like the fellow on the Beefeater's bottle. Flowered red jerkin, hammerhead shoes and a white pointy beard. I laughed till I peed. I never knew he had this side to him.

Cash, South Carolina

There are many towns by the name of Cash. Actually every town is somewhere else as well. Except, I have heard, for Edgartown, which is only in Massachusetts. This has never sounded right to me and perhaps it is not so. This is the only Cash I've seen though I imagine the others are the same. Birds nesting in neon lettering (for birds are mean and dumb everywhere). Movie houses taken over by Chinese restaurants. Mister Softees and rags in the streets. One has to make one's own joy. To travel through America you have to be in love. I am in love again! He is twice and a half my age but sound. He has become aggressive. We've stopped for the night at one in the afternoon. He embraces my yummy legs. I hold him tight but he's a different man from yesterday. He is confident and has a feathery touch.

I become a whimpering rag.

Nonetheless, opposite the motel is an electrical supply company which we can't help but notice. He says to me. Do you recollect Gerald Gee?

Of course, I say. How could I forget. He came to our house once from the laboratory where he is supposed to be an electronics genius. He broke a dish and didn't flush the toilet.

Gerald's had his breakdown, he says. It seems he found that mathematical thinking was touching off violent erotic excitement, often culminating in orgasm.

He says he can't understand how knowing this can help him. I agree. I say it would seem to me that few are fortunate enough to get such pleasure from their work.

Dusk returns to Cash. In the windows across the street are hundreds of different lights, all lit. They've been shining all day and at night they're still on. It must cost them a fortune. And for what? What's there to use them? Who's to know?

Out of simple and ubiquitous human experience, this generous and committed man discovered that his life was imaginary. The only element in the entire dream of it which was really clear, the rest being clouded in extrapolation, was this person, prone in a series of revolving bedchambers, with lust in her heart and the clear seamless mind of an infant. Though the evidence of her in no way guaranteed her reality, he decided that he would travel with and through his vision of her. No longer would he wait humbly for the wisdom that can only be won at the autopsy table.

Lugoff, South Carolina

As anyone could see from any map they chose to, we have not progressed very far! Lugoff can't be more than twenty miles further.

He's torn my blouse—pushed his hand right through that chemical crap they make everything of anymore. We turned off the highway and sped down a deep black piney road. There are turkeys flying beside us. He is showing most of his mouth in a great grin. The car is rocketing away with our electricity. He stops before an abandoned house. It is really an awful place. Half built or half torn down. Ratty Johnny-Kwik erected crooked in the front yard. No door and as we run in we can see the pink Southern sky through the roof. He tells me to get on my stomach. I am so excited. The last time he suggested this, naturally I complied but then he didn't do anything. Or rather he was very quiet for awhile and then he picked up a magazine. Then he became very engrossed in that. I went out for some Campari and a green pepper sandwich. I must admit I made the acquaintance of someone there.

This time I know it will not be the same. Fate has made a shambles of us.

My eye is on the knot-hole.

But then we realize that we are in someone's dining room and that they are having breakfast. Their backs are to us, thank goodness. A little family eating from blue bowls. We leave immediately and no one's the wiser. The car's engine as a matter of fact, is still running.

Atlanta, Georgia

His left arm is sunburned but his face is becoming pale. Last night I felt his ribs for the first time in many months. When he spoke to me, I found that I did not know what he was saying. This is not unusual, although now we fear that what was true before has become true now because he is rabid.

When he comes around again, we discover that he is talking about sharks. I am more understanding now. I have matured a lot. He is a little boy again with the soft wet lip of a little boy. He wants a milkshake. We buy milkshakes and pour a pint of Scotch into them. He says that even as a little boy he wanted to invent a shark repellent.

I can see this, I say. Make a good shark repellent and the world will beat a path to your door.

His experiments have only been partially successful. The sharks keep right on eating the protected food even while they're dying. Feeder and feedee are both out of luck. Such things have to be ironed out.

No he hasn't the time.

We kiss.

We are making it in a bank's parking lot. Santa Claus is walking back and forth. He's rather thin but it's him all right, holding a box of candy canes. There's a tiny person in front of him sucking on a pacifier and wearing a harness and a long leash as though he was a cocker spaniel. I find the situation . . . bittersweet. Two hippies come up, all arrayed in motley and dancing around, ringing bells. Fuck off, says Santa. The tiny starts to cry. Santa walks away. I am outraged. The hippies look astounded. They pick up one end of the leash. This is where we left them. I am shocked as though struck. Fuck off, said Santa Claus.

We also had bad meat in the bottom of a hotel here.

Valdosta, Georgia

Now this town was very sweet and cool with leaves and trees. We met the Governor at a vegetable stand. He is not the Governor of this state but of another one. He was buying peanuts and carrots. We are buying endive. Up the road I plan to make a salad and we'll drink Pouilly-Fuissé. It's very European. For example, we've decided to eat from a hamper. The Governor says, Well you sure look as though you had a good secret and I wish I had it too.

Well, we say.

Let me give you folks a little something I got right here, the Governor says and he hands over a license plate which says arrive alive.

A gimmick, my husband says, a sop!

I agree. I look right into the Governor's sunglasses. You're cow-old, I say. You're freezzzzzing. I must admit I say this girlishly and coy.

Well, the Governor says, shaking hands all around. It sure was pleasant meeting you for the first time. He has a beautiful Cadillac car. They leave.

He was certainly a well-put-together man wasn't he, I say. But I don't mean anything by it. I show my husband this by socketing my hip to his. We step back into our crummy Buick and a very judicious thing happens. All hell breaks loose. The car falls apart. I would not speak figuratively. I never do. It falls apart. Its time had come.

A worn battery cable shorted out on the frame, setting fire to the engine at the same time an electrode from the spark plug fell into the combustion chamber, disintegrating the piston. The tires went flat the transmission fluid exploded the gas tank collapsed an armature snapped shooting the generator pulley through the hood the brake shoes melted the windshield cracked and the glove compartment flew open spilling my panties into the street.

My husband is unflustered. A crowd gathers but there's not one dog. I used to have such a way with animals. Dogs don't come near me anymore. I say to him, I think I'm pregnant.

We walk across the street to a car dealer and on the spot he pays in full for the meanest machine I've ever seen.

Lakeland, Florida

We are at a stoplight, breakfasting hurriedly on gin and orange biscuits. There's a Court of Appeals in this town. Judges in robes are everywhere, eating barbecue, emerging from hardware stores and so forth. We couldn't care less. He wants only to get somewhere where we can lie down. His collars are too big for him. His cheeks have lovely malignant hollows.

Our car is snarling and burbling at the stoplight. It has air extractors, a shaker hood, six spoilers, four pipes, a 400-cubic-inch Ram Air V-08 and 4-barrel carbs. In black and plum.

Of course we're mad for it. I am dying to drive it but I can't push in the clutch. The Governor is in the next lane. We destroy him, of course. We stomp the accelerator and five seconds later we are doing sixty. We dust him good.

But I know not forever.

We are in a cozy white cabin on a lake, swinging on a white porch swing. He is asleep but he is loving me up regardless. He is comatose almost always now but he performs beautifully I must say. We talk about sharks. He says he can't understand what he ever had against them. I say, They keep the ocean clean and I thank them for that.

He finds my remarks incisive.

We watch the lake and a fellow and a girl fishing from a little motorboat. They are having a wonderful time but are not catching any fish. Then a big speedboat with a star on it smashes right into them, scattering wood and cushions and hair and sandwiches all over, disrupting the scene to an extent which we would not have thought possible. The girl was a casserole. The fellow went mad. They'd been married only an hour and a half. The deputy sheriff, everyone said thankfully, was unhurt. It could have been a real tragedy. He charged them with having no lifejackets.

We leave immediately for they were innocents and we are as well. Now I have nothing against sheriffs for I am American to the core, but we were innocents, riding and drinking and loving our way to the sea.

Key West, Florida

We are here at Mile 0. I feel sick about it. He is almost gone. We eat lime pie and snapper. The restaurant isn't much. There was a popular restaurant here but it burned down in 1940. We do not look for lodging. I help him down to the beach. All the streets are dead ends naturally. People are selling sponges and shells and baskets made of opossums. A woman comes up and shouts in his ear, for he has lost most all his faculties. She points out west into the water and screams, Out there was where Dr. Mudd was at. He agrees. I feel that he has given up.

Key West is a pit of salt. And then there is the water. The Governor is on the beach surrounded by constituents but his eyes are just on me. I see us reflected in his silver sunglasses. He asks an aide for a Dr. Pepper in a returnable bottle. He gets a Coke in a can.

He is not so hot.

We wade out—to where the green water becomes just blue. My man, and how can I say I have regrets? tends to me. He moves from desire to object.

So do I. We all do.

Oh!, I say. Be mine. And he does. Right where the Gulf of Mexico looks like the Atlantic itself and all around us is seaweed in the shape of little hearts and the sharks are almost where you can see them—swimming and smiling at all the good things there are to do and eat.

That's the advantage of this. For they can't get here too soon.

We kiss.

Tennessee Williams

The Diving Bell

I want to go under the sea in a diving-bell
and return to the surface with ominous wonders to tell.
I want to be able to say:
>"The base is unstable, it's probably unable
>   to weather much weather,
being all hung together by a couple of blond hairs caught
in a fine-toothed comb."

I want to be able to say through a P.A. system,
authority giving a sonorous tone to the vowels,
>   "I'm speaking from Neptune's bowels.
>   The sea's floor is nacreous, filmy
with milk in the wind, the light of an overcast morning."

I want to give warning:
>   "The pediment of our land is a lady's comb,
>   the basement is moored to the dome
by a pair of blond hairs caught in a delicate
tortoise-shell comb."

I think it is safer to roam
>   than to stay in a mortgaged home
>   And so—

I want to go under the sea in a bubble of glass
containing a sofa upholstered in green corduroy

and a girl for practical purposes and a boy
            well-versed in the classics.

I want to be first to go down there where action is slow
            but thought is surprisingly quick.
            It's only a dare-devil's trick,
            the length of a burning wick
            between tu-whit and tu-who!

            Oh, it's pretty and blue
but not at all to be trusted. No matter how deep you go
there's not very much below
            the deceptive shimmer and glow
            which is all for show
of sunken galleons encrusted with barnacles and doubloons,
an undersea tango palace with instant come and
            go moons ...

ABOUT THE EDITOR

George Murphy's most recent book of poems is *Rounding Ballast Key* (Ampersand Press). He has edited *The Poet's Choice: 100 American Poets' Favorite Poems*, four annual volumes of *The Editors' Choice: Best American Short Stories (Bantam)*, and (with Paul Mariani) *Poetics: Essays on the Art of Poetry*. He was the Founding Editor of *Tendril Magazine* and for ten years has been the editorial director of Wampeter Press. He has received various fellowships and awards including a Bread Loaf Fellowship in Poetry in 1987 and the first Shaw Award from Boston College for "Outstanding Contributions to American Literature"

He currently lives on Houseboat Row in Key West where he hosts both a daily radio talk show and a weekly television program.